The Mon

The Moment

Claire Dyer

W F HOWES LTD

This large print edition published in 2014 by
W F Howes Ltd
Unit 4, Rearsby Business Park, Gaddesby Lane,
Rearsby, Leicester LE7 4YH

1 3 5 7 9 10 8 6 4 2

First published in the United Kingdom in 2013
by Quercus

Quotations in the text

'Tango', *Writing King Kong*, Robert Seatter (Seren, 2011)
'In Thread', *Love's Loose Ends*, David Tait (Smith/Doorstop Books, 2011)
'Thinking of Holland, III. The light on the water at Rhenen',
Nocturnes, Will Kemp (Cinnamon Press, 2011)
'In Athens', Bernard Spencer, *Complete Poetry,*
Translations & Selected Prose (Bloodaxe Books, 2011)
'XXII', *Marriage*, David Harsent (Faber and Faber Limited, 2002)

A CIP catalogue record for this book is available
from the British Library

ISBN 978 1 47125 679 0

Typeset by Palimpsest Book Production Limited,
Falkirk, Stirlingshire
Printed and bound by
www.printondemand-worldwide.com of Peterborough, Englan

This book is made entirely of chain-of-custody materials

For
Jez, Jared & Liam

Then I go backwards into love,
foot behind.

'Tango', Robert Seatter

CHAPTER 1

So, this is how the day begins.

A man is running across the concourse at Paddington Station. He is obviously late for something. Maybe he caught the eight sixteen instead of the eight ten from somewhere and so is hurrying towards the steps of the Underground, his suit jacket flapping like wings, his briefcase knocking against his thigh. At the moment he skirts the noticeboard alerting passengers to the fact that skating and cycling are forbidden and that thieves operate in this area, the girl, who is actually an art student from the University of Greenwich trying to earn some extra cash, and who is dressed, much to her distress, like something out of a Thomas Hardy novel, turns abruptly to walk back to the gazebo that bears the name of the company who have decided to give out free yogurts on this March morning, thus bumping into the man, causing the tray she's carrying to crash to the floor, the man to shout, 'Oh!' and Fern Cole to look back over her shoulder, one foot poised at the top of the escalator on her way down to the Circle and District Lines.

It is at this moment, this particular, tiny, breathless, coin-edge moment, that Fern sees the man she used to love standing on the far side of the station under the departure boards, gazing in her direction.

Fern's decision now is whether to lift her foot, turn and walk towards him while conjuring up something debonair and sophisticated to say; something like, 'My goodness, Elliott, how wonderful to see you,' and proffering her cheek in a way she's studied during long afternoons at the hairdressers' flicking through the society pages of magazines, or whether she should carry on down to the Tube, get her train to Victoria, meet Juliet, pretend she hasn't seen him.

Would it be better if she swiped her Oyster card over the sensor at the barrier, strode purposefully along the corridor, pretended to look at the advertisements on the walls? After all, she's managed not to remember him quite successfully over the past twenty-five years, hasn't she?

But she has time to walk across the station to where he is standing; she's not due to meet Jules at Victoria for another hour. It's just how the trains worked out; Fern's from Reading, Jules's from Kent, then their plan to take the District Line out to Chiswick. How odd, she thinks, as she looks down at her boots – they're new and still slightly too tight – that the studio changed the date of their pottery class to today. If it had been last Tuesday as planned, she wouldn't be here now like this, in this state of limbo, faced with this decision. On any other day she wouldn't be here now, like this.

It's a decision she doesn't want to have to make. She had woken that morning nestled in the certainties of her life: Jack's steady breathing next to her, the shape he made in their bed, the knowledge that when the alarm sounded he would stretch to turn it off, then reach out and rest his hand lightly on her hip. This was familiar and right. It is what she had chosen.

Later, when he'd left for work he'd touched her arm as she stood by the sink rinsing out a milk bottle. 'I won't be late tonight, I shouldn't think,' he'd said.

'Oh, OK,' she'd replied, turning quickly to smile at him. She didn't need to study his face; its features were printed on to the back of her eyes.

'Hope you have a good day,' he added, hesitating by the door.

She knew he was trying to remember what she was going to do today but that it wouldn't matter if he didn't. She would tell him about it later. They would be OK anyway.

'Thanks,' she called out happily to him as he closed the front door. Waiting in the quiet that followed, she heard him start the car, heard its distant purr and the sound of him reversing it out of the drive. She put the milk bottle on the draining board and dried her hands. She did not feel his absence because he was still everywhere.

Now, at the station, Fern considers what to do. She knows that her sons, whatever they are doing, do not think of her as she does of them and that this is as it should be. They don't seem to carry with them the same kind of inbuilt barometer she has grafted just under her skin; the thing that seems to allow her to sense how they are across the miles that now separate them. It's as though she has a slide show in her head which plays constantly: pictures of them running, the soundtrack of their laughter, the shapes they too make in her life. They wouldn't mind her saying hello to an old friend on her way to meet Jules; it wouldn't mean anything to them. It shouldn't mean anything to her either and it wouldn't matter to Jack. They all had enough together anyway; this would not threaten anything.

So, she unpauses her foot from its position hovering over the top of the escalator and swings around saying, 'I'm sorry,' as she dodges a cross-looking woman in a bright red coat who's bearing down on her. The woman's hair has been badly dyed a shade of stale copper that clashes with her coat and makes her look somewhat bilious.

Crossing the concourse towards where Elliott is standing, Fern feels a bit like an iron filing being pulled towards a magnet. She's curious, she admits, and in the face of this curiosity the certainties that underpin her life seem momentarily to wobble. This she hadn't expected.

It also seems as though the air is heavier than

normal here this morning. It is, she knows, always a little strange, as though someone purposely pipes in a supply of made-up air: recycled and grainy, falsely warm. Paddington is, to her, a halfway place. No one ever stays here; it's a destination or a starting point, a place for greetings, farewells and passing through. And now the new platforms have been unmasked, making it vast and much, much lighter, the station has even more of a temporary feel; everyone owns it and no one does. It is, Fern thinks, as she makes her way to the departure boards and Elliott, the perfect place for this moment; one she has to admit she's only very occasionally imagined in the tiny silent spaces that have sprung up in amongst the wonders of her life with Jack and the boys.

Elliott keeps shifting his feet and looking impatiently at the screens as if willing his platform to be announced, and Fern wonders if he has, in fact, seen her and is trying to get away quickly so he can avoid her. Perhaps he doesn't want to be reminded, however obliquely, of what passed between them; how once upon a time he had lain on her, she had wound her legs around him and he'd kissed the soft skin on her neck, made promises he didn't keep.

These are not good thoughts, she tells herself and notices instead that, from this distance at least, it seems that he hasn't changed much; he's still tall, still broad, and this she finds oddly comforting. His hair, peppered only a little with grey, has been swept back from his face with the same unselfconscious gesture he used as a young man and, for a second, as she risks looking away from him to the card displays outside Funky Pigeon, she wonders who it's been who has seen him do this during all the years between then and now and, unexpectedly, feels an absurd surge of jealousy course through her; an unwelcome sense of exasperation at all the unknowing that now separates them. She has no right to feel this, no right at all.

With about twenty paces to go, she catches a scent that, for some reason she can't explain, reminds her of Jack. It's a sweet, meaty smell, like closeness under the covers and the lingering odour of Tube trains that clings to his shirts as she sorts them for the wash. If she's going to stop, it should be now. Jack is, after all, a good man. Doesn't she owe it to him to leave the past alone?

She imagines their conversation over dinner that evening. 'Oh, by the way,' she'll say, 'guess who I saw at Paddington this morning?'

Looking across the table at her, he'll say easily, 'No idea. Who?'

'Oh, just an old friend from uni. Made me realise how long ago it all was!'

And she will laugh as she says this and take a sip of wine and the certainties would settle around her again and she would be safe.

With this image of Jack in her head, Fern hesitates, pretending to look for something in her handbag. Her breathing is stupidly heavy and she feels a prickle of sweat under the collar of her coat. Suddenly she wonders where the youth and beauty have gone. She is aware that a boy about her son's age with ragged hair and frayed, low-slung jeans is bounding by in front of her, a guitar slung effortlessly on his back, a glow of confidence and joy around him like a Ready Brek shield. Watching him go, she looks back in her bag, moves her purse, finds her lipstick, touches its smooth shiny case and then feels a hand on her arm. She looks up.

'My God, Fern?' It's Elliott. He's there. He is smiling at her.

'You!' is all Fern can say in reply, the lipstick still clasped in her fist.

'What are you doing here?' His smile is like a smile a parent might give to a child who has just got top marks in a maths test. This makes her angry for some reason. How dare he stand there, look at her that way!

'Just a day out. Meeting a friend.' She waves the lipstick in the direction of the Tube. 'I was –' she pauses, putting the lipstick in her pocket and wondering how to explain why she's heading in the wrong direction, away from the Tube – 'going over there.' She points to the Ladies' sign, hopes she's said it with enough bravura to appear as young and carefree as she likes to think she once was, and not the middle-aged woman with a family, mortgage and cat that she is now. Not that this should matter, though, it is who she is after all, isn't it? 'What about you? Where are you going?' she asks, instinctively looking up at the screens as if trying to divine which train he is planning on catching.

'On my way to Wales,' he says, not offering any further information, which Fern resents immediately, thinking that after all they once meant to one another and how much it has cost her to have made the journey across the station towards him, albeit one he doesn't yet know she made because of him, he owes her a fuller explanation than this.

'Oh, Wales.' He's going home then, back to visit his parents, back to the house where he'd taken her, where they'd made slow, quiet love in front of a damped-down coal fire after everyone had gone to bed and only the house's night-time clicks and stretches had kept them company. 'Where've you come from?' she asks, purposefully keeping her voice light, a little peal of self-conscious laughter on the rim of it.

'Hastings. I'm based there now.'

The way he says this makes it sound like a military posting, not a home, and she can't tell from his tone whether this 'base' means a family house, with a white gate, a sit-on lawnmower and a dog, probably a Labrador cross; or a bachelor pad in the city with frosted glass doors and thick cream rugs. The unwanted bubble of resentment in her chest grows larger.

'How are you? What's your news?' He asks these

questions like an interviewer would, and for a second she sees them on either side of a small coffee table, both in black leather chairs, him in a sharp grey suit and her in some floaty film-star number. In this picture he leans towards her conspiratorially, and she is Emma Thompson and he is Michael Parkinson and they know they are playing Let's pretend and that it doesn't matter.

But how can she really answer him? How can she summarise all the years, the weeks, the moments that are hovering between them now? Should she tell him that yesterday had been a caramel-soft spring day, that she'd bent slowly over the acers in her garden and seen their leaves unfurling like the tiny hands of newborn babies? Should she describe how Jack had touched her arm this morning before he left for work; how he'd smelled of toothpaste and how she'd watched him walk across the kitchen, his shirt tucked into his trousers, and she'd remembered how she'd smoothed it flat before ironing it last Sunday? And then, what about her sons? How can she describe the connection she has with them, how she drinks in the beauty of them, experiences sheer, sharp moments of panic that something dreadful might happen to them? No, she can't tell him any of this, so instead she says, 'I'm fine, thank you. Really well.'

'You look well,' he offers.

But she doesn't, not compared to before, when she was stretched out on their bed in Turkey, covered in nothing but a leather jacket and a tan. Now she feels smaller, fatter, with a neck that rightly belongs to her grandmother.

She makes a *harrrumph* noise, scrabbles her mind back to something tangible, something she can hold on to. She returns her lipstick from her pocket to her bag. Her hand feels strangely empty without it. 'Hastings?' she asks. 'How long have you lived there?'

The crowd around them ebbs and flows like in movies where the central characters remain frozen and the action around them is speeded up. To Fern it seems that the minutes are hurtling and crawling; both rushing and creeping towards a deadline she didn't know she would have to meet, a decision she wasn't expecting to have to make, certainly not today, maybe not ever.

'Look . . .' he says, not answering her question but checking his phone instead, picking it out of his pocket with a practised move. His hands still have the same sturdiness they had before and unbidden comes the memory of the time she'd tried to get a splinter out of his thumb and how he'd flinched like a child and then how he'd brushed his free hand across her nipples and how they'd put off getting the splinter out until after-wards. 'Look, would you have time for a coffee? It seems silly just standing here. If you're not in a rush, I mean,' he says.

She has, she realises, blushed at this memory.

Surely she has to be in a rush; it's the only way

to be, Fern thinks. Surely, these days, everyone has to be busy and occupied, each minute filled to the brim with satisfying things? This is how her life with Jack has been up till now. But not this morning. Today Fern has an extra half-hour, one she was going to spend reading her book on one of the benches in the alcoves on the Circle Line platform. She was going to watch the pigeons bob by and make up stories about the people waiting for their trains. She was going to catch her train to Victoria, where she would meet Jules and they would hug each other and settle into their seats and travel to Chiswick, the tops of their arms touching. Of course, she could have driven to Chiswick, but she and Jules were bound to drink wine later and it would be difficult to find some-where to park and this way she'd have more time with Jules. This is what she really wanted; their times together recently have been so slight and fleeting.

She answers Elliott, 'That would be nice. If you're sure *you* have time. What time's your train?'

'Oh, I can get the next one. I'm not on a strict timetable today.'

Again he doesn't give any details and for this Fern is now relieved. If he had it would seem like she would now know too much, have got too close, and this wouldn't be allowed, not now, not after everything. But as he says, 'Come on then, let's go over there, shall we?' and points to the Sloe Bar up the escalator next to WH Smith's, she wonders what would have happened in *Brief Encounter* if Trevor Howard had said, 'Darling, don't worry. I'll get the next train,' and that this one gesture, this small delay had given them time to change their minds. Would Celia still have gone back home and sat by the fire and finished the piece of sewing she'd been working on? Would Trevor have stayed in England? Would Celia have left her family for him eventually?

Fern and Elliott walk in silence and she remembers other walks, like their first around the lake on campus. How little they'd known then! And then that final time when they hadn't walked but she'd run out of the room and he'd followed, tried to talk to her, failed.

She hasn't thought about that day for years, but now realises that the pain of it, the weight of 'what if' has never really gone away. Maybe it's just been covered over, repaired almost but not quite. Underneath, it is still pink, healthy and gently stinging. This is a shock, an unwelcome shock, and Fern wishes hard that it would go away.

'Here we are,' Elliott says, standing back and letting her get on the escalator first. He steps on after her and she can feel the heat of his eyes on her back. She wishes she'd worn something else now; not this old thing, but something a little bohemian, arty. The instructions from the studio had said comfortable clothing, something she wouldn't mind getting splattered with clay, but they'd also said overalls would be provided, so she's wearing jeans, her purple jumper, sensible – if rather tight – boots. At least she'd done her hair and make-up and, in a concession to the fact that she and Jules were going to Chiswick she'd put on some jewellery, but not a ring on her wedding finger of course, she rarely wears one there these days; she doesn't seem to need to; Jack's like her own fingerprint now, bedded so deep down as to be immovable.

They find a table on the mezzanine level; Elliott sits facing the back of the station, she's facing the front. At the table next to them is a man tapping at the keys on his laptop. Fern is curious about what he's writing, wishes he would look up, smile and say, 'Hey, come and read this; would love to know your thoughts.' But he doesn't, and all she sees is the top of his head, the ceiling lights bouncing off his bald patch. She looks across at Elliott and smiles, or at least she thinks she does, she's not quite sure whether she has any real control over her facial muscles at all. What is she doing here? How has the course of this day changed so much, so quickly?

'Right,' he says, 'what would you like?' He picks up the menu and scrutinises it.

'A latte, please,' Fern says, rummaging in her bag to pick out her phone. 'Look, do you mind if I just text someone? It's fine, really. I'm fine for time. Just want to let them know, that's all.'

Why did she say *'them'*, not *'her'*? Was it an instinctive thing, self-defence maybe? Maybe it was because it's Jules; would she have said anything different if it had been anyone other than her? Or maybe it's because the greater part of her still wants to stay mysterious and detached, while only a small bit of her wants to put her hand on his, say, 'Look, let's just stop this, shall we? Let's stop pretending we're polite strangers who've bumped into one another by chance at Paddington Station on a Tuesday in March and just pick up where we left off? You see, Elliott, if I'm honest, and although I didn't realise it until just now, I'm still bloody furious with you, and actually always have been.'

But of course she doesn't say any of this; she just says, 'It's fine, really. I'm fine for time. Just want to let them know, that's all,' and he replies, 'Sure, go ahead,' as he waves to a waiter who arrives at their table with an accomplished slide.

'An Americano and a latte, please,' Elliott says, pointing a finger at the writing on the menu.

In a host of unchanged things about him, his voice is the least altered. If she closes her eyes, she could be back to when it all started. 'Yeeees,' the waiter replies. 'Any cakes or pastrieees?' He's obviously from eastern Europe and his accent is deep and guttural; it makes the skin on the back of Fern's neck tingle.

Elliott raises a quizzical eyebrow across the table at her and smiles and her heart does a strange bellyflop – she'd always found this particular gesture of his breathtaking. Is that the right word? It sounds a bit of a cliché to her, but how else to

14

describe that sharp, blade-like feeling that stops her breath when she sees the corners of his eyes crinkle again, the slow burn of his smile? It is a look she treasured once, felt a kind of ownership of. She shakes her head. She couldn't eat anything, doubts she will ever want to eat anything ever again.

Her phone buzzes. Her text to Jules has been sent. 'Might be a tad late,' it had said, 'but c u at Victoria as arranged.' Fern now has about fifteen minutes before she should go. The waiter glides away.

'Do you know when your next train is?' she asks, toying with a sachet of sugar, tapping it against the palm of her hand so that all the sugar falls to one end in a hard lump.

'I think there's another one at nine thirty. I've got an open ticket, so it doesn't matter.'

'How long are you going for?'

'Not sure. Maybe I'll come back tonight, maybe tomorrow morning.'

'How are your parents?' she asks. To her they are round, busy people with soft lilting voices and kind hearts. They were the first people Fern had ever met who convinced her that love had a chance of lasting. She'd always been too close to her own parents to be able to gauge their relationship properly, but Elliott's parents, yes, they had been light, laughing people and she'd envied him them.

'Mum died about five years ago,' he replies, looking down at his hands as he says this.

'Oh my God, I'm so sorry,' she says, the words totally inadequate. There is a pause. The waiter comes with their coffees. He puts them on the table. Elliott picks up his spoon, taps the side of the cup.

'Heart disease.' He whispers the words. 'She kept it from us for ages. Until it was too late really. Not sure –' he winces – 'I can ever really forgive her for it.'

Fern has no idea what to say. 'Your dad,' she ventures, 'is he still . . .?'

'He's not so good actually. That's why I'm going down there today. He's in a home now; there are some things I need to sort out at the house. It's going to be a bit crap, I imagine.' He laughs a small humourless laugh as he says this.

'Could no one else go with you? To help, I mean? What about your brother?' Fern leaves a gap, wants to say, 'Your wife?' but doesn't. Instead she says, 'What about family?'

'Dan's in the States at the moment. He's got a contract with NBC. Not really something he can leave. I understand that, I don't mind, really.'

Again he doesn't mention the presence (or not) of a wife, of children, but their absence is a solid thing; it sits on the table between them, rests its elbows on the rim of their saucers, smiles a little mockingly up at Fern. She wishes she could brush it away. She has no need of it.

'Anyway,' Elliott raises himself up, his shoulders filling out his dark green jacket. He stretches his legs. He too is wearing jeans, but his look more like a second skin than hers feel, the hem of the right leg is frayed slightly. Ah, so, she remembers, his left leg is still slightly longer than his right. 'Anyway,' he says again, 'enough about me. What about you? What are your plans today? What's been happening to you? You still married?'

Still? How does he know she got married? She looks up at him, feels a bolt of impatience burst out from under her ribs. Oh, she thinks, let's just get this over with, shall we? 'Yes,' she says, 'still married. How did you know?'

'Dan told me. Piers told him, I think. They're still friends, you see. Dan told me you'd got married. It was years ago, right? His name's . . . Jack, isn't it? I never knew your new surname though. Dan didn't tell me that.'

Yes, his name is Jack. He is Jack. He is her husband and he is a good man. She nods. 'Yes,' she says, 'Jack. We live in Reading. He runs his own business managing large construction projects, mostly in London but elsewhere too. We have two sons; they're both living away from home at the moment. They're at uni, you see. We also have a cat!' She laughs out loud when she says this, thinking, Ha! You know everything now; wonders if he sees the irony in what she's just said, whether he remembers. She picks up her coffee with two hands, not trusting herself to use just one, and takes a sip. It is warm and smooth; it makes her feel like sleeping. She is, she realises suddenly, very, very tired.

As she drinks she wonders if Elliott ever Googled her or searched for her on Facebook. She's never looked for him but, sitting here now, isn't sure whether that's because she had no need to or because she'd been too afraid of what she might find.

And she feels watched, not only now by his grey-green eyes, but always. It's like she's carried a camera around with her all these years and this camera's beamed back pictures to him, showing him her thoughts, her deeds. She shivers.

His mobile rings. He presses a button. 'Yes?' His voice is soft, conspiratorial. Fern can hear that it's a woman at the other end; she can't catch the words but it's a light tinny sound; young and breathless. 'Uh-huh, yes, OK,' Elliott peppers answers into the stream of words coming from the other end of the line. He raises his eyes to Fern's and shrugs apologetically. Finally, he says, 'I'll call you from the train. When I've had a chance to think about my plans. Is that OK? . . . Right, well, OK. Yes. Goodbye then, love . . . Yes, speak later.'

He puts the phone down on the table. Fern catches sight of the time. Five minutes to go.

'My daughter,' Elliott says. 'She lives a very complicated life. Everything has to happen now, right this minute. You know the type?' He laughs self-consciously and brushes his hair back from his face. He doesn't tell her anything else: not his daughter's name, nor her mother's, whether he's married, to whom. If he is, he's not wearing a ring;

18

she seems to have noticed this earlier when he was on the other side of the station from her. She's not sure how this could be.

But, yes, she does know what he means. Her sons, when they're home, fill the house with their large feet and even larger priorities, but there's so much about them she doesn't know; their friendships happen via Facebook and text, not by people ringing the house phone or calling by on their bicycles any more. All she gets are rare insights from them, the occasional hug, and, when they're not looking at her, she studies the contours of their faces for clues, her mind like fingers exploring them as though they are maps, tracing any shadows of doubt and worry and trying to remember what they'd been like when they were small.

She smiles at Elliott. 'Yes,' she says. 'I know.' She pauses; her coffee cup is empty, so is his. 'Look,' she says, 'I guess I'd better go, and you've got your train to catch. It's been lovely to see you, really lovely.' She stands, pushing back her chair. He stands too, coughs, searches in his pockets for change and leaves some in the silver dish with the bill which had appeared without them noticing. Perhaps, Fern thinks, it was when he was taking the call. They'd both been too wrapped up in the same moment then, oblivious obviously.

'It has,' he says, 'been really lovely, and you look . . . well . . . you look so well. I'm pleased.'

This last comment makes her angry again. How dare he! How dare he sit in judgement on her, give her a virtual pat on the back for surviving so well without him! *However has she done it?* she wonders caustically. Against all the odds she's managed to live a reasonable life, a successful life, after he left her at that street corner and turned back, after he decided not to stay and fight to keep her. It's bloody marvellous, she thinks. I've obviously surprised him!

All she says though is, 'Thank you,' and the air is heavy with what's left unsaid; the sounds from the bar are muffled, someone is announcing that the nine twenty-eight will depart from Platform 3, but their voice is soupy, far away.

'Can we . . . can I . . .?' he says. She senses he's struggling to find the right words. 'Can we keep in touch? You know, now we've met up again. It would be such a shame not to, don't you think?'

She's been dreading this. *Yes!* she wants to shout. Yes, of course we must. But, buried deep at the base of her skull something is tugging: doubt, guilt, the word 'wrong'. Wouldn't it be better to let it lie? Keep today as what it should be, just a tiny oasis, a frozen moment, how he'd decided it should be when he left her when they were young. She has no need of him now; she has so much else instead.

'If you give me your number,' he's saying, 'I'll text you later, maybe. See what you're doing this evening or something. Maybe if I come back tonight, we could meet for a drink, finish catching up properly. There's still so much I don't know, about you, you know, about what you've been doing all this time.'

This is so like the first time, when he'd asked her out; a concert at the students' union it was. The tone of his voice is exactly the same; it's just his face is so much older – far wiser, she would hope.

'Oh, OK,' she says, not sure if it is OK at all, and she fishes a pen out of her bag, plucks a serviette out of the dispenser on the table and quickly scrawls her number down. She thinks of wrong-numbering him, like they tell you to do in she's-just-not-that-into-you-type movies, but doesn't. She's still curious about him, still wants to try to make him understand. Understand what, she's not sure, just understand some of what it's been like, this life she's lived without him in it. She guesses she also wants, eventually, to be able to sit in judgement on him, give *him* marks out of ten for the life he's lived without her in it. She shouldn't want to do either of these things but it's like being on a roller coaster; now she's on, she has no idea how to get off.

'Thanks,' he says, folding the serviette and putting it in his pocket.

She readies herself to walk away, can feel the forward momentum of her body, sense the distance already getting larger between them. She can see herself meeting Jules, him getting on his train to Wales, knows this episode is almost over, fears what might come next.

He leans across the table and kisses her lightly on the cheek. 'It's been lovely to see you,' he says. 'Really lovely. I'll text you later, OK?'

There is no right answer to this question. Fern hooks her bag over her shoulder, turns and walks away from him. Her face, where he kissed her, is singing quietly. She resists the urge to touch it, doesn't look back.

CHAPTER 2

November 1986. 'Hey,' Fern said, skipping down the stairs as Jules was walking back into the kitchen.

'Hey yourself,' Jules replied, looking back over her shoulder, her hair a tumble of curls. 'You had a drink yet?'

'Nah, not yet.' Fern had to raise her voice above the sweep and beat of A-ha.

Earlier, Fern had stood in her bedroom gazing at the clothes hanging in her wardrobe. She had half an hour before the first people were due to arrive. The house was as ready as it ever could be; the table in the kitchen was piled high with plastic cups, various bottles of spirits and cheap wine, and Jules had scattered bowls of crisps around the lounge. The music was already pumping.

Fern had run her fingers through her dyed cropped hair, picked out a lacy white blouse and a long velvet skirt in a kind of maroon colour and tugged on her DMs. For some reason she couldn't explain, her skin was singing.

She'd been aware of the pulse of discontent, from the rooms of the other two girls she and Jules shared with. They'd told them about the party but, for some bizarre reason, they'd preferred to stay in than go out. Maybe they'd join them later. Fern kind of hoped they would but would be equally relieved if they didn't.

The sweet fug of cannabis smoke was already sifting through the air of the house. Jules's brother, Piers, was sitting on the sofa. He'd been staying for a few days and had brought all sorts of things with him that Fern had never seen before. 'Whatcha,' she said to him as she stepped over his large feet.

He mumbled a reply, flicking ash from his joint into an empty lager can balancing on the armrest of the sofa. The ash fizzed as it hit the dregs of liquid at the bottom.

'Oh,' he said, as Fern reached the door to the kitchen, 'I've invited a mate I met in Hackney to come along; his name's Dan. OK? I think he's got a brother studying here or something.'

'Sure,' Fern said, not knowing what else to say. Jules's brother had always been an enigma to her; he seemed unpredictable – exciting, but dangerous. He shifted in his seat and in the pause between tracks the leather of his jacket creaked.

People arrived in a steady stream and soon the house was full of denim and heat and there was laughter and the thump of music. Fern found herself in the hallway at one point, a glass of warm white wine in her hand, her head reeling and that strange singing of her skin dulled to a steady hum.

24

She was talking to someone but couldn't really hear properly and then this person must have said, 'Hey, I fancy another drink. You coming?' and she followed whoever it was into the kitchen.

At the moment she crossed the threshold she heard someone in the room say something about New Order and another voice answered and then the voices faded as she looked over to the window and the music started up again from the lounge.

It was dark outside and the condensation streaming down the glass made her think of the Santa's grottoes she'd visited when she'd been small. Swaying slightly, she reached out to hold on to the door frame; she must have drunk more than she'd realised. The movement of her arm, the tiny silence after the New Order discussion, the slither of a pause between tracks must have all happened at the same time, and a boy leaning against the fridge – a boy with grey-green eyes and brown hair, which he was sweeping off his forehead in a seamless gesture with the hand not holding a pint glass – must have chosen that moment to look across the room at her. He smiled and she smiled back.

It was like being drawn in on a piece of elastic, Fern thought as her feet took her across the kitchen. The floor was sticky with spilt drink and she could hear Jules laughing, see her shake out her hair, and then she was standing in front of the boy with the grey-green eyes and he said, 'Hi, I'm Elliott,' and she said, 'Fern, my name's Fern.'

'I'm Dan's brother,' he added, his voice like warm water, 'Economics, second year.' And then he laughed and his face lit up and something in her snapped, her skin began to sing again, more loudly this time, insistently. She had no idea what was happening. She'd never felt anything like this before. Then, 'Hey,' he said, 'do you fancy going somewhere a bit quieter?'

She must have nodded because the next thing she knew she was following him upstairs, driven by instinct and a need she didn't recognise. She was running on empty. At one point he reached back and took her hand; the touch of him was like electricity. She stumbled and he said, 'You OK?' She nodded.

They were in her room; her bed was piled high with coats. Outside she could hear the faint sound of a siren and the pound of the music from downstairs. It was dark and the coats on the bed looked like some sort of slumbering giant. He closed the door and walked over to stand behind her. Then she felt his fingers moving her earring aside and his lips brushing against the skin just under her ear. She shivered.

'Do you want this?' he asked, moving to stand in front of her. Still he didn't hold her, didn't rest his hands on her.

It felt like she'd travelled a thousand miles, had known this boy for a hundred years. 'Yes,' she managed to say and she leant forward until her head was on his chest. It was broad and warm and he smelled faintly of washing powder and cigarette smoke.

He tipped up her head and kissed her mouth. Then with both hands he cupped her breasts and rubbed his thumbs over her nipples; her stomach tightened. 'Fuck me,' she whispered. She had no idea where the words had come from, or really what they meant. She'd had sex before, in her first year; cautious, unsatisfactory sex with a medical student, had started taking the Pill then, hadn't stopped, but had the feeling that what she'd got herself into now was going to be something completely different. The need was primal, it started between her legs and her brain was filled with heat and the colour white.

'Thought you'd never ask!' he said, laughing a little.

And so he guided her to the bed, lay on her, moved over her, down her, lifted up her skirt and pushed her knickers aside with his tongue and then he circled her and it rose in her like the sea. It was hungry and salty and was huge until it crashed and she pulsed, gasping into the darkness, her hands in his hair.

He shifted up and she pulled him into her. 'Do we need anything?' he asked, kissing her neck.

'No, I have it covered,' she said, and he came in her, his hands pushing against the pile of coats, and when he came there was a noise at the back of his throat of capture and release; something halfway between joy and despair.

They didn't talk much afterwards but dressed quietly and slowly, glancing up at one another and the room stayed dark and the music must have kept on playing and there was the sound of voices and her heart was lit up like it was full of fireworks; it was beating so loudly that at times it was all she could hear.

Later, downstairs, he got her a drink, stood in the lounge by the window with his hand resting on her waist and she had fitted up against him and felt she had arrived someplace she hadn't known she'd needed to visit, but that now she was there, it was the only place on earth she could ever be. People had come and gone and some had talked to them and some hadn't, and Fern couldn't see Jules or Dan or Jules's brother anywhere. Maybe they're outside, she thought, and imagined their breaths clouding the cold November air, imagined them looking up at the stars.

'Can I see you again?' Elliott asked as the last of the guests began to drift away and all that was left was dim light, empty bottles and two people dancing to an imaginary soundtrack in the lounge. 'There's a thing on at the union tomorrow night. Fancy coming?'

'Yes,' she said. 'I'll meet you there. OK?'

He nodded, kissed her on the mouth, his tongue skirting her teeth and with one hand on her shoulder, and later she slept in her clothes because they smelled of him and she remembered his mouth on her and she wanted it all again, a hundred thousand times, she wanted it again.

The next night she went to the union, climbed the stone steps up to the front door, paid her money to go in, searched the bar for him. She didn't let herself think he might not be there and then she saw him, sitting by a table under a window. The seat on the bench next to him was empty.

'Hi,' she said, standing in front of him.

'Hi, yourself,' he replied, smiling at her, and seeing him smile again was like lightning, her heart leapt; it was just how she had imagined it to be, just how she needed it to be.

Later, he walked her home and the night was clear and cold. The banks of the lake were speckled with frost and the air clung to their faces; it felt like leather on her skin. The water was ink black and still. It looked ancient, mystical.

This, she thought, as they crossed the bridge to take the short cut up to Abbey Road and the house she shared with Jules, is it. This is the moment around which all other moments will orbit. I will never have this moment again. And she believed it, but when he said, 'Penny for them,' she replied, 'Oh, I wasn't really thinking about anything.'

'Go on, you must have been. You looked miles away.'

'Oh, OK, I was just wondering.'

'Wondering what?' He stopped her and looked down at her face, then pushed her gently against the cold railings of the bridge and pressed his legs against hers; she could feel the warmth of his body, his breath on her neck.

'If it gets any better than this,' she said quietly.

'Oh, I'm sure it will! I promise you it will!' He laughed then and kissed her. 'Come on, it's late. I'd better get you home.'

Linking arms, they walked on in silence and during this silence she let herself start believing in him and the promise he'd just made her. There was a whole life of her and him to live through. There'd been the chance meeting at a party, the hook of his eyes and his smile, the sex they'd had in the dark of her room and now, this evening, there was the sureness of him and this walk in the cold of a November night, these steps she was taking with him, because of him. This was perfect, but there would be other perfect moments. She believed this with every atom in her body as she put her key in her front door and he said, 'I'll see you tomorrow, OK?'

'OK,' she replied, pleased she would have the night alone to remember him and to imagine all the nights she would know him, the never-ending line of them.

'My God, girl,' Jules said when Fern walked into the lounge, stepping over a couple of stray cans which hadn't been cleared up yet, 'you look like you've seen a ghost.'

'Nah,' said Fern, 'not a ghost, but I've seen something; something I think is going to be good.'

'You do talk mush,' Jules said. She was sitting

on the sofa. Her legs curled under her. 'Total mush, but I love you for it!'

That night Fern dreamed of the smell of grass and could see seagulls soaring high above her. She was seven and on the dunes, with her parents somewhere nearby. The world tasted of lemon and she was wearing blue shorts and was running was with the wind in her hair.

Next there were horses, vast stamping creatures with coats the colour of conkers. They were galloping and she was flying above them, her wings beating to the rhythm of their hooves. She could see the rise and fall of their heads and their tails streaming out behind them. More than anything she wanted to land on one's back and and grasp it around the neck, feel its heat on her skin, hold the thick hair of its mane in her fingers and ride it out to where the land meets the sky.

Then she was lying next to Elliott. She could sense him rather than see him. He was a presence and a shape. There was his heart beating and she could feel his hands on her. He was everywhere and he was nowhere and she wanted to cry out, but when she opened her mouth no sounds came.

Her alarm clock woke her and she stretched out in bed, tried to recall her dreams, briefly touched herself where he had touched her two nights before, wanted suddenly and urgently to have done it all; to have lived her life with him, be in her forties and to have it all sorted, to know that there were going to be moments better than that one by the lake. She wanted, more than anything, right there, right then, on that morning when the frost was hard and sharp and deep, to be sure of this.

CHAPTER 3

Of course Elliott had seen her. His eyes had been radars for years. Not consciously maybe, but somewhere deep down he'd half expected, half hoped to catch sight of her again, have at least some of his 'What if' questions answered. And now, after the years he'd resolutely refused to ask Dan for her married name or search for her on the Internet, there she was walking across Paddington Station, exactly how he'd imagined her to be.

But he'd hesitated a second too long. As soon as she came through the barriers, he should have set off, aiming to meet her halfway. He could imagine tapping her on the shoulder, saying 'Fern?', his voice gentle, kind, so very sorry, and she would have turned around and smiled, her chocolate-coloured eyes fixed steadfastly on him, and said, 'Elliott! How wonderful to see you!' and he would know that he was, in some ways at least, forgiven, that the pain he'd caused her didn't hurt any more.

But this didn't happen. She walked, concentrating on her feet, not glancing round, unaware of the bustle of the morning, and then as she reached out to hold on to the escalator and raised her foot, a woman in a red coat just behind her obscured his view of her.

At the same time, however, Elliott was also aware of the man running across the concourse, his stride lopsided, his briefcase swinging out, banging back in against his leg. He noticed the girl in the milk-maid's costume with her tray of freebies, from that distance he wasn't sure what they were, and he saw the two of them converging, heard the crash of the tray on the ground, the man shout, 'Oh!' and then saw Fern stop, pause, her foot in mid-air, saw her turn and look straight at the man, the girl, and him. He willed himself not to lower his eyes. She turned and started to walk towards him. He scrutinised the departure board, had no idea what to do.

Outside the card shop she stopped, rummaged in her bag for something, and while her head was bowed, he started walking. It was, he thought, like travelling down a kaleidoscope; multicoloured fragments of the past bumping up against him, until at last he was standing in front of her, saying 'Fern?' and she was looking up at him.

Then there was the stilted conversation, nothing like how it is in the movies. There was no music, no camerawork making them look other than they were: two middle-aged people in a crowd on a Tuesday morning, searching for the right things to say. And then there was the coffee, him having to dig deep into the memories of first-date disasters and recalling the awful, pained conversations he'd had with Meryl over recent years and working out how he could survive this occasion intact, not give too much away. And finally, the call from Chloe; again he had to make sure he said the right things, doubts now that he did.

When Fern leaves the Sloe Bar, she doesn't look back. He sees her disappear, her body so familiar, yet so strange. He sees her jeans, low heels, her bag slung over her shoulder. He sees all of it fade, be swallowed by the Underground, and he feels an intense, sharp stab of disappointment; not at her, but at himself. He should have, could have, done so much better. And now he's sitting on the train, at a forward-facing table seat, opposite a woman who looks like his mother used to look. She's doing a wordsearch puzzle and looks very content. He wants to lean over and say, 'Hello. My name's Elliott. Will you keep me company, talk to me?' But he doesn't, naturally. She's probably getting off at Reading anyway, he tells himself.

The train manager makes his announcements about the destinations they'll be calling at, that the safety cards are available in Braille format, that he'll be progressing through the train so Elliott should please retain his ticket for inspection, and Elliott is proud that he hasn't thought of Fern, not directly, for quite a few minutes. He takes out his BlackBerry, ignores the star next to the email icon which means he's got unread messages to deal with and calls his daughter's number. She answers after eight rings but this isn't unusual; he's spent quite a bit of time recently waiting for Chloe to answer him, both directly on the phone or by email, but also indirectly. Since he left her mother, he's been trying to connect with his daughter on quite a number of levels.

'Hey,' she answers.

'Hey, yourself – calling back as promised.'

'Yeah, cool,' she says. 'Where are you? Why couldn't you talk earlier?'

He doesn't know what to say. How can he explain? Her voice is somewhat strident, a bit like an angry bee. 'It was just very noisy where I was, so I thought I'd wait until I was on the train. Anyway, what exactly do you need me to do? What's wrong with it?'

With Chloe, the call could have been about anything from deciding to leave university to needing money for a music-festival ticket to asking if he can pick her up at the weekend and take her and some friends to a party in London. Recently he's had all these and more and, if he's honest with himself, as much as he loves her, he's grown a little weary of this constant emotional power play from her, of being battered by her. Perhaps he'd been naive to think that when she'd gone to Bath Spa to study photography, she'd suddenly transform into some sophisticated, capable woman; not the flaky, changeable girl he's always known.

But when he'd been having coffee with Fern,

trying to stop the world he'd lived in since he lost her from spinning totally out of control, he'd promised his daughter that he would think about this latest request. Her laptop's not working – can he get it repaired? 'How?' he wants to say. 'Shall I use my magic wand to unfurl my wings and fly over to where you are, pick it up, fold it carefully into a sack made from the softest goat skin, which I shall hook around my neck, swoop over fields, in between the pylon wires, until I land softly in the car park of PC World where I shall wait patiently, my wings folded back in, while they repair it with their own spells and incantations and then return it to you while you sleep?' No! He wants to shout, 'Just get it sorted yourself. Get a friend to go with you, stand in line, pay with the credit card I've given you, promise to pay me back when you get a job. Be hard, businesslike, driven. Be all the things I had to be at your age.'

He doesn't say any of this, naturally. Instead he listens as she regales him with a list of its faults, how doesn't start up properly and how, if and when it does, its connection to the Internet is rubbish and that she can't possibly be expected to work on it.

'Have you backed everything up?' he asks.

'Duh,' she replies. 'I'm not stupid,' and the way she says this makes it sound like 'stooopid'. 'Of course I have, what d'ya take me for, Dad? Everything's on the uni system anyway, all my pictures, my coursework, you know.'

Well, that's a relief, he thinks. 'Sounds like it just needs a clean-up, perhaps Windows has got itself in a knot,' he says. 'Can you take it to PC World yourself, or maybe there's a place near the uni that other students use?' He's clutching at straws and he knows it. She wants him to fix it, no one else. It is part of his duty and his responsibility, part of the enormous task he needs to perform to make up for the fact that he's left her mother and moved out of their family home into a small flat above his office near the Priory Meadow Shopping Centre.

What Chloe doesn't know, of course, is that as well as the whole Meryl thing, every day he goes down to his desk, he tries to match an overwhelming number of candidates to an alarmingly shrinking number of jobs, bears the bemused and pitying looks of his staff *and* is dealing with the Susan issue the best way he can.

'Dad,' Chloe says, her tone wheedling now, 'you said you'd help. Please, I just need you to sort it.'

She could be five, wanting the stabilisers off her bicycle, or Barbie's leg reattaching, or her forehead soothing after a nightmare.

'Can it wait until the weekend?' he parries instead. 'I'm heading off to Wales today. You know, I told you. I have to visit the old house, see Grandpa.'

'Why can't you stop off on your way back, pick it up?'

In reply he shifts in his seat, looks out of the

window, sees Middlesex Hospital rise out of the ground all square and blue, and then it's gone. His daughter obviously has no idea of his priorities, of how much he's dreading today, how he wants to do what he has to do and leave: one mission, one journey. It's the only way to protect himself, he thinks. Fern's number, written on a serviette, is burning a hole in his pocket. He should be ashamed, but he wants to stay a free agent, to have the chance of meeting up with her again this evening to find out more, tell her more. This has nothing to do with Chloe or her mother and, although he can't help it and probably shouldn't, he feels a certain resentment towards both of them for getting in the way and, to his surprise, isn't sorry about this at all.

Instead he says, 'I'll be too late, love. I've got to get back to Hastings tonight. Busy day tomorrow. Meetings, you know. I'll come over at the weekend. We can get it repaired together; have lunch – would that be OK?'

She lets out a small whine, like a spoilt dog. He feels a prickle of anger, breathes deeply. How come Chloe doesn't know how far Hastings is from Bath? They're opposite sides of the country, for fuck's sake. Surely his daughter should have some compassion. Has he failed so entirely with her?

He knows the woman opposite him is listening, can tell by the way she's cocked her head to one side, hasn't circled a word for a number of minutes. He wants to throw the phone over to her and say,

'Look, you deal with my daughter. You deal with all the guilt and what's happened and the fact that her mother seems to spend most of her time these days dissing me to her, cataloguing my failures. Chloe once loved me unconditionally, you know. She used to call me "Superdaddy".'

His offer of visiting at the weekend is a generous one and Chloe should accept it as such. Their negotiations have reached crisis point. At the other end of the line he can imagine the glint of the stud in her nose, the small butterfly tattoo on the inside of her left wrist. She's probably wearing black or purple, she normally does. And her hair will be a mess, spiky with dye and lack of sleep and, despite everything, he wants to fold her into his arms and hug her until she says, 'OK, Daddy, you're right. You were right to leave Mum. Your happiness is important. I love you. Thank you, yes, the weekend is fine. I'll look forward to seeing you. Thank you, Daddy, thank you.'

'Oh, OK,' is all she says. 'I guess so.'

He can sense her shrug, the slight turn of her head. She has already finished with him. Perhaps she's seen somebody she knows across the campus, or someone's walked into the kitchen of the flat he's paying her bit of the rent for. He's being dismissed. He was set some kind of test and although he thinks he's passed it according to his own shaky set of rules, he has the sinking feeling that he's failed her somehow, that whatever he did right now wouldn't be good enough.

'I'll call towards the end of the week then,' he says, 'and we can make a plan for Saturday. Just make sure you keep backing stuff up, and use the library or photography-department computers if you have to. If you need more money, just say, won't you?'

As if money can help. Hurt and tears soak through twenty-pounds notes as quickly as through tissue. Trying to patch up the wounds he's caused with money isn't the answer. He knows this, and so does Chloe. It helps, but it's not the answer. There is no real answer. He can't rewind time, make it all OK again.

She hardly says goodbye; it's more of a noise, just a faint breath of air and then she's gone and the screen on his phone is blank for a second before the screensaver with his company logo on it reappears. The star next to the email icon is still there. The time is now nine fifty-five.

The woman with the puzzle magazine gets off at Reading as he predicted. She shuffles across to the aisle seat, squeezes her ample frame out of the gap between the arm-rest and the table and raises her eyebrows at him, smiling a comforting smile. He's mid-way between wanting to shout something he shouldn't shout and rest his head against her chest and sob. But, in a swirl of sensible gabardine and tapestry bag, she's gone. He's aware of her progress down the carriage, of her climbing carefully down the steps, of her walking slowly past the window where he's

41

sitting. She doesn't look up at him and for this he's grateful.

The train chuggers on, swaying on the rails, making clickety-clack noises, and the conductor makes his announcements again. Elliott reaches into his pocket, lifts out the serviette, flattens it on the table and studies the numbers as though they are the key to some ancient code.

He's in a position of supreme power, he realises. He has Fern's number; she doesn't have his. But, he wonders, what if she's given him the wrong number, either purposefully or by accident? The balance of power shifts again. It's about twenty minutes until Swindon. It's too soon to text her, to test her.

His BlackBerry buzzes with yet more emails. He reads them, starts answering some. The countryside flashes by like a film reel: backs of houses, parcels of gardens, washing on washing lines, queues of cars at traffic lights, kebab and carpet shops, fields, sky; the world in miniature, the world sped up.

He's exhausted, tired to his bones, and it's been like this for a year or so, ever since a kind of weariness took up residence at the base of his neck, just under his voice box, and spread throughout his body. He brushes his hair away from his face; it falls back exactly as it was before. He puts his phone and the serviette back in his pocket, leans his head against the window and, after a while, dozes.

His dreams stutter. He is watching himself walk down the street. He's nine or so, wearing shorts, a green-and-white striped T-shirt. Dan is beside him carrying a stick. They're late for tea again. Dan isn't worried; he twirls the stick. To Elliott, it could be a sword or a band-master's baton, but to Dan it has magical powers. He's smaller than Elliott, less afraid. Maybe it's because he's always had Elliott to stand behind when faced with Dad's scoldings for being late, for worrying their mother, for making the tea spoil, or maybe it's because Dan still believes in magic.

Then there's the sound of the sea and there's sand, gritty between his toes. He's surrounded by a certain breathlessness and the cack-cack of seagulls. He can see his mother's yellow dress, the one with the small white flowers; she is laughing as the waves eddy around her legs. She's tucked the skirt up into the hem of her underwear and Elliott feels both embarrassed and afraid. He doesn't want his mother to be mortal, visible, to show the veins on her thighs to strangers. Dan is crouched low over a sandcastle; their father is asleep in a deckchair. If Elliott concentrates really hard, the world could be only the four of them.

Lastly, there's the house. Mum's downstairs in the kitchen, battling the pans. They clatter against each other like something which could pass for music, and smells of baking waft up the stairs. He's sitting cross-legged on his bed, a tin of keep-sakes in front of him: buttons, a strong red elastic band, a catapult, a box of matches. Next door's cat is basking in the sun on the path next to Dad's marigolds. It's late summer. The cat's sides are rising and falling gently. It licks its lips, its eyes tight shut. Its fur is getting hot.

Elliott wakes with a jolt. Feeling he might have dribbled, he hastily wipes his mouth with the back of his hand. It takes him a second or two to focus. The train's slowing. Must be Swindon. Reaching for his phone, his fingers touch the serviette again. Yes, he thinks. I'll text her now.

The message takes a long time to draft. The train leaves Swindon, heading for Bristol Parkway. People get on, including a couple with a baby boy. They are holding him as though he's made of china, as if they are the first people in the world ever to have had a child. There is something about them, Elliott thinks, something that reminds him of how he used to be. He remembers his call with Chloe, how it could have gone differently, what he expected from her after all the years he's loved her, how fundamentally disappointing his life seems to be.

Chloe could have said, 'Oh, Dad, poor you. What a horrid day you have in front of you. Is there anything I can do to make it better, easier for you?'

'No,' he would have said. 'It's OK. I'm OK, but it's nice to be asked.'

'Why aren't you driving?' she would have asked. 'Surely it would be easier.'

And he would confess to her something he has only half confessed to himself, that he's taking the train because he daren't take the car, daren't risk filling it to the rafters with gleanings from the house. If he'd still been with Meryl, it might have been different. He could have stored the stuff in the garage, but she's put an exclusion zone around the house, his house, so dense and tight and he has so little energy with which to beat it down, that he's decided it's easier just to leave it there to grow thicker and denser, like the forest around some kind of bizarre Sleeping Beauty's castle, one that contains no Beauty and one he stands in front of not as a prince, but as a pauper. Neither does he have the option of storing stuff in his flat or the office, however worthy the memorabilia, however sentimental. And Dan's in much the same position. He has a tiny loft apartment in Manhattan which costs a queen's ransom each month, and when they last spoke about Dad, Dan gave Elliott *carte blanche* to do what he needs to today. Elliott hates everything about this, even has the bizarre wish that Meryl was with him. She'd know what to do; she would take the emotion out of the occasion. In recent years she has reminded Elliott of a Dementor in *Harry Potter*; as if she too was sucking the life out of his hopes and dreams.

He laughs quietly to himself as he thinks this, and the couple with the baby look up at him, then look at one another in alarm, thinking maybe, Oh no, we've got the nutter on the train! He smiles at them and their baby, bends his head back down to the screen on his phone, continues to try to compose the text to Fern.

Eventually he sends it, 'Good to see you,' it says. 'Let's keep in touch! I'll text if I'm passing through London tonight and if you're free . . .' He detests the three dots as soon as he presses 'Send'. They make him seem seedy, the sort of man he was when he did what he did to her. He isn't that man any more; he's learnt the hard way that it doesn't pay. Now all that's left is her forgiveness. Is that why he wants to see her again, to seek redemption? If it is, he doesn't want to admit this to himself, not quite now, not at this precise moment. He needs time, a few hours perhaps to sort his thoughts, allow him to recalibrate his day, from the one he'd expected to have to this one, the one when he's seen Fern again, has texted her, has no idea yet whether she will reply.

The minutes and the miles tick on. He's turned his phone to silent because he's afraid to know if she hasn't replied, or even if she has. It's strange, but it's nice being in this state of limbo, on this train, on this day. He feels very much halfway through everything; his life, his relationship with his daughter, halfway through the end of his marriage and halfway through knowing Fern, both the girl he'd once known and the woman she could be to him from now on. Yes, of course she's married, he knows that, but she wasn't wearing a ring. He wonders whether this is significant, finds it frustrating that he doesn't know the answer.

The train reaches Bristol; the couple with the child get off and an elderly man wearing a hat gets on and sits where they were sitting. He has a military bearing, Elliott thinks; an old soldier, someone with battle experience. He's tempted to touch the old man on the arm and say, 'Tell me. Tell me what it was like for you. I want to learn, to know,' but he doesn't; he's too embarrassed. Instead he lets himself think about work and the meetings he's got lined up for the rest of the week and then there's this thing with Susan in the office. At times she reminds him of the secretary in *Love Actually* – he can't remember her name offhand, but the one who sets her sights at poor, bewildered Alan Rickman and whom he tries so gallantly not to hurt and stay faithful (in deed anyway) to his wife. Talk about a rock and a hard place, Elliott thinks. Susan has even taken to sitting with her legs a little bit open as if he needed help directing his cock in the right direction. He isn't tempted, of course he isn't. It would be a very foolish thing to do and there would be absolutely no way that they could both end up undamaged by it. But saying no, without actually saying no, is, he's growing to realise, very hard to do. It's just one more thing that's harder to do now he's no longer really married.

Oh no, here come thoughts of Meryl again, and for a second he sees her pinched, disappointed face, the crispness of her hair, her faultless body, which it takes most of her energy and his money to maintain, and wonders, not for the first time, how she can have turned out so differently from the girl he met that night, the girl he gave Fern up for, how significantly he too must have disappointed her.

Just before Newport he goes to the toilet and gets a coffee and a bacon roll from the buffet. The drink's tepid and weak, but it's sort of warm and the roll is welcome; it's been a long time since he left the flat and drove to the station. As well as bacon, he can taste Wales on the air; it's a sweet, downy taste and suddenly he seems to be able to breathe more easily, is reminded of the familiar space between the skyline and the hills. He's nearly home.

The train draws into Cardiff Central at eleven thirty. He tucks his litter into the bin at the end of the carriage, lets the old gentleman get off first. He tips his hat at Elliott and makes him feel like a schoolboy again, and then Elliott steps into the station and its swirls of travellers. He's tempted to look at his phone, but he doesn't. Maybe he'll check it in the cab. The engine pulls out, on its way to Port Talbot, Neath and Swansea. He watches it go with some sort of affection, as though they'd made friends with one another on the journey.

As he waits in line for a cab, it starts to rain. Pit-pat drops fall on the perspex shelter and people start running, opening umbrellas. It's a short-lived squally shower and a moment later the sun blasts out from behind the steel-grey edge of a cloud. Elliott is anxious to get going, is dreading it too. The cab door opens for him. It's his turn. He climbs in.

CHAPTER 4

January 1988: it had snowed and a white light glowed through the curtains. It was too early for cars or for the wheeze and hum of the house's central heating, and Elliott lay in bed listening to the silence. Fern had her back to him; he could feel the delicate ladder of her spine through her T-shirt as she pressed up against him.

He dozed as the dawn grew sharper outside the window. At about seven o'clock the heating came on and he crept out of bed and pulled back the curtains. The snow looked like icing, or cotton wool, or clouds; he couldn't quite decide which. There was a muffled quality to everything and, despite the cold, he felt unaccountably warm. Neither he nor Fern had lectures; they could stay in bed all day if they wanted while outside the world clicked into life, people cleared their paths and windscreens, kids pulled on their wellies and threw snowballs at one another on their way to school and he and Fern could stay here, just them.

Slipping back into bed, he pulled Fern closer to him. She murmured in her sleep. He loved looking at the tapering of her hairline and her slender neck, wondered, not for the first time, how it could hold the weight of her head.

'Morning,' she mumbled.

'Hi there, you. It's snowed.'

'Mmm, has it?'

'It looks like a Christmas cake outside.'

'Don't be such a girl!' she said, snuggling down into the pillow and laughing quietly to herself.

'You know I'm not,' he replied, cupping her hip with his hand. He was hard and she would know this; it was like this every morning. She moved a fraction closer to him. Gently he pulled up her T-shirt and slipped her knickers to one side. She moved again, centering herself for him, and he held on to her hips with both hands, sinking into her, drawing out, circling her. She moaned quietly, turning her head so his lips were on the soft skin under her ear and, gripping her tightly, he came. It was quick and pulsing. It was needful and wonderful. It was like every time; so private, so easy.

She reached out and grabbed a tissue from the box on her bedside table and wiped herself. Then he wound his fingers between her legs and, opening her up, felt her arch against him, then stiffen and release as she came too.

'Mmm, that was nice,' she said.

He wrapped his arms around her again.

They must have slept because the next thing he knew the light outside the window was different;

there were soft noises in the street: voices, the whoosh of tyres on snow, a dog barking.

'What time is it?' she asked.

He looked at his watch. 'Just gone ten.'

'I'll make some tea, shall I?' she said, throwing back the covers, and, standing up, hauled on a sweater and a pair of his socks which he'd left on the floor by the bed.

He didn't answer. There was no need. She would know, and not having to say things out loud told him that where he was and who he was when he was with her were the best possible place and best possible person he could be.

He heard her use the bathroom and then go downstairs. He got up to pee too and then when they were both back in bed, they drank their tea. It was hot and strong and sweet, just how he liked it.

'Ah,' he said, 'this is good. So, what shall we do today?'

'I've got *Paradise Lost* to read. I just fancy staying in all day, just staying here, doing nothing but reading. What about you?'

'Sounds good to me. I've got some reading to do too. Maybe we could go for a walk later. Chuck a few snowballs around.'

'Maybe,' she said, sipping her tea.

They were both quiet, could discern other small movements elsewhere in the house. Someone must have put the heating back on. He hoped they would be able to afford to pay the bill when it came.

'Penny for them then,' he said, after a pause.

'For what?'

'For your thoughts.'

'Oh, I was just wondering, you know, what's going to happen next. After this. What we're going to do with the rest of our lives.'

'Why should you think that, today of all days?' He didn't mind the question, wasn't annoyed, not yet, was just puzzled, that was all.

'Oh, I don't know. It's just an idle thought.'

'Well, I think I still want to go into politics,' he said. 'I know it'll be like an ant carrying an elephant uphill, but I want to give it a go. I still believe I can make a difference.'

'Aren't you being a little bit idealistic?' she asked, cradling her mug and blowing on the surface of her drink. The steam snaked upward towards her face.

'Probably, but then if there weren't idealists in the world, no one would dare to try anything.'

'Guess that's true. Still, I have a sneaking feeling that real life's going to get in the way of any utopian vision you might have of making impressive speeches, fighting your constituents' battles, stopping motorways from being built, etc., etc.'

'What do you mean by "real life"? Surely these things are the things that make up real life?'

'Maybe,' she said, obviously losing interest in the conversation and getting out of bed. She walked across the room and grabbed her bag from beside the desk. She rummaged it in for a moment and pulled out her copy of Milton.

He watched her as she did this, suddenly wanting more than anything to preserve this moment, set it in amber so that in their later life together he could excavate it, look at it and wonder at it. At that particular moment, he believed they would be together forever; could not foresee a time when they wouldn't be.

'What about you?' he asked her as she clambered back into bed, the book falling with a thump on her outstretched legs.

'What about me?'

'What do you want to do that'll make a difference?'

She looked at him and her eyes seemed almost black against the strange light in the room. A sense of unease settled on him. This wasn't really the sort of conversation he'd wanted to have with her today. Actually, thinking about it now, he wasn't sure he ever wanted to have this sort of discussion with her, with anyone. Wasn't it better just to let things happen, not over-think them? There'd be time for the serious stuff later, when he was older. Not now, not now. His chest tightened as she began to speak.

'What I want,' she said, 'is to be with you, live in a house with you, fill it with furniture and pictures and have children and weave a busy life for myself around them; a life of routine and listening to the radio and those quiet moments when I can take stock and realise that things are OK. I want,' she said, tipping her head to one side and looking at him, 'I want cars in the drive and holidays on the Isle of Wight and maybe even a cat!'

For a second Elliott was unsure. Was she being serious, or was she playing with him? Did she expect him to be able to reconcile his vision of the future with her own? Which of them was the more right and which of their versions of the future was most likely to come true? When he thought of his, it was of him sitting behind an impressive desk in Whitehall, of earning a reputation for fairness and worthiness, for putting the good of the public before himself. The way into this life was, he believed, by getting an understanding of business first, so he'd applied for a place on HP's management scheme; before he could go about making the world a better place, he needed to know how it worked. But despite the details, this was all still a concept and he was happy for it to be so. He didn't need it to be real, not yet, not now.

And, for the first time since he'd met her, the thought that Fern might not be the right person for him to be with flashed across his mind and shook him to his core. Suddenly the whole of his adulthood seemed to yawn open in front of him and all he could see was a maelstrom of lights and movement; there seemed no way in nor any way out. How he wished this conversation had never started.

'Elliott?' she said, opening the book and smoothing the pages. 'You OK?'

'Sure,' he replied.

But he wasn't, not really. He'd finished his tea, so put the mug down on the floor and lay down again, put his hands under his head and stared at the ceiling.

'Listen,' Fern said, reading from the book. She was sitting cross-legged now, he could see the swell of her breasts under the sweater, her hair was tousled. She was smiling as she read:

So much the rather thou Celestial Light
Shine inward, and the mind through all powers
Irradiate, there plant eyes, all mist from thence
Purge and disperse, that I may see and tell
Of things invisible to mortal sight.

'Well?' he asked. 'What does that mean?'

'Milton was blind when he wrote *Paradise Lost* – did you know that?'

'No, I didn't.'

'Well, he's talking about literal and metaphorical blindness, his own failed eyesight and the lack of divine wisdom.'

'And?'

'Well, I think it's saying that sometimes we don't have to be able to see things clearly to know whether they're right or wrong.'

She read on quietly to herself after that. He heard the flick of the pages as they turned and he lay there while the slow-motion world outside stayed wrapped in snow. There are no answers, he thought; just me and her, and here and now.

'We'll be OK, won't we?' he said.

Marking her page with a finger, she leant across and kissed him. 'Yes,' she said, 'we will. I know we will.'

But he wasn't sure; he wasn't sure at all.

For how could they know each other? You met every day; then not for six months, or years. It was unsatisfactory, they agreed, how little one knew people. But she said, sitting on the bus going up Shaftesbury Avenue, she felt herself everywhere; not 'here, here, here'; and she tapped the back of the seat; but everywhere. She waved her hand, going up Shaftesbury Avenue. She was all that. So that to know her, or any one, one must seek out the people who completed them; even the places.

Mrs Dalloway, Virginia Woolf

CHAPTER 5

So there's no sitting and reading on a bench on the platform in an archway of honey-coloured bricks with the pink and grey bobbing of pigeons for company. Instead Fern gets on the first train that pulls in, is lucky to get a seat and folds her hands on her lap to stop them from shaking. As she'd walked down the corridor to the Tube, she had been so tempted to look back to see if Elliott was following her. She wishes he had, is glad he didn't.

She wants to replay every second of their meeting in her head, but it's like the tape has got jammed. All she can see is a flickering image of them at the table, looking down at their cups. It is silent in the film. He's already slipping away from her, has probably already left on his train like Trevor Howard did, and she has the feeling that she will never hear from him again, never see him again. This is it, she thinks as the train pulls into Bayswater, where a solitary lady gets on with a dog tucked under her arm. The dog looks at Fern knowingly.

This is it, Fern thinks again. I've had my second

chance with him. After all this time, it came and went in less than a flash. If all the minutes she's lived, all the words she's spoken since he left her on that corner on a spring day very much like this one are counted and divided by the time she's just spent with him, the number of words they exchanged, the ratio will be minuscule, like a pebble on a beach. She's reminded of Mrs Dalloway, and her need to seek out the people and places that completed her. Now Fern knows that she may need this too.

She shifts in her seat, looks at her reflection in the dark glass of the window, tells herself not to be so stupid; she has the weight of today to carry, the expectations of her family, of Jules, to live up to. She has no room for Elliott or the past to come surging in and taking over; they have absolutely no right to do so.

But at High Street Kensington she's tempted to get off and go shopping. She wants to touch fabrics, lift handbags off shelves and run her hands over their clasps. She wants substance, things to hold, things to earth her. Her phone is burning through the pocket in her bag. Will he have texted so soon? Will he text at all? The lady with the dog gets off. The dog is panting; it gives Fern one backward glance as if to say, 'I know you. I know what you're thinking.'

They pass through Gloucester Road, South Kensington and Sloane Square before Fern is brave enough to think of Jules, of whether she will be able to hide what's just happened from the one person who knows, who knew her back then, who helped pick up the pieces after Elliott did what he did. Fern has no idea whether she will or won't, or whether she should even try. But then the train stops at Victoria and Fern is carried in a rush of people up, along, through. Someone bumps into her, a wheeled case yaps at her ankles, a foreign voice says something which is probably 'Sorry' and then she's out, out under the fretwork and columns of the concourse, so like Paddington, yet so different, and the tiles of the floor are shiny and cream and there are signs and adverts and there, there under the departure board, is Jules. She is smiling. She is waving.

'My God, woman,' Jules says, enveloping Fern in a hug, 'you look like you've seen a ghost!'

Fern mumbles something into the voluminous lime-green scarf wrapped around Jules's neck. She is released, breathes.

'You look fab, as ever!' Fern says in reply, and it's true. Jules is one of those women who never seem to age. She's what's commonly known as statuesque, all curves and height and depth. Her hair flames in auburn corkscrews that reach halfway down her back and that bounce as she walks. She has legs that are long and shapely and covered today in faded blue jeans, scuffed slightly at the hem, unselfconsciously tatty around the knees and over which she is wearing a long scarlet knitted tunic, the lime-green scarf and a necklace of huge wooden beads. On her feet are turquoise cowboy boots which cause Fern to sigh a little with envy at her friend's gall. Jules is, and always has been, like a brave, permanent rainbow.

Jules is also exquisitely happily married to Bernard, a small balding man fifteen years her senior who spent his working years doing something complicated at a trading desk in the City and who has now retired to play golf, learn to ride a horse called Seren and sail his boat around the coastline of Kent, a substantial amount of which he and his family have owned, still own. They don't have children; 'Never seemed the right time,' Jules said to her once when questioned yet again by Fern, and Fern has often wished Jules would be just a tad more honest, let Fern know the real reason, let Fern try and staunch the grief that floods out on the very rare occasions Jules drops her guard.

Today is not such a day, however. Today Jules says, 'And you, you still look like you've seen a ghost!'

But Fern doesn't tell her about Elliott. The words are scalding the back of her throat, sitting heavily at the base of her brain, but she can't let them out. Instead she says, 'Just a bit stressed, that's all. Thought I was going to be late.'

'Nah,' says Jules, tossing her mane of hair and grabbing Fern by the arm. 'Nah, it's cool. Come on, let's go.' She laughs happily, linking her arm through Fern's and they make their way down to the District Line.

64

This train is crowded and noisy; it is full of discarded copies of *Metro* and people pressed up against each other, clinging on to poles and shifting uncomfortably, reading on Kindles. Fern and Jules huddle up, Fern leaning against Jules, drawing comfort from the smell of firewood and horses that emanates from her. They don't try to speak.

At Earl's Court the crowd thins and they get seats, one at each end of the carriage, and Fern wonders if any of their travelling companions have guessed at the length of history connecting these two so different women on this March morning. Fern risks one look at her phone; there are no messages, but then, she tells herself, that's not surprising, she's on the Underground, any message he might have sent probably can't get through.

She and Jules smile at one another occasionally. Fern is suddenly hungry; the buzz from the coffee she drank when she was with Elliott is wearing off now, leaving a hollow feeling at the pit of her stomach. The thought that she would never be able to eat again has long gone. She looks ruefully at Jules, who nods and points at the door as if to say, 'Yeah, when we get off. Definitely cake before pottery!'

They get off at Turnham Green and bear right out of the station, leaving the flower stall and bridge behind them and, in the crouched shadow of St Michael & All Angels Church they go into a coffee shop on the corner of Bath Road. Fern's back is aching. She knows the tension is because she's been trying so hard not to say what's upper-most in her mind, and she's glad to sit down again, glad of the croissant and coffee, the bowl of sugar on the table, the art on the walls, glad to be with Jules. Her phone is still silent. It's ten fifteen.

'So,' Jules says, leaning her head on her hands and looking at Fern, her blue eyes shining. 'What's news? How's that gorgeous husband of yours, and those sons? How are *you*?'

'I'm fine, we're fine,' Fern says, tearing off a bit of croissant and popping it into her mouth, the icing sugar dusting her fingers. She is surprised by her answer and realises that just then, just as she says these words, her family *are* fine, that the plates are spinning exactly as they should. Even though she has seen Elliott this morning, there has been no seismic shift in her life; its certainties are still in place, and for this she is grateful, very grateful.

'Wilf's finding the second term easier than the first,' she says to Jules. 'He's made some friends; they're talking about getting a house together next year. And Ed's great, in his last term or so; still with Sookie – doesn't tell me much of course, and has no idea what to do afterwards! Has told me though that his dissertation's going to be on the representa-tion of discovery in mid-nineteenth-century literature – you know scientific and medical inventions, evolution, that sort of thing.' She rushes this last bit, is afraid to commit it to the air because then it seems real; her son is soon to graduate, move on to the next Monopoly round, pass 'Go', give up yet another two hundred pounds rather than collect it. It is a terrifying thought. Her boys are still both so young and vulnerable, so debt-ridden. Yes, they might have driving licences and bank accounts and sleep with girls, but they are her children; she remembers them dressed in shorts, with sunlight glinting in their hair; remembers the heat of their skin as they ran in from the back garden throughout a hundred different summer days.

'And Jack? How's he?'

Oh yes, Jack, Fern thinks. 'He's the same,' she answers, glad that he is so. She wants to tell Jules that he still rests his hand on her hip in the morning as he wakes, still clears his throat a little too loudly while driving, still has an odd taste in music, which he likes to listen to while he's sitting at his computer working, still seems to desire her. Yes, he's the same. Although, she thinks as takes another mouthful of pastry, there are hidden corners in him that she'll never know. The facts, oh, she knows them: his first shag, how he nearly set fire to a barn when playing with matches as a child, how he always spells his surname out on the phone; 'Cole,' he says, '*C, o, l, e*, like Lloyd Cole and the Commotions, not the fuel.' But there must be parts that he doesn't share, and she admits she's relieved by this. Loving him, loving the boys, looking after them, working in the shop, and doing all the other things she does is a full-time occupation; she doesn't have time, or the room, for Elliott, or even the thought of him, does she? But perhaps she keeps busy so she doesn't have to admit to the things that worry her. She works part-time, does her garden, pays the bills, talks to her mother, tries to keep track of her boys. She reads and goes out with friends to swap stories about their husbands and children, and she watches Jack come and go, irons his shirts, cooks his meals, kisses him goodbye when he leaves for work, kisses him goodnight, but sometimes what she wants more than anything is to rest her head against his chest and say, 'Hold me. Just tell me everything will be all right.'

So she keeps busy because she's afraid. For more than twenty years her real job has been to be mother, wife, daughter, friend, colleague and she's done it well, or so she hopes. The stage has been set and kept static, the scenery only changing with the seasons and the arrival and departure of bit-part players; the main action has been simple, circular. Now, though, she's unsure of her role, afraid of the next bit. Will she really know how to be all those things without the ballast of her sons, the anchor their day-to-day need of her brings to her life? Does she actually want to spend the rest of it all with Jack? Do they have enough of each other left to be successful at this or is there something else she should be, could be doing now? Should she be someone else now?

Meeting Elliott again has brought these unwelcome and unsettling thoughts more to the fore; it is as if his return has given her an option she wouldn't let herself imagine up to now and this can't be good, it really can't.

This life, the one she's led up to now, has been so different from the bright, professional one she once thought she'd have: a life of pacing through office corridors in wonderful shoes and elegant clothes, saying, 'Yes,' and, 'No,' and, 'By Monday, please,' to the people who worked for her. Had she always really wanted to be as she is now: homey, slender, ordinary, unfinished, and is being so just fine and how it should be? Could she really have lived any other life than this? Had what she'd said to Elliott that morning it snowed all those years ago always actually been her destiny?

'Jack got chatted up the other night,' she says now to Jules, wishing at once she hadn't.

'He must have liked that!' her friend replies.

'Of course he did! But I was there, and actually it was a bit uncomfortable. This waitress, well, she kept putting her hand on his arm when he was ordering. He got all puffed up, like he does, you know? I thought it was odd though, as if I was wearing an invisibility cloak or something!'

They laugh, but Fern remembers the surprising bolt of jealousy she'd felt at the time, how she'd wanted to say, 'Oi, hands off. He's mine!', how astonished she's been every night since that he's come home to her.

Her phone buzzes. She picks it out of her bag and glances at the screen; it's a text from a number she doesn't recognise. It could be anyone, she tells herself, putting the phone back in the bag. It might not be Elliott. She hopes after what she's just been thinking that it isn't. How could she ever reconcile feeling something for Elliott again, reconcile being tempted to look outside the reaches of the life she's living now, when she's so deep within the folds of her marriage? Her marriage has, it seems to her, as she finishes her coffee, says 'Guess we'd better go then' to Jules, grown about her like an outer skin. It is made of soft leather and held together with silk thread. It is both impermeable and flexible. It moves with her, because of her, and this is how it should be.

After paying – 'Your birthday, my treat' – she holds open the door for Jules, says, 'I'm looking forward to today, aren't you?' and follows her friend out, adding, 'On the way, you must tell me your news. I feel like I've taken all the limelight so far.'

'Not much to tell,' Jules says, smiling. 'Same old, same old: Bernard, Piers, the horse, the boat, Bernard's mother.' She laughs loudly. 'Actually,' she says, '"Boat" would be a good name for his mother!'

They walk to the High Road and turn left, glancing in the shop windows as they pass. A bus stops at a set of traffic lights, humming diesel fumes at them. An advert for the latest Bradley

70

Cooper film is emblazoned on its side and he grins down at them, the gun in his hand lit up like a firework.

'Did you ever see *Limitless*?' she asks Jules.

'Don't be silly,' Jules replies.

Fern does feel silly, but it was something to say; something to stop her thinking about the unread text on her phone, the fact that earlier this morning Elliott had leant across a table and kissed her on the cheek. She should tell Jules, she knows this. She owes it to her really. They turn left into Merton Avenue. The pottery studio is in the back garden of number 4, a house belonging to a Tom and Mary Westbourne. She'd bought them a day's potting for Jules's birthday. She is, she realises, as they stop at the gate, stupidly nervous. Looking up, there's something about the way the light reflects off the front bedroom window, the way the sash frames are snug into the mullions, the size and shape of the window, the fact that early cherry blossom is falling like confetti around her, that reminds her of Elliott, of when they lived in a house, in a room with a window like this.

This thought takes hold as she follows Jules down the path by the side of the house, and it's as if the outline of Elliott, the indistinct shape she's carried around with her over the years, is becoming slightly more defined, slightly more distinct. They had lived in a house like this for a while and what happened there had mattered. Before seeing him today she wouldn't ever have

71

wanted to admit to this, but now, now perhaps she should. This thought is worrying and she dismisses it but has the feeling that it hasn't quite gone, that it's still lurking somewhere quite close.

The joining instructions said to arrive at eleven, so they have. The garden is shabby but somehow chic; it has history. Large trees nudge up against a brick wall which runs round its perimeter and the green of their leaves is a fresh, uncreasing green now that spring is here. There is a swing, the old-fashioned kind Fern knew as a child, painted light blue, and a tricycle abandoned on its side as if its rider had had an important mission to attend to, something to do with being a spy or an astronaut probably. They can hear voices from the studio. There is laughter.

Jules taps on the door, 'Hellooo,' she says in her bright, fearless way. 'Anyone at home?'

'Come in, come in,' a man answers, and they enter.

The studio is square and functional. It has shelves running round the walls on which an assortment of grey shapes are lined up; it has what Fern takes to be a kiln in the far corner, four pottery wheels, a sink, a gas heater and small, clay-splattered windows. It owner, Tom Westbourne, is standing by the sink beaming at them.

'Oh, you've arrived, wonderful,' he says. 'Let me introduce you to the others. This is –' he gestures to a small, pleasant-looking woman of about fifty – 'Linda, and –' he turns to a younger woman, exactly the same shape and size as Linda – 'her daughter, Rachel.'

Jules steps forward, her hand outstretched. 'Juliet Grimshaw-Smythe,' she says, 'pleased to meet you. Call me Jules.'

Fern wishes she had Jules's bravado, her confidence. She shakes Linda's hand, then Rachel's. 'Hi,' she says, 'my name's Fern, Fern Cole.'

She waits for the joke; somebody normally makes it. But this time no one does, so she says it to herself, 'Jules Verne, hah! If you put Jules and Fern together, you get Jules Verne!' This refrain had followed the girls all through university until it had stopped being funny and they'd always make sure they were introduced the other way around. However, Fern believes that Jules wouldn't actually give a damn any more, and that neither should she.

'Right,' Tom says, 'we have a busy day ahead of us, so let's get cracking. We'll kick off with a basic introduction to the clay, the wheel, the rules, a go at centring, an early lunch made by my lovely wife, and of course I'll let you loose to make something of your own!' He smiles broadly as he says this.

Tom's a lean, wiry man of about thirty-five, with large, capable hands and kind eyes which he hides behind a pair of red-framed glasses. His hair's almost gone, just a few wispy curls remain cropped close to his head; his overalls are dotted with clay and on his feet he wears clogs. The bottoms of his trousers are rolled up slightly to reveal his ankles and this makes him seem somehow vulnerable. He's a strange mix of energy and resignation and Fern can't quite decide which is the more dominant.

'Sorry,' Fern says, raising her hand and immediately feeling foolish, 'do you have a loo I could use before we start?'

'Sure, sorry, should have said,' Tom replies. He steers Fern to the door, puts a warm hand on her shoulder and points around the corner of the studio. 'There, the green door,' he says. 'It should be clean and stocked, but if not just shout.'

He's obviously happy showing off his studio and Fern is happy for him, hopes she doesn't let him down.

The air is sharp and damp inside the cloakroom and Fern peers at her face in the small mirror; her eyes look worried and clouded. There's nothing for it but to check the text. She's reminded of a poem she read once about an unopened telegram which the poet's great-aunt believed held news of her fiancé's death in the First World War. Because it was never opened but kept in a box for sixty years, the young man remained undead and the great-aunt never had to mourn him; she could believe that, somewhere, he still lived. Such it is now. If Fern doesn't read the text, she can tell herself it hasn't been sent, that she didn't meet Elliott this morning, that he's safely boxed up, unopened. He could still be in the place she'd put him so she wouldn't have to reconcile

74

herself to what happened, how it changed what came next.

'Good to see you,' it says. 'Let's keep in touch! I'll text if I'm passing through London tonight and if you're free . . .'

She hates the dots. What are they for? They seem pretentious and glib and her anger is refreshing; it pleases her. It is a text which says nothing real; it holds no import, no obligation. At this point of the day, she doesn't care if he does text again, is tempted to delete it and the number it came from, but she doesn't.

Instead she sends Jack a text: 'Arrived safely. Just about to start!' She adds a ubiquitous smiley face on at the end of the text, knows he will struggle to remember what she's doing, where she's arrived, and that he'll delete the message after reading it.

Washing her hands, she feels a little ashamed of her treatment of Elliott. Shouldn't she give him the benefit of the doubt? Isn't now just like before, when he asked her out the first time, and like his stumbling sentences this morning?

This is how she remembers it. Jules's brother knew Dan, Elliott's brother; Fern can't remember how or why. He just did. Jules had a party at the beginning of their second year; her brother came, Dan came and Elliott came, because Elliott, unknown to Fern or Jules, was at the same university as them. There was a huddle of people in the kitchen of the flat the girls shared with two other girls who had, rather alarmingly, become intensely Christian and judgemental, causing Fern and Jules to ricochet to the far end of the pendulum swing and party harder, smoke more, flirt quite unashamedly. It was a game; they made up the rules as they went along, and it was fun. It was a time of no consequences.

And there was Elliott leaning up against the fridge; his hair flopping over his eyes, him pushing it back with his hand in a practised move. There were his grey-green eyes, his lean sportsman's body, the cadences in his voice, and snap! Something broke, something else connected, and there she was lying on a pile of coats with his hands on her, his mouth on her; a world of promise before them, his clumsy 'Can I see you again?' question at the end of the evening: 'There's a thing on at the union tomorrow night. Fancy coming?'

These are the facts, and she'd thought she would always remember each second of the early days of him and her, but from this distance the whole picture of thoughts and words and how he touched her, is hazier than she was expecting, and now, after this morning, she's realised that it still matters, more than she would ever have expected, and it shouldn't, it shouldn't matter at all.

Fern steps back into the garden, hears the rumble of a jet overhead and a baby crying somewhere in the distance. There is a phone ringing inside number 4, and between her legs is tender from the

76

memory of that first time, and the one thing she does remember is the shock and abandon of it. It had seemed so right, so perfect. She doesn't want to think that she might never have felt anything like it since.

'Right you are,' Tom says as she pushes open the studio door, handing her an overall and a pair of plastic slip-on shoes.

Jules looks at her, frowns and mouths, 'You OK?'

Fern nods. Then, divested of their boots, jewellery, bags and jackets, which are hung up in a cupboard at the far end of the room and the door firmly closed on them, she stands in an overalled line with the three others like something out of *Nineteen Eighty-Four*. Her phone is in her bag in the cupboard and, separated from it, she feels free for the first time in a long, long time.

She becomes hypnotised by Tom's voice and the way he handles the clay, hears some of what he says.

He starts: 'Wedging up,' he says, 'gets all the bubbles out; squish it, push, make it into a ram's head shape until the pops have stopped.' He proudly holds up a lump of the clay: 'ES5 Original Earthstone, good for throwing, but remember, it's a tricky relationship; you have to show it who's boss!' He throws the clay on to the wheel, smoothes it lovingly. 'Each wheel is different, has its own quirks, you just have to feel your way.' He bends over the clay, turns on the power, the wheel hums. Then he dips a hand into a pot of water on the side, sprinkles the clay, smoothes it again. 'Remember, put the clay on the wheel head when it's still, use plenty of water and note that the clay will be cold. Then,' he bends further over, his voice becomes strained; his muscles tense, 'weld your elbows to your stomach, place the lower half of your hand here.'

The women look on. They are silent, transfixed. Laughter bubbles in Fern's chest. She feels wonderful. Being here is wonderful.

'Centre it to a pill shape.' The wheel spins. 'Swap hands and lock in to maintain the centre, then drag. There she goes, there she goes . . .' The clay changes shape; it looks like magic to Fern, it looks like sex feels.

'Clean up, flatten the bottom of the bowl with the tips of your fingers, sponge it clean again. Test the thickness, wire off. There, there, there.' He cups the bowl, gazes at it. 'Watch your chamois leathers,' he adds, holding up the strip next to his elbow, 'never, never, never get them mixed in the clay. I'm very strict about this!' He looks up at them; the wheel is still now, his eyes are shining.

The bowl sits before him, perfect.

'Looks easy!' Jules says. The tension breaks; the other women laugh, Fern laughs.

Rachel creeps nearer to Linda, rests her head on her mother's shoulder. Fern is aware of them but can't look. The laughter subsides. Would this be what it's like, she thinks not for the first time, if I'd had a daughter as well as the boys? She and

78

Jack had talked about it when Wilf started school. Could they – should they – try again?

'I really don't think,' Jack had said, leaning back in his chair at the dining table one evening when the boys were in bed and the house was quiet, 'it would be wise. Not now, and especially seeing how difficult it was for you, you know, with the births and that.' He put down his knife and fork, looked at her and then glanced away as if afraid of meeting her gaze. The cat they had at the time had wound her body around Fern's legs and purred.

She didn't care about wisdom. It was a primal urge, a feeling that this couldn't be it. However, time had passed: the boys had filled up all available space, she had grown older, she and Jack started to see the possibilities of a different kind of life, the one that now scares her so, and so at the time they'd got more comfortable, too settled maybe. So there was no other baby, not even a flicker, a murmur of one. There would be no daughter, just girlfriends who come, who go, who she can't let get too close, and there will be daughters-in-law who will claim ownership of her sons, take them further away from her, maybe give her grandchildren, granddaughters perhaps, whom she will love, hold tight, smell the innocence of their baby-soft hair and remember that she's had her time, that there will be no other here either.

'Right?' Tom says, picking up the bowl, squashing it in his big hands. The pot crumples, made ugly suddenly.

Fern wants to cry out, 'No, don't!' but she doesn't.

'Remember,' he says, wedging it up again, 'clay has memory. The second, the third throw will be easier. Just you and it, the two of you. Feel your way.'

He repeats the process; the centring, the dragging, and another pot appears, exactly like the first. 'Here,' he hands each of them a lump of clay, 'practice wedging up, getting to know the clay and then we'll have lunch. OK?'

The women smile self-consciously at one another, hold the clay as if it's something fragile, precious.

'Oh my God!' Jules says. 'I'm regretting what I said now – it doesn't look easy at all!' She straddles the seat of one of the wheels, looks down at her clay.

The clay is cold, ice-cold, surprisingly so. Fern touches it; it is slimy, a little hostile. She doesn't feel like she wants to get to know it, is afraid they won't get on. Unbidden comes the thought of Elliott reaching over the table earlier and kissing her. She lifts a hand to her face, touches it; the clay on her fingers leaves a pale grey mark.

CHAPTER 6

The cab driver is young, has a shaven head and a tattoo of the Welsh dragon on his neck. Elliott wishes he would turn around so that he can see his eyes.

'Yes, mate?' is all the man says.

'Llantwit?' Elliott asks.

'That'll cost you.'

'I know, it's OK.'

Elliott does know it will cost; it's a twenty-mile trip, then there's the journey to Cowbridge later to see Dad and then back here again. These are necessary expenses because he needs to travel light. He could have caught the train from Cardiff to Llantwit, but the connections didn't work out and it just seemed easier this way. His wallet, camera, the key to the house and the pad of sticky labels form comforting lumps in his pocket and he is proud of his forward-thinking. The lack of this skill was just one of the things Meryl had found annoying of late.

They pull away from the station and the driver says, 'My cousin Bryn's from Llantwit.'

'Ah,' Elliott says, thinking he should probably

know him, or his dad at any rate. 'It's a small place.'

'Where you to?' the driver asks.

Elliott translates 'to' into 'from'; the language sings in his head. 'Llantwit as well,' he replies, 'I grew up there. Left when I went off to study. Never really came back.'

'There's the thing,' the driver says too wisely for his years, turning the radio up, obviously not wanting to talk any more.

Elliott is relieved and takes out his phone, ostensibly to check work emails, but the text screen is blank. Fern hasn't replied. He gazes out of the window as the countryside flashes by; the phone is hot in his hand, his head is full of the music of Wales. He hasn't heard it for a while, but its sound is like an echo: familiar, persistent.

For reasons he can't explain, his thoughts veer towards Meryl. However hard he tries to get rid of her, she's still lodged there, just at the back of his eyes, and whatever he sees or does seems to be through the twisted filter of her disapproving view of the world. It hasn't always been like this, but he's kind of glad it is now; it makes him feel more justified for having left.

It was brutal at the end. What started out as just turning away from one another at night, sleeping without forgiving each other for the petty crimes of the day, grew and grew until a strange, purple beast moved into the space between them and became a living, breathing creature with a life of its own. Meryl did her thing, he did his: working, meeting his mates for drinks down the pub, reading the paper on a Sunday afternoon, and she would mince about the house and fuss and worry and shop and be dissatisfied with everything. The flashpoints, of course, were Chloe and money, both of which he felt he had no control over, and it was all so different from how it was at the beginning, how it should have been. And there were also always the enormous things they left unsaid; they never spoke about the baby Meryl lost or whether he ever regretted leaving Fern. Neither of them has ever been brave enough to face each other with either of these truths.

As far as he knows, he thinks as they pass signs to the airport on the A48 and the driver drums his fingers on the steering wheel in time to the music seeping quietly out of the radio, a track Elliott doesn't recognise, he and Meryl haven't been unfaithful, not in the traditional sense of the word anyway. He'd had chances but hadn't been bothered to see them through; it all seemed so much effort for so little reward, even feels that way now with Susan at work. He had thought of trying to find Fern again, of course he had, had sharpened his eyes for sightings of her in the unlikeliest of places, but overwhelmingly what he felt over the years was a kind of creeping paralysis, as if he'd lost connection with who he really was, and now, on this day, he has seen her again. All too briefly, of course, but his day has been thrown off track because of it and he's on dangerous ground now, the past rising up behind him and, sitting in the cab on his way to Llantwit, he's not sure if he's brave enough to turn and face up to it.

He thinks instead about his holidays with Meryl and Chloe, one long sweep of soggy campsites, interminable evenings playing Snap! with Chloe and that feeling that each breath he took couldn't quite reach the bottom of his lungs. These holidays had no beginnings, middles or ends; they just were what they were – mosaics made up of snapshots in which he never seemed to feature, or if he did, he was never smiling.

They'd also done the whole foreign package-tour option, when Meryl would establish herself next to the pool with that year's most-talked-about summer read unopened on the sun-bed next to her and he would trek around the quiet, ancient streets of some Greek town and take photographs of shutters or sleeping cats while Chloe would spend the day in a kids' club from which he would collect her at six when she would look up at him with her tired, pinched face and say plaintively, 'Daddy? Can *you* read me a story?'

It was as though she was really saying, 'You've brought me to this place, and each day I spend more time on my own than I do with you and I hate it, I hate it!' And he didn't blame her, but then he didn't have the energy to blame Meryl either. She would busy herself getting to know other people around the pool, would arrange to meet them for drinks in the bar and, having booked a babysitter for Chloe through the hotel's reception, she and Elliott would shower, dress in cool linens and drink cocktails talking to people he had no real interest in knowing and certainly with whom he had no intention of keeping in touch.

'Yes,' Meryl would say, twirling a paper umbrella around in some frothy yellow concoction, 'we have considered the new Jag, but I think –' and she'd look at Elliott with an admiration he knew she didn't really feel – 'that we always have been and always will be Mercedes people.'

It was times like these that Elliott wanted to run. He wanted to push back his chair, let it scrape on the shiny tiles of whatever hotel bar they were in and even maybe let it fall to the floor with a crash, hoping the tiles would splinter and crack, and run so far and so fast that no one would ever be able to find him, or catch him. He has, he's always felt, had a kinship with Charles Ryder in *Brideshead Revisited*, wishing that, like him, he could just take off to far-off lands and paint; or even be like Forrest Gump and just run, run until there is nowhere else to go, no landscape in the world he hasn't seen. But then, afterwards, when they'd eaten and Meryl had gone into the bathroom to apply creams to her burnished skin, he would tiptoe through the adjoining door into Chloe's room and watch his daughter as she slept and he would think that there should be nowhere on earth he'd rather be.

Maybe this only happened once but it seems now as he's travelling home that it could have happened a hundred times. And of course there were other holidays: those when Meryl got the camping bug and would send him to Carter's for the very latest in tents and Calor Gas stoves and they would load up the car, one of the Mercedes she claimed to be so very fond of, and map-read their way through tiny lanes, up steep hills to a farmer's field near a hamlet called Back-of-Beyond and, as dusk fell and the midges danced, he would struggle with ridge poles, flysheet and mallet, cursing under his breath until Chloe would skip into the snapping crackle of the tent's mellow, greenish light and beam her joy up at him, saying, 'Daddy, we are explorers!' It was then that all the effort would be worthwhile. However, after this, as he lay in his sleeping bag listening to early-morning rain pock the canvas, he would want to be able to lift himself high into the clouds and float far away. Holidays with Meryl and Chloe always seemed to cause this elastic tension between who he really was and who he wanted to be.

And there was that Christmas holiday they spent at Disneyland Paris when it poured with insistent French rain the whole time and there was no magic anywhere. He'd hated the way the French smoked in the queues, hated the plasticness of it all and the false bonhomie, as though a man dressed up as a mouse could make the pain disappear. But the holiday he remembers most is when they rented a cottage on a farm in Devon one September.

It must have been when Chloe was about four as she hadn't started school but was itching to go; she'd even made Meryl buy her a school uniform to wear around the house and had taken to lining up her toys in a row to teach them how to count to ten. When he got home from work Elliott would take on the role of the headmaster and test these creatures and then give his daughter a gold star for being the very best teacher in the world.

These toys and her mini blackboard all came with them. Their cottage was nestled up to a farmhouse on a quiet hillside and the weather was balmy and kind that year. During the day the three of them visited museums and parks and one warm, unusually damp afternoon they went to the RHS garden at Rosemoor near Great Torrington. He remembers walking a few steps behind his wife and his daughter, watching as Chloe listed slightly in towards Meryl and noticing how, from the back and only separated by a few inches of horizontal air and a foot or two of vertical air, they looked so similar, as though cast from the same mould. Their footsteps matching, he could see his daughter's thoughts span the space between her and her mother, and could see Meryl gazing steadfastly on, looking neither left nor right. It was at that moment that Elliott realised how very much alone he was. It seemed that neither of the people walking in front of him really needed him, and, as he stopped to gaze at a bed of ferns, at the tight fists of those leaves which had yet to uncurl and the delicate green stretch of those that had, the awful thought that maybe he didn't really need them either crept insidiously into his mind.

The next morning he got out of bed and had to bend down low to peer out of the small window in the cottage's bedroom. This window looked out on to a lane dug deep between two hedgerows and along it an elderly man was walking with his dog. It was misty, that sort of wet, silver mist that had a wire-mesh quality to it, and the man was walking slowly, the dog's body swaying as he shadowed his master, and as Elliott envied them their closeness he allowed himself to think of the plants he'd seen the day before and how the name Fern could still, even after all this time, cause the bones in his body to shift, readjust and reassemble themselves into a different order. He wished it could be other-wise, but it wasn't. He'd turned back from the small window to look at Meryl asleep in the bed. Her brow was puckered slightly into a small frown.

That morning has stayed with him ever since and is, perhaps, his most vivid holiday memory. It's as though he's spent the rest of his life up to now looking out of that small window, wishing he was on the other side of it, wishing he was anywhere other than where he actually was.

And now he's officially separated from his wife, gearing up to fight over the assets of their marriage: the memories, chairs, money, collateral, and until things are sorted, they'll live each in their own fortress, defending it savagely.

Probably the worst time was when, just after he'd moved out with her words 'Well, thank God for that, about time too' ringing in his ears, and Chloe so very angry at him for going, he'd taken delivery of some flatpack furniture for the apartment and had realised that his tools were still in the garage at the house. He'd had to ring home.

'Meryl, it's me.'

'Yes, what is it?' She seemed to spit out the words as if she'd just bitten into a lemon.

'I need to come and take some tools.' He'd chosen his words carefully. The word 'take' was significant. 'Take' meant to keep, claim ownership of. He thought of his garage, the workbench, the rack of screwdrivers and drill bits, his pots of nails. How he'd collected them he had no idea, but they'd arrived over the years like orphans. Dad had given him some of his father's, saying, 'There, lad, I've no use for them. You take them – part of your inheritance!' and he'd laughed his raspish smoker's cough. They both knew, however, that there was no other legacy, just the tapestry of memories and these now-blunt saws and chisels, the handles of which his grandfather had turned himself on the lathe at his work when he'd been a young man.

The rest had been gifts from relatives who had no idea what else to get him, and then there was the Black & Decker Workmate Dan had given him for his fortieth birthday as a joke. 'Hey, man,' the card had said, 'now you're really middle-aged!' But the real joke had been that Elliott had loved the gift, had seen it as a rite of passage, and now it, and everything else, was trapped behind the garage door, the key to which he no longer had the moral right to keep.

'What tools? Why?' Meryl had sighed as she said this.

He wanted to say, 'None of your fucking business, you miserable fucking cow,' but he didn't. It had shocked him, though, to realise that he could have. Instead he said, 'I ordered some furniture, for the flat, you know. I need tools to assemble it with.'

He'd tried to sound sarcastic, worldly, but the word 'need' was a bad choice; it gave her the upper hand. Recently she'd been able to sniff out his need from a hundred paces and in tiny dagger-like moves find ways to pierce it, make him bleed.

But this time all she said was, 'Fine, if you must. I'll leave the key in the pot by the gate. Put it back when you've finished. If I'm in, don't bother knocking. I won't answer.' And she'd hung up and he'd listened to the dial tone for a moment, feeling like he was drowning in blood.

As it was she wasn't home when he went round after work later that day. It was November; dark, wet and cold and he'd had to get a torch from the car and scrabble around the pots to find the key, thinking all the time that he looked too much like a thief and that surely someone would put a hand on his shoulder, say, 'Stop right there. What do you think you're doing?' and he'd have to say, 'This is my house, *my* house, you moron, now fuck off.' But no one came and he unlocked the garage door and crept in, turning on the light and surveying his realm like a king back from exile.

He could smell sawdust and oil and the faint scent of white spirit and he remembered mending broken toys here and the punctures on the bike Chloe used for her cycling proficiency test. The spare fridge purred in the corner. He opened the door; it was empty, just white light and plastic shelves. It used to be full of wine and extra cheese and the turkey remains at Christmas. Cars whooshed by on the wet road outside and far away a siren sounded. The key was now warm in his hand. He took the tools he wanted, putting them in a canvas bag that used to be his grandfather's, and left feeling as though he was walking away from the grave of someone he hadn't taken time to mourn sufficiently. He locked the door, took the key, got a new one cut and, like the criminal he felt he was, put the original back in the pot later that evening. Meryl had still been out, so, even now, she doesn't know he has the key on his key ring and that, should he want to, he could return at any time and claim the rest of what is rightfully his.

As they approach Llantwit the driver says, 'Nearly there then, mate,' and Elliott's phone buzzes with another email.

He ignores it, saying 'Right you are,' and then, 'Look, can you take me down to the beach and drop me off there? I can walk back to town.'

'If you want to, that's fine. If you're sure though – it's quite a trek,' the man says, turning left into Llantwit Major Road. The car winds through the narrow lanes, stopping to let a tractor go by, then it's past St Illtyd's Church, through the square and down Colhugh Street, passing the house Elliott grew up in.

This house still has its pale yellow door, its steps up from the street, and there are daffodils in the tiny flower bed under the lounge window. Elliott feels the house is asking him questions as the car drives by it on its way to the sea. 'Where are you going?' it seems to say. 'Why aren't you stopping?' Elliott looks back and thinks, Just give me a moment, please.

Mill Lay Lane goes off to the left as the road bears round to the right, winding through the valley to the beach, and Elliott is besieged with memories of elderflower, a girl under him on the cliff top, cycling too fast round the bends, racing Dan with a sharp winter wind in their hair.

When the taxi driver stops the car he turns round, his hand outstretched for the money and Elliott can see that his eyes are the palest blue imaginable. They are almost translucent, ghost-like. He tries not to recoil. 'There you are,' he says, handing over the notes. 'Thanks. Hope you get back OK.'

'Yeah, cheers, mate,' the driver says. 'Did you want a receipt?'

Elliott nods. 'That would be great, thanks.'

'Hope you have a good day now.'

'I doubt it, but thanks anyway,' Elliott says.

He takes the receipt and puts it in his pocket. Then he steps from the car and watches as Bryn's cousin drives away, regretting that he didn't ask who Bryn was, wishing he'd found out after all whether he'd known this man's mother, father, uncle or whatever at school. He rather has the feeling that he would have done.

The wind hits him like a hammer. It funnels up the Bristol Channel in between the cliffs and into the valley. It is a wet, salty wind, and Elliott's hair is pushed back with the force of hands. There's a new Coastguard station, toilets and shop and some money has obviously been spent on sea defences: huge grey boulders have been placed at the top of the beach. The tide is halfway out.

He struggles to catch his breath, has to let himself relax into the wind, thinks back to the heat wave summers of '74 and '76 when he'd spent every day here with Dan, their friends and a girl named Jane. They'd grown 'brown as berries', as his mother had said, and each day had held a tiny miracle, whether it be a rock-pool crab, all orange and sideways-moving, or him riding a wave on his belly or touching Jane's hand as he climbed back on to the rock where she sat, her chin on her knees, her eyes smiling into the sun.

The waves tumble and moan in the distance and the sands glisten with the reflections of the clouds as a lone seagull struggles against the wind, its wingtips flexing and straining, and he turns around to face land, his face stinging, bunching his jacket collar around his neck to ward out the chill. This sea is the right sea. The sea where he lives now is just not the same. He starts to walk back up the valley to the house. He is unaccountably angry and feels the force of his rage pulse through his veins. He walks quickly, beginning to sweat slightly under his coat.

He doesn't know where this fury has come from but it is refreshing; it seems to give him a new purpose. There is no room in his head for Fern, nor Meryl, nor even Chloe at this moment. Now is about the things he wanted to get away from: Mr Hughes, the headmaster at the Junior School, with its Boys' Entrance and Girls' Entrance and classrooms separated by a wooden partition with glass windows at the top that the boys would clamber on to their desks, when the teacher wasn't in the room, to look through and make faces at the girls on the other side. Then there was Batman, the headmaster at the Comprehensive School, so called because he strode about the campus in his college gown, its black wings flapping. He was portly, florid, constantly scowling. Elliott remembers lying on the sports field behind the school in a circle with his friends and the girls they fancied and feeling that the sky was too vast a thing for him to comprehend, that he was too tiny and powerless underneath it ever to make a mark. These things didn't matter now though; what actually mattered was that what came afterwards: his time with Fern, his time without her, his role as a son, husband and father and this is what should matter, what should count.

The hill is steep and he's panting by the time he gets to the top. Eventually he stands on the steps of the house, gets the key out of his pocket and lines it up in the lock. He's nine, he's fifteen, he's twenty-two. Dan is there, then Fern, then Meryl, and his mother's in the garden hanging sheets on the line. They whisk white in the breeze and his dad is coughing his smoker's cough, sitting behind the paper in the lounge-room. The daffodils nod in the breeze. He unlocks the door, steps inside.

The house is so obviously empty, as if it's been holding its breath since the last person walked out of it the day they moved his father out. Elliott has entered through this door many times, but never like this, never to this complete and heavy stillness. The hallway is narrow, the flecked wallpaper is scuffed and the carpet underfoot is worn in patches. He can't remember it being like this before either. Maybe he's just never noticed; always moving forward instead, towards the people, towards the beating hearts that lived here. He slips the key into his pocket and walks past the lounge-room door further into the depths of the house.

There's a noise somewhere. He stops, breathing quickly – so quickly that the blood pumps in his ears and he can't hear properly. He's not angry now; suddenly he's scared. It's stupid, he knows, but then he realises, it's Sid and Peggy next door; the familiar sound of their footsteps, the murmur of their voices. He releases the breath he hadn't known he was holding and makes his way to the kitchen.

A fitful sun is battering the window, and the garden rises gently up to the row of trees at the back. The grass probably needs mowing, he thinks. Sid does what he can, but he's not as young as he once was and it's a lot to ask of him to look after this garden as well as his own. However, it's here, in his mother's domain, that he misses her most keenly. Normally he can reconcile himself to the fact that she's gone, but not in this place, not when she is so powerfully here, with her hands in the sink, an apron tied around her middle, her house shoes on, the backs of which she's worn down.

The Formica worktops are bleached clean and the cooker seems expectant, lonely. He runs his finger along the edge of the kitchen table; it is smooth with use, from the years of being leant up against at mealtimes. Next he goes into the dining room; there is a quiet layer of dust here, illumin-ated by the angle of the sun through the French windows his parents never opened. The furniture in this room is muted and he feels like weeping; it is all so much shabbier than he remembers. In the lounge-room he rests his hands on the back of his father's chair, imagines his dad's weight in it, the rustle of newspaper, the commentator's voice on TV announcing the three thirty from Haydock.

Upstairs, he can't face his parents' bedroom, with its pale pink counterpane and the triptych of mirrors on his mother's dressing table. The room is full of her bustle and goodwill. Somehow he can't visualise his father here, not just now, at this particular moment.

In his and Dan's room he stands by the window and looks out on the back garden. He can see next door on both sides; the sun is bouncing off the glass in Sid's greenhouse, making it look white, like asbestos, and, on the other side, the new people have laid the vegetable patches down to lawn and put a slide there; it is big and red and very plastic. It doesn't look at all right to Elliott.

And it's here, sitting on the narrow single bed in which he spent his youth, that he remembers the first time he brought Fern home, how his parents had liked her instantly and how she'd slotted comfortably into the rhythm of the house. It helped that she was small and wiry, bubbling with life, and he remembers making love to her in front of the fire embers one Saturday night after his parents had gone to bed. Her skin had glowed like gold and as he'd entered her she had moaned and he'd put his hand over her mouth and she had kissed it and taken a finger gently between her teeth and he had come in her. He checks his phone again. It's twelve thirty; still no text, but the email icon is flashing busily.

Between the beds is a chest of drawers. Elliott opens the top drawer, expecting to see his boyhood relics still there. He'd collected stones and comics and had had a catapult of which he'd been especially proud. But these things have gone and the drawer is empty. It is lined with newspaper and he picks it out and reads the date: 13th May 1994. He wonders what he was doing on that day. It would have been after he'd met Meryl. You'd think, he says to himself, that the significant dates in his life would be firmly fixed in his head, but somehow today they are eluding him. The scenes are flashing in front of his eyes. One minute it's Fern, the next it's Meryl, and the huge 'What if' question is there too. He feels like he's standing in amongst the falling pack of cards in *Alice in Wonderland*.

He knows it was in March on a day like this one when he'd run after Fern, then left her at the corner, still beguiled by the memory of Meryl sitting up in bed, her breasts full and pendulous, her nipples tender from where his mouth had been. This had been before the shame set in, of course, and before the baby, when not one but a thousand reasons stopped him from going back to Fern like he should have done. But the facts are hazy; he can't recall the exact timeline, not after all these years. Maybe it's because he doesn't want to. But he does know that his mother never took to Meryl the way she had to Fern; even at their first meeting, downstairs in the kitchen when his mother stood with her apron tied around her middle, her hands in the sink and the backs of her house shoes worn down. Without saying anything or even turning around, the set of her shoulders had told Elliott that he had most probably made a very grave mistake.

A knock at the front door startles Elliott. Who can it be? For some strange reason he checks his pockets. Yes, he has his phone, the key and his camera, the labels. He goes downstairs: there's a dark shape on the other side of the glass.

'Elliott, my boy,' Sid says, beaming up at him. 'The wife thought you might like some coffee, and a sandwich.' He proffers a thermos and what is obviously a bread roll covered in greaseproof paper.

'Oh, thank you,' Elliott manages to say. His voice seems inordinately loud in the silence of the house. 'Will you come in?'

'I'd rather not, my boy, if that's OK. The wife's got my dinner on the table. It's steak and kidney pie today. My favourite.' He smiles shyly, his eyes almost disappearing in the wrinkles of weathered skin. His teeth are brown, a gap where an eye tooth used to be, and his jacket is patched and there's a button missing. He is, however, wearing his going-out shoes. Elliott recognises them from before.

'Are you sure?'

'Yes, absolutely,' Sid replies. 'I'd better not keep you. You probably have a lot to do.'

For a moment Elliott can't compute what he's seeing. There is a small, wizened man in front of him who seems in awe of him. How did he know Elliott was there? He hadn't told them he was. Maybe he should have done.

But no, that wouldn't have been necessary. He can imagine the conversation that's just taken place.

Sid would have said, 'Do you hear that, Peggy?'

'Mmm? What's that, love?'

'There are sounds next door. Shh with your clattering, woman. That's Elliott, isn't it?'

And Elliott would know that the noises he's making are like lifeblood to them. They are the cadences that Sid and Peggy have lived with throughout the years and it's their absence, not their presence, that they find difficult to bear.

'Sounds like it,' Peggy would have replied.

'Shall I pop a flask round to him?'

'Good idea, love, but don't keep him talking. I bet he's busy, and dinner's almost on the table.'

Now Sid is awkward and over-polite and he's holding out his offering as though he's one of the Wise Men in Bethlehem. This isn't how it should be. This is the man who used to terrify Elliott and Dan when they were younger. Dad would say,

'Behave, boys, or I'll get Sid,' and Sid would be huge and stern and unfathomable and have all the answers because he didn't have children of his own. He would look down from his own doorway at the boys when they went round to apologise yet again for breaking a pane of glass in Sid's greenhouse, and later, when the boys were in bed, Dad and Sid would sit in the lounge-room of Elliott's house and drink beer out of bottles and smoke a pipe each and murmur, laughing occasionally, and his mother and Peggy would talk over the garden fence, bundles of washing in baskets at their feet. Elliott and Dan would listen to these sounds as they fell asleep and believe that their childhoods would last forever.

'Well, thank you so much – for the food, I mean,' Elliott says haltingly. 'I'll drop the thermos round when I'm done, if that's OK.'

'Just leave it on the step, my boy,' Sid says. 'The wife and I are likely to be having our afternoon nap!' He chuckles as he speaks and a tiny bit of spit gathers in the corner of his mouth. He reaches out a hand to shake Elliott's. Elliott quickly tucks the thermos and sandwich under his left arm and holds out his right hand. 'Give my best to your dad,' Sid mumbles.

'I will, thank you.' Elliott wishes very hard that it doesn't have to be like this. He wishes his father was sitting in his chair calling out, 'Tell that man to come in, for heaven's sake. The twelve forty-five from Ascot's about to start,' and that he could leave them together talking about the going. 'Good to soft, they say,' his dad would say, and Sid would reply, 'It's that rain they had yesterday, mind you,' and they would settle, watch and comment and be again the friends they were when they were working men in the steel plant at Port Talbot.

'You must miss him,' Elliott says, not realising he's said it out loud.

Sid loosens his grip on Elliott's hand and lets it fall. 'Yes,' he says simply. 'I do, of course I do.' Then he kind of shakes himself, turns on the spot and waves as if dismissing Elliott. 'Well, better get back or the wife will start her complaining!' and he laughs, coughs and is gone. Elliott can hear their front door close and Sid's steps in the hall through the wall and he can hear Peggy call out, 'Is that you?' from the kitchen, and Elliott shuts the door to his parents' house and makes his way through to the back, unlocks the kitchen door and sits on the wall outside the French windows his parents never opened and pours himself a cup of coffee from Peggy's thermos. The steam rises and catches the back of his throat and he reckons this is what must be making his eyes water. He rests the cup on the warm bricks, unwraps the grease-proof paper and bites into the roll, but finds it difficult to swallow.

After he's eaten and finished the coffee he feels a little stronger and a little more able to face what he has to do. He starts in the lounge-room, putting labels on things, taking photographs to send to Dan so they can decide what to sell, what to give and what to throw away. They both know they have to sell the house to pay for their dad's care and that this heartbreaking fact is unavoidable. But more tragic will be the dismantling and the stripping bare that will come beforehand, the careful deconstruction of everything their parents built up. If the house isn't ours, Elliott wonders as he puts a 'Sell' sticker on the mirror above the fireplace, does that mean the memories we made here aren't ours either?

It's just then, at that very second when Elliott is feeling unanchored and bereft, that his phone buzzes again. It's a text this time. Could it be Fern? he wonders. It seems like synchronicity if it is; that he is here so very alone and that she should choose now to answer him. Is it a sign? He sits down in his father's chair; the springs are soft and the fabric on the arms is stained. Funny I've never noticed that before, Elliott thinks. He opens the text and reads what's written there.

CHAPTER 7

When she washes her hands in the sink at the studio, the skin is tight, reminding Fern of childhood holidays by the sea, of swimming in saltwater and the grittiness of sand. She picks remnants of clay out from underneath her fingernails and, getting her bag out of the cupboard, follows the others into the garden. There's a conservatory on the back of the house she hadn't noticed when they arrived. It's old, made of wrought iron and thick glass, and has the skeleton of a plant trailed over it, a Virginia creeper maybe. She crosses the lawn; the grass is thick and springy under her feet.

'Right, here we are,' Tom says, shepherding them into the conservatory. 'Mary's just picking up our littlest one from nursery. She'll be here shortly, but in the meantime have some lemonade and oh, she's left us some olives too. How yummy.'

To Fern the word 'yummy' seems incongruous; like he's reading from a script or something. She wishes he would speak as he normally would and not feel he has to put on this act, pretend that everything in his life is perfect and smooth and designed for their pleasure. Why can't he sit down, put his head in his hands and say, 'Oh it was so not supposed to be like this. I'm supposed to have my own gallery, win prizes, be able to charge a fortune for my work. People are supposed to write about me in books, study me at college. I shouldn't have to make dinner services for wedding presents, put on courses, have my wife rush our children through their day so she can serve you this lunch. This isn't art, this is compromise'?

The four women sit in wicker chairs. The cushions are hot from being in the unexpected sun and Fern rests her head back and closes her eyes momentarily. The words of Elliott's text seem to have printed themselves on the inside of her eyelids.

Tom is hovering over the table, a jug in his hand, and Jules is talking. 'Yes,' she's saying, 'Peter Beard, I've heard of him. A friend of mine has one of his pieces. She bought it at an exhibition, carried it home on her bike; it cost over a thousand pounds, you know.' She laughs her deep throaty laugh and pops an olive in her mouth, chewing on it with vigour. Fern picks up the glass of lemonade Tom has poured for her and sips. The liquid is cool and slightly bitter. It is perfect.

'So where do you sell your work?' Linda asks, looking up at Tom. Her legs don't quite reach the ground and her feet jiggle up and down as she speaks.

'Shows, craft fairs, the Internet. You know, wherever I can, really,' Tom replies. He's standing in front of the door into the house with his hands on his hips, leaning slightly backwards. All Fern can see is his silhouette. 'This job kills your back,' he says. 'I normally do Hatfield Show in August, Farnham Market in November and Winchester at Christmas. But it's not so easy now to leave Mary and the children.'

'What made you decide on being a potter?' Rachel asks, and Fern wonders what it is that Rachel does. She looks like she would be a good doctor, Fern thinks. She has that air about her: capable, sturdy and kind.

'I fell into it by accident,' Tom says, cocking his head as he hears voices coming down the pathway. 'Oh, that'll be Mary and Benjamin.' He seems nervous now, on edge for some reason. 'I was,' he continues, taking a step nearer the garden and turning back to speak to the ladies so that Fern can see him properly again, 'a bit of a rebel at school. Then the art teacher persuaded the head to let me throw pots during detention and, well, I guess I just fell in love with it. From there I went to art college, then a degree at a local college. I worked at a pottery, making garden pots for a while, and hey presto, here I am!' He beams at them; the last words have rushed from his lips like a car speeding around a corner so that he's finished when his wife and son arrive.

She's whippet-thin and dark-haired. Her skin is porcelain white and she's smiling. 'Hello,' she says brightly. 'How it's going?'

'It's fine,' Tom says. 'We're fine, aren't we, ladies?' He seems anxious to please her, then bends down to the boy who's hiding behind her leg. 'So, Benjamin,' he says, 'did you have a good morning at nursery?'

The child nods the head that's buried in the denim of his mother's jeans and for a second Fern can't breathe. She remembers when her boys were hip-high, their hot hands in hers; when she knew them inside out.

'I'll bring the lunch out in a jiffy,' Mary says. 'Let me just settle Benjamin first. Hope you're hungry!'

'Mary is . . .' Tom hesitates as if it's not possible to sum up what his wife is in mere words, 'a wonderful cook. I am . . .' he looks about him, at his house, his garden, his studio, the retreating backs of his wife and child and says, 'a lucky man.'

Jules reaches over and grabs another olive. 'Do you have other children, Tom?' she asks.

He pushes his glasses up his nose and says, 'Yes, a daughter. She's at school. She'll be six next birthday.'

Linda chimes in, saying, 'What's her name?' and Fern can hear Tom answer her but not what he's saying, because her mind has suddenly emptied and she's in the car. It's last Friday evening and she's waiting for Wilf's train.

'Pick up at 7?' he'd texted.

'K' she'd texted back, feeling a degree of cool using the shorthand language her boys seem to speak in, but not sure if it was actually a bit lame to do so at her age.

She'd left the house at six thirty and had plenty of time. It had been a blustery day and she'd finished work at one, done some washing, been to Waitrose and had called her mother but she hadn't been in so she'd left a message, thinking she should really go and visit on Sunday, it being Mother's Day and all. But what with both boys coming home and Ed bringing Sookie and Jack's mother staying overnight, she just didn't feel she had enough energy for her own parents as well.

The roads were busy with rush-hour traffic and she tuned the radio to Classic FM, letting the music sweep over her; it felt like fingers in her hair. At the entrance to the station two cars were having a squabble. The driver of one of them, a man with a cigarette hanging from his lips, was waving his arms in the air at a young girl in a pink Ford Ka who was having trouble turning into the underground car park. She kept getting the angle wrong and hitting the kerb so she had to reverse and try again and the man with the cigarette was waving and shrugging and banging his fist on the steering wheel as if doing this would help. But the more he waved and shrugged and banged, the more flustered the girl got and the worse her driving became. Fern wanted to get out of her car, tap on his window and say, 'For fuck's sake, leave the poor girl alone. How would you like it if this happened to your daughter?' She was about to open her door and do just that when the incident was over and both cars had disappeared down the ramp.

The final notes of Mahler's Fourth Symphony were fading as she drove into the concrete gloom of the car park. The girl in the pink Ka was parking up, the cigarette man must have already locked his car and gone. Fern switched off the engine and in the hush between tracks she could hear the boom boom of a car's stereo and the thud thud of an engine and a bright orange, customised Astra revved its way up and out. It was wonderful when it had gone. Then the music started up again in her car and she watched the doors out of which Wilf would come, suddenly afraid of what the next few minutes would bring.

Why should she be scared? He was her son; she had been the touchstone of his childhood. Surely this was enough for them to get through the awkwardness of his getting in the car, turning to her, saying, 'Hello, Mum,' and her wanting to but not touching his hand and replying, 'Hello, Wilf. Good journey?'

But for a second she had no idea how she was going to get through it. Would she even recognise him when he walked towards her? The doors opened and a man walked out; he was young and was carrying a bag, but it wasn't Wilf. She was sure he wasn't her son, yet still she scanned his face, searching out some feature she could recognise. The track on the radio hit a strident note;

the music surged and struck her hard between the eyes. She turned it off, heard someone shout, 'Oi!' and then there was laughter.

A private hire cab drew up in front of her and four passengers got out. There was much discussion about luggage and paying and then the car drove off and the people disappeared through the doors. When the last one had gone, Wilf appeared as if by magic. She hadn't seen the doors open, or him walk towards her, but here he was, taller than she remembered, wearing a jacket she'd never seen before, but still smiling his father's smile at her. He tapped on the car bonnet as he walked around it, opened the back door and threw in his bag, then got in beside her, turned and said, 'Hello, Mum. Ta for this.'

And then it was all right. Having him there was just as it should be and she was able to relax. There was nothing to be scared of, nothing they couldn't cope with. She'd been everything she could have been to him over the years and, in the final reckoning, she was sure he wouldn't stand by her grave and say, 'You know what? I think she could have done better.' No, he still trusted her and she trusted him. She was in the right place, doing the right thing, being the person she was always meant to be and maybe, just maybe, this next bit was going to be OK after all.

'Hello, Wilf,' she said. 'Good journey?'

★　　★　　★

'Fern?' she hears her name and is shaken back to the present, to Tom and Mary's garden, to Jules, who is leaning forward touching her on the knee and saying, 'Here, wakey wakey, lunch is ready.'

'I'll be with you a minute,' Fern says as the others follow Tom into the shade of the house and to the dining room, where she imagines there is a pine table, a tureen of soup and homemade bowls and freshly baked bread and it is there, at one fifteen, that she replies to Elliott's text. She holds her phone – the plastic is surprisingly cool to the touch – and she types, 'OK', hesitates, then adds an exclamation mark and presses Send. She doesn't let herself wonder if it's the right thing to say, whether it was right even to reply, and has no idea what will happen next.

The dining room is just how she imagined it: dark and homely. There's a huge oil painting above the fireplace and, with the skin still tight on the tips of her fingers, she wants to trace the brush strokes, the sweep and curve of them. She feels that this act will give her some degree of comfort.

'Right, here we are, here we are,' Tom says, pulling out a chair at the head of the table and nodding to the others, saying, 'Sit, sit. Enjoy.'

And then Mary comes in with a pile of bowls and puts one down in front of each of them; Fern's is warm and she wants to cradle it, nestle it against her chest. Then there's the tureen but it's not soup, it's some sort of goulash; the scent of it is pungent and spicy and it reminds Fern of that holiday with

Elliott in Turkey at the end of their second year; before Jack, before the boys.

She and Elliott had spent the day with the lithe, dark-skinned boatman they'd met in a bar. He'd laughed a lot, had taken them around the coastline in a battered motorboat and then had steered them into the cool fresh waters of a river. They'd watched the two currents meet: warm seawater, cold river water from the mountains – the surface had burbled and swirled. Elliott had dangled his hand in the triangle of churning water, laughing joyfully. Then they moored up by some trees, sat on blankets while the boatman played his guitar, and they'd eaten stew, dipping hard Turkish bread into the gravy and drinking rough wine out of tin cups. When they'd got back to their hotel she'd lain on the bed with Elliott's leather jacket draped over her and he'd peeled it off so very slowly and had made love to her to the sound of the market being packed up outside their window and everything had been wonderful, beautiful.

She thinks she hears her name. 'Sorry?' she says. 'Oh yes, lovely.' She holds out her bowl; it has cooled slightly. Tom fills it. She helps herself to some bread and looks around the table. Jules is chatting to Linda and Fern can hear fragments of their conversation. She makes out the words 'Kent' and 'City' and 'horse' and 'mother-in-law' and knows that Jules is doing what she does best; she's making Linda believe that she is knowable; it's her 'Here I am, love me' act and one she's perfected over the years. But Fern knows – she knows there's more to it than that. Yes, Jules is big, confident, wealthy, still in love with her husband, doesn't have children to stretch and confuse her, but deep down Fern knows that this friend, this one she loves so very much, is inherently lonely and, if only she would admit it, has also lived a 'What if' kind of life. But then, Fern argues to herself, who is brave enough to admit this? Certainly not herself, not today, not now she's just sent a text to Elliott, has maybe started something which should not have been started. By replying it seems that the day, which was supposed to be straight-forward and ordinary, has shifted slightly on its axis. She is running on instinct now. She takes a mouthful of stew. It is delicious.

Mary slips out of the room, saying, 'I'll have mine with Benjamin, if that's OK' and in the background Fern can hear the tinny sound of a faraway TV, the familiar strains of a cartoon. There is a short clattering of pans from the kitchen and then it's quiet.

The women eat, Tom absent-mindedly strokes the rim of his bowl and in between mouthfuls Rachel asks, 'Can you explain the firing process to us, like – what happens to the pots?'

And so Tom talks about bisque firing and glaze firing. His face suffuses with happiness as he explains about elements and cones and knowing your kiln and how he fires at night because the electricity is cheaper then. He tells them about

Raku firing and the Raku Master and that it takes twelve hours for the kiln to heat up and two days for it to cool down and that there's the soak period and how he admires Mick Casson's work. Then he describes the recipe he follows for his glaze, how he uses cobalt oxide and cobalt carbonate and, knowing she should be listening but isn't, Fern lets his voice drift over her as she remembers Saturday night when she was at a table like this one with the boys, Jack and his mother, and how then she'd had no idea that by Tuesday she would be sitting here, like this.

Had she, she wonders, even thought about Elliott that night? Had he been somewhere in her subconscious? Had she scanned the restaurant just in case he was there? She can't recall – maybe she had, maybe she hadn't. She hadn't needed to because she had everything she'd wanted right there.

When she got home with Wilf on Friday night, he'd stood in the kitchen for a while as she started to prepare the dinner and then she'd said, 'It's OK, you can go, you don't have to stand on ceremony, you know!'

He hadn't been home since Christmas and, as he shifted his large feet and leant up against the counter and cleared his throat, she'd wondered if he'd forgotten that this was his home too and that he didn't have to be a visitor here.

So he'd gone upstairs and soon she could hear the bass notes of his music and it was like he'd never been away. But after they'd eaten and Jack was clearing away while she closed the curtains around the house she'd walked past his bedroom door and had been surprised to think he was just the other side of it. She'd grown so used to the silence that both he and Ed had left in their wake that momentarily she bristled with annoyance.

Stop it, she'd said to herself, but a slither of impatience remained. How was it, she wondered, as she put a towel on the guest bed for Jack's mother, that when the boys were at home she was so fearful of what it would be like when they left that she was impatient for them to leave so that they would be gone and the worst bit of their going would be over, and yet when they were gone, she wished more than anything for them to be at home again?

She and Jack were in bed when Ed and Sookie arrived. She heard the car pull in on the drive, the mumble of voices and the bunch of keys drop on to the table in the hall. Jack snuffled in his sleep, but didn't wake. He'd stopped worrying years ago, but Fern? Well, she still saw twisted metal, the rip of rubber on tarmac, the heart-stopping awfulness of a crash, every time she imagined Ed in the car. She knew she shouldn't, but it was just how it was.

'Hey,' Ed whispered, tapping lightly on their bedroom door. 'We're back.'

Should she get up, she wondered, do what she wanted to do, which was to lean up against the solid shape of her firstborn and scour the threads of his clothes for the scent of the boy he used to be? No, she thought, what would be the point? He wouldn't want her to. He had Sookie; small, Oriental, quietly intelligent. What need had he of his mother right now?

'Hey,' she replied softly. 'See you in the morning.'

Jack moaned and turned over in bed, taking the duvet with him so that a cold draught sliced down Fern's legs.

'It's good to have you all home,' she whispered into the darkness as she edged the duvet back over herself and Jack's breathing steadied.

As she lay there listening to the house click and settle, she thought of the holidays they'd taken after the boys had been born. She'd always felt that being away from home provided her with an opportunity to redefine herself, establish a different order, be someone other than who she actually was. But it never quite worked out that way.

When the boys were young, she'd never had the courage to take them abroad, until that first trip to Menorca when they were eight and ten and they'd spent days splashing in and out of arcs of beaded water in the hotel's swimming pool, eating chocolate ice creams and playing their version of snooker with Jack in the bar – their version, of course, being the one where they won each time and Jack always lost!

It was en route to Menorca that she'd first realised she was scared of flying. She'd never been so before and had taken many trips abroad when she'd been young but, she came to realise, this was one occasion when there would be nothing she could do to save her children should the worst happen; all she could be was brave and quiet and comfort them as the plane plummeted down. This was, of course, before 9/11 when everything changed anyway. After 2001 it only got worse, not better. The boys, however, grew more daring. They pointed at the landscape as the plane rose sharply on take-off and loved to follow the ribbons of motorways and rivers as they circled Gatwick on the way home and she would sit, her eyes fast shut, being neither brave nor quiet nor comforting. Wilf would reach across to wherever she was and touch her on the hand as though he was the parent and she the child. It was a strange time.

And then there were the summers they spent in Malta, witnesses to the hordes of ancient Ford Escorts and Hillman Imps and the unreliable throaty yellow buses that wove in and out of the traffic. The buildings there were pale and shuttered and crowded in amongst the fine, solid ones the Victorians had left behind.

They'd loved Malta, its history and its modesty, and Fern would sit on the balcony of the hotel and gaze over the rooftops of Sliema, imagining Jack, Ed and Wilf cutting through the hot alleyways of Valletta on the far side of Manoel Island and picturing the market stalls they had visited and the dust that would be gathering on their shoes on the journey back.

The sun danced silver on the water during those summers and the sky was every shade of blue imaginable, and she, Jack and the boys would spend hours trying to figure out the coded pealing of the town's church bells, wait eagerly for the sounds of the fiestas being held in distant villages each day at dusk and then watch the firework displays as they punctured the night sky. Each time there was so much to celebrate, or so it seemed.

And one day they visited the Blue Lagoon and the boys swam in the turquoise water and, laughing, had pressed their wiry tanned bodies against hers as she rubbed them dry with a towel and Fern believed that the days they spent in Malta and the nights she lay with Jack in huge, cool hotel beds should have been the happiest of her life. Her boys were close by and she loved the way they played in the pool, their unconscious abandon and total trust in one another; she had thought then that it would always be like that.

Then there was the year that George Best stayed at the same hotel. Ed was football mad in those days and had persuaded Jack to buy him a huge array of the replica shirts on display in Valletta Market and she remembered Ed arriving breathless in her hotel room one morning and gasping out the words: 'You'll never guess who's downstairs?!' It was like they had been visited by a god, but what a fallen idol he was.

Despite the panning he got in the press, however, and his death, which happened a short while afterwards, George was kind to the boys; he sat with them and chatted quietly to them and had his photo taken with Ed and, more than anything, just seemed sad and uncertain, like he knew somehow that it was going to be his last summer.

When they got home and Jack caught up with the coverage of this, George's last fall off the wagon, he'd said as he walked by Fern as she was gathering in the washing, 'I wonder what would have happened if he'd been better supported when he was young, not thrown to the wolves of fame like he was?'

Fern had nodded her agreement into the white of one of Jack's shirts and his words had ricocheted around in her head for days after. Each time she gazed out of the kitchen window or heard footsteps on the stairs or caught a glimpse of her unusually tanned face in a mirror, something uneasy lapped temporarily but terrifyingly at the outer reaches of her life. George might have been saved, but all the 'might have been's' might also have meant that this life she was living had never been. The thought of Elliott had been there then, it must have, but she'd brushed it aside, had had no need of it, did not want it.

So it was during the weekend just gone, with both boys back for Mother's Day, that, in a flurry of chatter and bangles, Jack's mother, Rosemary, had arrived.

'Hellooo,' she trilled, stepping through the back

door as if she'd just returned from a short visit to the corner shop.

'Oh, hello, Rosemary,' Fern replied, drying her hands on a tea towel and going over to her, bending down to kiss her on the cheek. Rosemary's skin was always so surprisingly soft.

Since Jack's dad had died, Fern had been waiting for Rosemary to fall apart, but she hadn't. Instead she'd bought a bright yellow Mini, had her hair cut, started to wear clothes made from linen and hemp and had festooned her arms with bracelets and her fingers with rings. She'd taken up quilting and acquired an allotment and was, she said, to Fern over the phone one evening, thinking of getting a dog.

This woman was, Fern had been thinking recently, an example of how to survive; a bit like Jules, she thinks now, as Tom leans across and says, 'More water, Fern?'

'Thank you,' Fern replies, holding up her glass. The water flows into it and she can still hear Linda and Rachel chatting to Jules. Everyone's plate is almost empty and Mary comes in carrying a cake on a platter.

'Pudding, anyone?' she asks, smiling at them. 'It's banana loaf and I've got some homemade ice cream coming too.'

For a second Fern feels a flash of envy. How come this woman can be so slim and yet so homey, so Jamie Oliver? When her boys were younger, surely she hadn't been this capable and generous? Sitting here, handing her empty plate over to Tom, she's sure she was cranky and harried most of the time, that she hadn't deserved the attention she'd got, however brief it had been, at the meal on Saturday night.

Jack had been at one end of the table, she at the other. Next to Jack on his left sat his mother, and then Wilf next to Fern. Ed sat on her left, with Sookie next to him. She'd felt cocooned by her sons, tiny in their presence.

'Cheers. To Mum,' Ed had said, raising his pint glass.

'Cheers,' Jack had replied, adding, 'To my mum too!' and had smiled at Rosemary, who had blushed very slightly and rested her hand briefly on his arm.

It was then that it had hit Fern, this feeling of being so very provisional. It was as though she was one of an ever-changing cast. There were Rosemary and Jack being how she and her boys would be in years to come, and there was Sookie, if she stayed around, ready in the wings to take over from her as she had taken over from Rosemary. It was like playing a weird kind of musical chairs and this thought made her dizzy for a second. It was a privilege to be there, but her impermanence also made it so painful, so poignant.

'You OK?' Wilf asked, still holding his glass up towards her.

'Yes, sure!' she'd replied, chinking her drink against his. 'Thanks, everyone. Now let's order, shall we?'

And the moment had passed, the cards had been exchanged, her family had laughed and the boys chatted about something called *IMDb* on the Internet, and in one of the pauses Ed looked at Sookie and said, 'What d'you fancy, love?' and Sookie whispered her reply to him so quietly that Fern couldn't hear it.

She'd had her time with them; that brief second when they'd held their glasses up had been her accolade, her bit in the spotlight. It could be no other way. Jack looked at her over the top of his menu, and although she couldn't see his mouth, she knew he was smiling at her; it was the way the skin crinkled around his eyes, the tilt of his head.

This is how it should be, she'd thought. How could I want anything else?

Now she's in Chiswick and she's poised, fork in hand, watching her plate, and her ice cream is softening at the edges. She sinks the fork in; the banana cake is moist and light. She eats, smiling across at Jules.

'Good here, isn't it?' Jules says, raising her glass and saying, 'To Tom and Mary. Thanks for a lovely lunch.'

Linda and Rachel nod in agreement, and outside Fern can hear a jet trundle through the sky to Heathrow, birds shout in the trees and Mary laugh in the kitchen.

I am very lucky, Fern thinks, to be here like this today, to have all this, all of everything and, she

122

pauses, her fork once again in mid-air, to have seen Elliott this morning, to have the chance, finally, of laying the ghosts of the past to rest. It is luck, she thinks. Isn't it?

CHAPTER 8

Is that it? Elliott looks at the two letters and one punctuation mark of Fern's text. Is this what I've been waiting for? Surely she could have said something more, given me some hint as to what she's really thinking. But then, as he gathers up the thermos and greaseproof paper and walks back into the kitchen, he realises that maybe this is all she could have said. It is encouraging after all, isn't it? She's agreed to him letting her know if he's passing back through London tonight. Maybe they will be able to meet for a drink and he'll be able to study her some more, try to find out what her life has really been like, see whether she's anywhere near forgiving him for what he did to her.

He needs this, he realises, and this is something he hadn't known for sure this morning when he'd set out from Hastings. Maybe it had always been an implicit wish, but not something he could have articulated. But now? Now he's seen her again, spoken to her, and everything has changed. Yes, he still needs time to get used to this fact, but what is certain is that now he has the chance to seek the atonement he so obviously needs he should not let it pass him by, should he?

The sun goes in behind a cloud and there's a chill in the air; the house is preternaturally damp from the sea wind that channels up the street. He had forgotten this. He takes the thermos outside and leaves it on the step of Sid and Peggy's house. Inside they are still eating; there is the faint sound of cutlery on crockery and the air around the house is full of steak and kidney pie and, despite the fact he's just eaten, Elliott's mouth waters for the taste of it.

Looking up, he sees a man approaching from the direction of the town. The man is young, is wearing a suit, has a look of bewildered anxiety on his face, but is walking the walk of someone who is pretending to know what he's doing. It seems an odd mixture to Elliott, but then he can remember acting like this when he started out on Hewlett-Packard's graduate training scheme; how every day had been a matter of survival, worrying about clean shirts and wanting never to have to go back to Wales. This, he felt, would have been something akin to surrender. Now it is the one thing he wants to do. Coming home for good would be the best thing he can imagine, but is the one thing he can't do, because of Meryl, his divorce, his daughter and his business.

Elliott straightens his back, pushes his hair off his face and smiles. The young man smiles too. He's carrying a clipboard, and then Elliott remembers. Shit, he says to himself. The sodding estate agent.

It had been so quiet in the house that Elliott had forgotten about this. Getting the house valued for sale was fucking heartbreaking. But, as Dan had said in their last email exchange, it was necessary. 'We can't go on indefinitely footing the care-home bill,' he'd written. And Elliott, reluctantly, had agreed. There was no way Meryl would understand or agree to factor this into their negotiations over money, so selling was the only option, but it felt to Elliott then when they made the decision, and even more so now, when he's standing in front of this raw-faced boy from Foxtons who's wearing a shirt that's slightly too large for him around the collar, so totally and unremittingly unfair.

'Good afternoon. Mr, er, Morgan?' The agent slips the clipboard under his left arm and holds out his right hand. It is, Elliott notices, trembling slightly.

'Yes.' Elliott is unnecessarily brusque, he knows this, but can't seem to help it. He takes the hand; it is warm and limp and Elliott wants to crush it in his own. He does try to soften his voice for the next sentence, but it doesn't entirely work. 'You'd better come in then,' he says, letting go of the agent's hand. He wants to wipe his own hand on his jeans, but doesn't. Not doing so is excruciating.

'My name's Ryan Edwards,' the agent says, following Elliott into the hallway. 'I think you might have known my dad at school? When I said I was coming here today, he said he remembered you, knows the house, you know. His name's Alun.'

This boy's voice is all Welsh; it rises and falls but seems to do so self-consciously, as if stressing the differences between them. Elliott can visualise this boy standing in the kitchen of his parents' home that morning, eating his bowl of cereal, careful not to spill milk down his suit. He's probably never left Wales, neither has his father lived anywhere but here, has lived here all his life in fact. This Ryan probably joined Foxtons straight from school, as an office boy or something, has worked his way up to this, to standing in his father's old friend's house on a March afternoon, preparing to put a value on all the history and love that have over the years seeped into its floorboards and walls.

'Alun Edwards?' Elliott can't think, can't remember. He should, he knows. There was a boy called Alun in the First XV, maybe it was him? 'He played rugby, right?' It's a safe guess.

'Yeah,' Ryan says. 'So he says!' He laughs, but it's a shy, tinny laugh which makes Elliott feel uneasy.

How can this boy know enough to value this house, make sure it's sold to people who will understand it? But then Elliott doesn't know what sort of people buy houses in Llantwit any more. Are they exiles from Cardiff looking for a retirement place by the sea? Are they the English from places like Cheltenham or Worcester looking for a holiday home? Or are they people like Ryan, wanting to buy their first home, bring a girl to it, have children, stay close to family? He'd never thought of it this way but, maybe this is what his parents did. How could he not know what they'd thought when they'd stepped over the threshold that first day back in the late 1950s? He should do, they should have told him. He is cross with them for this.

It feels like the village is holding its breath while this decision gets made, and Ryan shifts his feet in the hallway, obviously anxious to get on. The resentment in Elliott's chest bubbles yet more.

'Right,' he says. 'Guess we'd better make a start. Do you actually need me to come round with you?'

He both wants to and doesn't; he feels over-protective of the house and yet doesn't know if he can face the prospect of seeing it through Ryan's eyes. He knows he shouldn't be angry with his parents; it isn't their fault he's here today doing what he's doing, the thought that his parents had always really been strangers to him lodged in his head.

'It's up to you,' Ryan replies. He's obviously been trained in how to deal with householders reluctant to sell, but Elliott can sense that, even so, the dynamic between them is not an easy one. It's an uncomfortable relationship; they are separated by age, by the rules of customer and supplier, by the fact that he went to school with this boy's father, probably stood in the showers with him after a match, fought for the attention of the same girls but wouldn't recognise him now if they met in the street.

'I'll be here if you have any questions,' Elliott says, turning so he's looking out of the front window. 'Don't mind the labels. They're just for me and my brother. We need to sort out what's going where.'

Ryan doesn't reply. There's a man on the pavement outside; he's bending down, plastic bag in hand, to scoop up the mess his dog has made. Elliott can hear the man talking to the dog, not the actual words, but it's a kind of conversation anyway. The dog looks adoringly up at its owner as if in answer. The street is otherwise quiet. There are few cars this time of day.

Elliott senses Ryan's progress through the house; sees him scan the kitchen, make a note in his file that probably reads: 'Good size, in need of modernisation.' He then pops his head around the door into the bathroom that leads off the kitchen, and his disappointment is palpable. 'Downstairs bathroom,' he writes. These are not popular, not now. This small extension to the back of the house should be knocked through, the kitchen made larger and the box room upstairs which his mother had used as her sewing room should be converted into a bathroom. A third bedroom could be made in the loft space if anyone was willing to go the expense and trouble. This is what modern families want. Elliott knows this and he knows it will affect the price.

The box room was always a place of mystery to Elliott and Dan. They rarely ventured into it, but now he wonders, as he hears Ryan's footsteps scuff up the stairs towards it, what his mother thought as she sat there, the evening sun falling in pools on the floor, her head bent over her sewing machine as she made curtains for neighbours, mended suit pockets, took in the waistlines of wedding dresses. Perhaps it's because he never really took notice of her in there that he can't visualise her now: she's still in the kitchen, her hands in the sink, her back to him, the patterned material of her dress stretched over her hips. Did they really need the money his mother's sewing services provided? He'd never thought of this before and is winded temporarily. How can he have been so spectacularly selfish? he thinks. Should he therefore not be so cross at Chloe? Is this how we all are when we're young, maybe? A door closes upstairs and Ryan walks into his parents' bedroom. Elliott feels like weeping.

It's soon over. Ryan comes downstairs, says, 'Can I take a look outside?'

'Sure,' Elliott replies. 'There's not much to see. Just the back garden, and parking in the lane up there.' He points to behind the trees. 'There's room for a car and a—' he can't think of the word, there's a painful pause— 'turning circle,' he says at length.

'No garridge?'

The way Ryan pronounces the word makes the skin on the back of Elliott's neck burn.

'No.' Elliott really can't be bothered now. It won't make any difference, but he does add, 'Visitors normally park opposite, in Spitzkop – they don't normally mind, or didn't in my day anyway.'

The name 'Spitzkop' has always flummoxed Elliott. Why on earth should a road in a Welsh village be called this? It had annoyed him intensely when he was younger, he just couldn't understand the connection, but now, well, now he doesn't have the energy to care all that much about it.

Ryan makes his way up to the top of the garden; Elliott watches him from the kitchen window as he looks down at his shoes and the footprints he leaves in the damp grass, watches him write something else down in his file and then look up at the sky. Just for a second Elliott is curious as to what this boy is thinking. Can he smell summer on the air, or the threads of salt coming up from the sea? Is he listening to the chorus of birds or the wheeling of seagulls? Or is he just pausing, his mind empty other than wondering what his mother'll make him for his tea later and what score he'll get on the Slot 777 fruit machine in the King's Head tonight?

It's like waiting for an exam result, Elliott thinks as he goes back into the lounge-room. Ryan comes into the kitchen, wipes his feet on the doormat and slinks round the door so that he's now standing in front of Elliott.

'Mr, er, Morgan?' he says.

'Call me Elliott.'

'Oh, OK, well, er, Elliott,' Ryan is obviously uncomfortable with this. Perhaps he hasn't covered this bit in his training. 'I think I would advise you to put the house on the market for . . .' He stalls. The seconds stretch. He names a figure. 'It might not reach that, but we can try.'

He has the grace not to the mention the kitchen and bathroom and for this Elliott is thankful, but the price isn't nearly enough; it's not what the house is worth to Elliott, nor will it pay for his dad's care for long. Elliott does a quick calculation in his head; that's just over four and a bit more years. Both the thought of his dad living that long, and the thought of him not, make him feel nauseous.

'Just do what you think best,' he says to Ryan. 'I'll leave it up to you. You've got my contact details, right?'

'Yes.' Ryan is obviously relieved. This ending is better than he had feared. Maybe he'd expected Elliott to haggle, or punch him, or something. The fact that Elliott has capitulated so completely and so quickly has surprised both of them. 'Email and mobile. I'll send you the draft details for approval and let you know when it goes on our website. And I'll give you a weekly update on enquiries, viewings, that sort of thing.' He pauses, holds out his hand, coughs a small cough. 'If I could . . .' he says.

'Oh yes,' Elliott replies, passing over a spare key, and has to close his eyes so he can't see Ryan put it in his jacket pocket. 'Thank you,' Elliott adds at last as he starts to steer Ryan out of the house. He's had enough; he needs to be alone now. He needs to leave, lock the door, walk up into the village and get a cab from the station and get to The Grange. Time is passing too quickly. It's almost two thirty. Will there be time to meet Fern? Will she want to meet him? He feels as though London is a thousand miles and a hundred years away from him, and Hastings and Meryl are yet further and Chloe is somewhere on the moon, totally out of reach.

Ryan goes. No doubt he'll tell his dad later that he valued this house today and that this Elliott Morgan guy had been a bit weird, but that's what happens when you go to university, stay away, isn't it? And Alun Edwards will nod, remember some boyhood error of Elliott and say, 'Yes, son. It is. He was always a strange one.'

The thermos is still sitting on the step next door as Elliott locks up the house and starts walking up to the square and into the incongruously named Commercial Street. There is nothing commercial about it any more. The shops have all changed hands; what used to be the electrical-goods store is now a restaurant, the newsagent's is a hair-dresser's, the clothes shop on the corner is Foxtons.

Elliott can imagine the photograph of his parents' house in the window; can hear the villagers say, 'So the boys are selling up then. So sad, isn't it? Shame they didn't stay around. The younger one, Dan, he's in America, you know. New York, I think. How about that?' Elliott can see them standing there with their macs and shopping trolleys and feels that somehow they'll also know that his marriage is over. They'll know that today, when he's back here, it's as though he's holding the last twenty-five years in his hands, and like water, drop by drop, they're seeping through, falling on to the pavement below, evaporating in the fitful afternoon sun. They will be able to see all this so much more clearly than he does.

'Can you take me to St Hilary's?' he asks the cab driver outside the station. 'To The Grange?'

'No problem,' the driver replies. He grins at Elliott, turns on the ignition and they drive away. Elliott doesn't look back as they leave the village, but picks his phone out of his pocket. It has crumbs on it from the sandwich wrapper. He brushes them off, presses a button to read his emails. He needs silence and occupation. He hates the thought of what he'll find at The Grange; hates the prospect of seeing his father; is still far too full of love for the man he used to be.

The driver is mercifully quiet, but Elliott can sense the questions seeping out of him. 'Who are you? Why are you here? Why are you going to where you're going?' Drivers must be curious, mustn't they? Otherwise their jobs would be boring. Elliott thinks he should have brought a short questionnaire with him, with the answers filled in. 'My name is Elliott Morgan,' it could say. 'I am fifty years old. I lived here as a boy but now my brother and I are selling the house to pay for our father's care. Yes, the father who's living in The Grange. I have one daughter, a soon-to-be-ex-wife, my own business, a dead mother and I haven't had sex in months.' Oh, and finally, under 'Any other comments' he could add, 'This morning I unexpectedly met the girl I once loved and everything now feels different. It's also possible I might see her again soon and this might change things yet further.'

Going past the Llandow Industrial Estate, he thinks of Fern and of sex, both the sex he hasn't had lately and all the times he and Meryl made love. To his surprise, he can't remember any individual occasion; they've all merged into one great long intake of breath; the waiting, the wondering, the feeling afterwards that, somehow, he's done something wrong. It was so different with Fern.

There was the party where they'd met and the almost chemical spark that seemed to ignite between them as he stood by the fridge in the house she lived in with Jules. Fern had been small and fiery, with those deep brown eyes and close-cropped hair; she'd been energy and fizz and intelligence and, as she'd swayed in front of him, a little drunk, he knew he wanted her and he'd

135

taken her upstairs to a bedroom with the lame line, 'Do you fancy going somewhere quieter?' and he'd put his mouth on her, circling her clit, and she had come quickly, gasping and grasping him and pulling him into her. 'Do we need anything?' he'd asked, his lips on the soft skin of her neck. 'No, I have it covered,' she'd said, and he had come in her, his hands pushing against a pile of coats. That had been the first time, and then there were all the others; the soft slow times, the urgent fucks in train toilets and the laughter and sleeping and waking to find her there.

It's uncomfortable sitting in the taxi thinking these thoughts and he wishes he hadn't done so. It has been a mistake. He has to cross his legs, glad again that the driver's not looking at him in his mirror, but then the driver says, 'Almost there,' as they turn off the A48, adding, 'It's been a nice day so far, hasn't it?'

Elliott is relieved. Talking about the weather is a safe thing to do and he's grateful to the man. 'Yes,' he replies, 'it's been good.'

The driver sighs and seems to gather himself up to say, 'Have you seen that Rhod Gilbert on TV?' but from the tone of his voice, it's as if he can't really be bothered, isn't really interested in Elliott's answer.

Elliott also wishes he wouldn't bother. He can't think. Has he seen this man? Hasn't he? Does he really care? 'Think so,' he says non-committally.

'I love that one, you know, when he asks the

audience if anyone there has lived in Wales and some guy says yes, and Rhod asks, "So how old were you when you first realised you could take off your cagoule?" It's a killer, that one, isn't it?'

'Mmm,' Elliott says, thinking back to his walk to school, the constant push against the wind, the rain slanting in his eyes, the wet rustle of his coat and sitting in damp clothes all day. He had tried to forget these things. He wants to say something insightful about the funniest jokes being based on real life, you know, and that they work because they're clever observations of what it's really like, but he can't frame the sentence, pick out the right words. So he says, 'Mmm,' again and, 'I'll look out for him on TV.'

'*Live at the Apollo*,' the driver says, turning into the driveway of The Grange.

This is a strange thing for Elliott to hear at this moment and he can't reconcile the two images; the thought of a stage and lights and heat and applause and this, this mellow-stoned building with its gravel car park, its woodland and the sulphur-coloured cloud above it that has appeared as if from nowhere. He also thinks of his father sitting in a chair somewhere inside, his hands crossed on his lap, staring into space.

The driver doesn't seem to require an answer so Elliott leans forward and says, 'How much?'

'Ten?' the driver suggests.

'Great.' Elliott gets out the money, hands it over.
'Do you want me to wait? I don't mind.'

Does he? Would it be good to have a car waiting, know that that his visit is to be timed, that he has an excuse to get away?

'No, it's OK,' Elliott says. 'I've no idea how long I'll be. Wouldn't want to keep you hanging about.'

'Righty-o then.'

The driver puts the car back into gear and Elliott gets out. Neither man makes the effort to look at the other, and the cab pulls away, gravel spinning from its tyres. Elliott waits until the sound of the engine has faded, then turns towards the house. The cloud has gone and sunlight is slammed up against the front of the building. He starts walking.

The doorway is wide and squat, the door itself heavy and old. Elliott always feels a little bewildered when he comes here. Part of him wants it to be safely municipal, smelling slightly of disinfectant and lavender; he wants the nurses' shoes to squeak on the tiled floors. But it's not like that; instead it's a polished place, with carpets and dark wooden furniture. There are always flowers in the hallway; it's lilies today, and the light is the colour of lemons.

'Ah, Elliott.' The manager appears out of her office to one side of the wide staircase. 'It's good to see you.'

She is dressed in navy: a skirt and a jacket with a white blouse underneath. Her make-up and hair are perfect and her shoes are smart and shiny. She doesn't talk about the details of his father's

138

care, or money, or anything official; that's all done by letter and gracious email correspondence, so that when he comes here it's like visiting with friends. It was a good choice of place, the only choice really, because neither he nor Dan could have taken their dad away from Wales like Meryl had wanted them to, it would have been like taking away the air he breathed, but not for the first time Elliott wishes that Dan could come with him, just once, just to see it for himself. He also wishes his mother could know this place, but then, if she was still alive, his dad wouldn't be here at all, would he?

The manager is talking about some building work they have planned – a new summer house in the garden and an idea for art classes – but Elliott isn't really listening. He doesn't want to; all he can see is his mother as she was at the end, lying beached on stiff hospital sheets. She's parchment pale, stick thin, is wearing a mask over her mouth and her eyes are glued shut. Her chest rises and falls in time with the machine at her side and there are monitors and suction noises. There is a bleeping from somewhere; it is insistent and unwelcome.

His dad was sitting in an armchair by the bed when Elliott arrived. 'Hello, there,' he said, looking up at his son, an expression of total confusion on his face. It was like he was saying, 'I've no idea what I'm doing here. Who is this person in the bed? Where's my Annie gone?'

And all Elliott could do was touch the woman's hand, feel its slight warmth and the faint pulse in the crease of her wrist and wish harder than he's ever wished before that he could turn back the clock and have her standing at the sink, her head turning to look at him, her eyes seeing through his skin to his bones and muscles and his innermost thoughts. He would, he knew, as he pulled up a chair to join his father in his vigil, miss being so known by someone else. It was as though with her death he would lose that part of him that she had loved, and at that moment, as a nurse came in, picked up his mother's chart from the end of the bed, looked down at it and flipped the lid of her pen up with a click to write something, this part seemed to be the biggest bit of him; that when she went he would be left less than half the person he used to be.

Her death was so wrong, far too quick and merciless, and now Elliott cocks his head to one side in an effort to concentrate on what the manager is saying. He can see her mouth moving, her eyebrows lifting and falling. She is smiling and she laughs as she waves a hand in the direction of the garden. 'So you see,' she says, 'it's going be a busy time. But we will, of course, make sure that our residents are disturbed as little as possible. Your father has been so well of late. He will be delighted to see you, I know he will.'

How can she? How can this woman in her suit and with a computer in her office and charts on the wall know what his father, or he for that matter, is thinking? Was she there with Elliott in the house with Ryan's clipboard and unease? Was she at Paddington this morning watching Fern lift her coffee cup to her lips with two hands? Did she take the call from Chloe about the sodding laptop? No, these things were Elliott's, just as the man in the armchair at the hospital on the day his mother died and the man in the armchair now in the care home lounge with its lemon light and soft music are his gift and his burden.

But now all he can think to say is, 'Thank you. I guess I'd better go through then?'

'Sure, sorry, Elliott. I shouldn't have kept you.' She uses his name again deliberately as though she's revised it and he leaves her with her as much a stranger to him as when he arrived. He has spent five minutes in her company and doesn't know her at all, and she doesn't really know him, and this is how it is meant to be.

And he makes his way to the sitting room and his father and remembers sitting with his mother's body after she died. He'd looked over at Dan and his father; they were standing with their backs to the wall and the weight of something incredibly heavy was in the air between these three men and he'd searched and searched his mother's face for some sign that she would be able to lift off the weight and carry it away with her, but her face had remained resolutely still, totally empty. It's up to us now, Elliott had thought, and he hadn't cried. He had never actually cried.

It's twenty past three and his dad's in a chair by the window. Elliott steps nearer, puts his hand on the old man's arm, says, 'Hi, Dad, it's me.'

CHAPTER 9

In the kitchen of the house in Merton Avenue, Mary is bending down, looking in a cupboard. As Fern enters the room, she stands, straightens and looks at her.

'Oh, thank you,' she says, glancing about her and adding, almost apologetically, 'I never seem to be able to get straight!'

Fern puts the pile of bowls she's carrying down by the sink. The kitchen's a jumbled kind of a place, with laundry overflowing from a basket in the corner by the back door, paintings of strange green and red beasts stuck on the fridge with the name Benjamin written in large round writing underneath each one and, on the table, a doll is surrounded by her discarded wardrobe.

'Don't worry, I know!' Fern says. 'I was just the same when my boys were small. Well, actually –' she pauses, laughs a little self-consciously and looks down at her boots – 'when they come home now it's a bit like the house has been hit by a whirlwind! They never seem to put anything down in the same place twice . . .' She lets her voice trail away.

143

The younger woman looks exhausted and Fern wants to say, 'Here, rest your head on my shoulder for a moment,' but she doesn't. Instead she says, 'Well, I guess I'd better get out of your way and join the others,' but as she walks out of the room she feels Mary's eyes on her back and it seems that there is a whole conversation they haven't, but should have, had.

Is this what Elliott's wife's life was like when their daughter was younger? Fern wonders. Was she the woman he left her for, and did she have a kitchen like this? Did she collapse in a chair with a glass of wine in a conservatory, like the one Fern is walking through now, when her kids were in bed? Elliott mentioned a daughter, but maybe he has other children too. There is so much Fern doesn't know, but she can see a younger Elliott stepping into his house at the end of the day, putting a briefcase down in the hallway and making his way through to where his wife is sitting with her feet tucked under her and, leaning over, kissing her tenderly on the top of the head. Is this what Fern wanted for herself when she lay in that bed in Turkey replete with foreign spices, sun and Elliottt's touch? Is this what she gave up when she let him walk away from her that day?

It's true, she's had so much else instead, but still, on the way back to the studio she checks her phone but there are no messages, no missed calls. She feels somewhat disappointed by this. She'd had a small need to be needed. Also, she'd wondered if

144

Elliott had texted again, but he obviously hasn't and she doesn't want to wonder why this might be. She automatically slips her phone into her jeans pocket, follows the others back into the studio, puts her bag back in the cupboard and hauls her overalls on.

The others are chatting; Linda's emptying her water bowl and filling it with clean water and Tom is wedging up some more clay. The small studio is a busy and happy place. They have been well fed, the sun is still shining and time is going at just the right speed. Fern had worried briefly, as she helped clear the dishes from the table, that the day would go too quickly and that she wouldn't have time to do everything she wanted; that it would suddenly be six o'clock and she and Jules would just be leaving to go back to Victoria and that Elliott would be somewhere else, somewhere she didn't know, returning to whatever he'd left that morning, the life he's made for himself and which she knows nothing about and now won't have the chance to and that, although it shouldn't matter, suddenly and fiercely it does. This is surprising, but the surprise is getting less with each passing hour. Elliott's presence back in her life is becoming more of a given, and she's amazed by how quickly this transformation is taking place.

She bends across her wheel and switches it on; the studio fills with humming, like bees, she thinks, as she flicks water on to the wheel head. I have, she tells herself again, so much, and it has to be the only life I could have lived because otherwise there would be no Ed, no Wilf, none of what I have lived through with Jack, what I've loved.

Tom comes over to where she's sitting and says, 'Right, here you go. More clay! Now it's your turn. I want a bowl. You can do it, I know you can.'

The clay is cold again so she wraps her hands around it to warm it and, as she does so, moisture trickles through her fingers. Looking across at Jules, she smiles and Jules smiles back and then her friend dips her head towards her own clay, tenses her shoulders and starts to centre. Fern does the same.

The clay fights her at first; it's stubborn and lazy, but she finds herself talking to it in her head; she whispers to it, cajoles, says, 'Come on, it's just us,' and the pill shape starts to emerge; it is a perfect circle but slightly off-centre and suddenly she feels Tom's arms around her. His hands are covering hers and he's pushing her and the clay together, shifting them subtly towards the middle of the wheel. He's breathing heavily and she can smell a trace of cologne on his neck; it's bedded down under the scent of the clay, the lunch he's just eaten, the heat that came from his son's head when he touched it earlier. Fern feels uneasy. This is like something she's done before; this closeness, this sense of strangeness and of doing something wrong. She struggles to remember. It was such a long time ago.

146

'There,' Tom says, stepping back, and she feels cold without him.

His hands had been strong and hot; it had been a wonderful kind of intimacy, not what she'd been expecting at all, and then it comes back to her. It was, she thinks, about twelve years ago now. She'd tried to parcel up the memories, store them like she had those of Elliott, but with Tom's hands on hers, they'd rushed back.

She'd met Lars at work. They'd both worked for ABN AMRO; she in London, he in Holland. For her it had only been a short-term job and she'd hated the commute, leaving the boys, having to set up after-school care for them, taking time off when they were ill, but it had been his way of life. She remembers the precise way he spoke, his efficiency and how he'd touched her briefly on the arm the first time he came over to meet with her boss, how he had seemed to soak her up with his eyes.

He was so totally different from Jack. Jack was big and soft and familiar and Lars was lean and wise and unknown. After his first visit they'd started to email, just innocent exchanges, like, 'How are you?' and would swap news about their children, work gossip, lots of talk about the weather and it was safe and at a distance. But then he came over on secondment for a month. She'd booked his hotel room, sorted out his transport to and from the office each day, used to lie in bed with Jack asleep next to her imagining Lars reading papers, dictating reports into his Dictaphone for her to type up, and at work she would plug in the tape, put her headphones on and listen to his voice; it had felt like a caress. She hadn't really appreciated at the time just how lonely being a wife and mother could be, and Lars gave her a kind of escape, a harmless one, she had thought at the time.

However, things changed; without her really knowing how or why, there was a shift and it seemed dangerous. They were at an offsite meeting at a hotel just off the M25, there'd been dinner, wine, and some sort of flash had lit the air between them, and on her way out of the room at the end of the evening he'd followed her, stood in front of her in the corridor, said, 'Will you come to my room, share a coffee with me?' She had looked round to see if anyone was watching; laughter came from the function room behind the closed doors, but the corridor was empty. 'It would be good to be able to talk away from the noise, from the other people,' he'd added, and so she'd found herself in his room at midnight, sitting on his bed and holding a cup of coffee which was burning her fingers and he was standing in front of the mirror so she could see him reflected in it; it was like there were two of him.

'Could we?' he'd said, his eyes on her, fixing her.

'Could we what?' She was struggling. It had been years since a man other than Jack had looked at her that way and she knew, of course she knew, what he was asking of her.

'You know what it is I would like?'

'I think so, yes.'

'It is possible? Yes? No?'

His eyes were the colour of honey, his hair prematurely grey at the sides and his forehead was creased with worry lines, yet, looking at her that night, he had seemed almost boyish, very vulnerable and shy.

'Oh, Lars,' she had said. 'I don't know. I just don't know.'

She'd put the coffee down on the floor by the bed and stood up and made her way to the window. She pulled back the curtain. The moon was low and huge; it hung in the sky like a weight. It was the colour of custard. She felt an overwhelming sadness because she'd never be able to explain what she felt at that moment, not to him, not to anyone. It was a mixture of fear and gratitude: fear at what might happen and gratitude that she had the opportunity and the strength to say, 'I'm sorry, so sorry,' and she dropped the curtain back into place and went across the room towards him. He held out his arms and she moved into them. He fitted around her perfectly and she drank in the fresh laundry smell of his shirt, sensed the muscles of his chest and legs tighten as he held her. She felt him stir, felt the length of him against her and tipped up her head so she was looking into his eyes. 'I can't – you know

I can't – and really, if you think about it, you can't either. Maybe, well, maybe if things were different . . .'

'This is correct, you are correct,' he'd said, his mouth moving around the words so tidily, and even though he was still there, and she could still feel his breath on her skin, she'd started to mourn him then, knew that she would do so for a long time, and now her wheel is spinning and she shifts her hands very slightly, presses down hard to form a crater in the clay, then rests her fingers against one side of it as she starts to lift the pot. She can feel the clay move and stretch, is connected with it at a basic level. She holds her breath, watches the bowl grow slowly, so slowly. It is like sex, she thinks again, and eventually, reluctantly, she lets go of the clay, pulls a length of wire under it and turns the wheel off so that it too slows, and looks across at Jules, who is staring at her, an expression on her face that seems to say, 'I know what you're thinking,' and all Fern can do is smile back at her friend, damp down the bolt of grief she has felt and stare at the pot in front of her. It is, she thinks, quite simply one of the most beautiful things she's ever done.

In the quiet of her stopped machine, she can hear her phone buzz; it vibrates inside her pocket and she's glad; she's glad that whatever is it will bring her back to now. She hopes against hope it isn't Elliott. She wipes her hands on the seat of her overalls and delves through the layers, picking

150

out the phone, leaving grey fingerprints on it. She looks at the screen. It's Wilf. Despite everything, her instincts kick in; he might be nearly grown, but this boy, this boy who is calling her, is her son. Oh my God, she thinks, what's wrong?

She hurries out of the studio, leaving her pot drying on its tile; the sunlight outside is bright and blinds her for a second. Peering down at the screen she struggles to find the right button, presses it and lifts the handset to her ear, 'Yes?' she says, not wanting the need to be needed that she felt earlier to feel like this. 'Wilf? What is it? What's wrong?'

'Hey, chill, Mum, it's OK, nothing's wrong.' There is a pause, 'Well,' he adds, 'not really.'

His voice is deeper on the phone than it is when she's speaking to him face to face, and he's more of a stranger to her now, like this. In her mind he's not the man who got into her car last weekend. Instead he's seven; small and bony, full of wild enthusiasms and temper. She remembers his face as he rushes out of school at the end of the day to find her standing with the other mums and him planting his feet squarely in front of her, his hands on his hips, ready to share the injustices of the day with her; 'Miss Stephens said I wasn't allowed to use the glue twice in a row when I was making my robot, but that I had to let Toby share it.' And it was as if he'd said, 'There, you own the problem now. Sort it,' and she'd done what she always did with him, said, 'Gosh, Wilf. That must have been tricky, but it's sausages for tea tonight. Your favourite!' and he would skip back to the car, always a few steps ahead of her, and she would hurry to catch up with him.

Ed, meanwhile, seemed to have sauntered through his childhood; always late for swimming lessons, cubs, trips to the supermarket. She must have spent years waiting for him in the hallway, with Wilf sitting on the bottom step of the stairs, his fists clenched, always ready, always alert, like a match just about to flare.

Now they are both at a distance from her and she seems constantly to be reaching out and touching the hems of their clothes, but there's never enough material to hold on to.

'Go on,' she says, 'what is it?'

'Well,' Wilf says, 'you know we – that's the others and me, Si and that lot – are planning on getting a house together next year . . .' His voice falters.

Is this, she thinks, one of those times when he expects her to have all and every possible answer? Does he want her to conjure a house for him, say, 'Here, my love, is the key. Live here and be happy!'?

'Yes?' she says cagily.

'Well, we've found one – a house, that is; the only thing is he needs the deposit by Thursday and it's Tuesday today, right?'

'Yes, it's Tuesday today,' she says, and with a hint of impatience which she doesn't want to feel, adds, 'And I presume by "he", you mean the landlord?'

152

'Yeah, he's some guy we found through the uni, all looks OK – the house is all right too.'

'How much do you need?'

This has been a familiar refrain over the past few years. Each time either boy rang it was normally to ask for money or a lift or the answer to some obscure question, like, 'Remember that time we went to that lake? Where was it?'

There had, of course, been nights when she'd stayed awake listening for one or other of them to come home; waiting for the sound of a key in the door, footsteps on the stairs, and then there'd be the phone call, the 'I've lost my keys' or 'My wallet's been stolen' one, and she or Jack would haul on warm jumpers and boots and head off out into the night to pick one of them up from some country lane, or from the station where they'd pay the excess due on a lost ticket. Then the boys would stumble into their rooms and they would go back to bed. Jack would fall asleep almost immediately and she would lie there with the weight of the dark pressing down on her eyelids but still awake, still watchful.

Was it always going to be like this? she wonders now as Wilf tells her the amount, says, 'We get it back at the end, so it's only a loan. I've got enough for the rent, well, almost.'

He'd insisted on getting a job to help with the costs of university, but his wages were just a drop in the ocean really and one day they'd have to sit down and work it all out, but now they just lurch from one financial crisis to another. Ed's money situation is more mysterious, but then Ed is more mysterious generally; he has moved so far away from her and Jack that all she can do is feast on the scraps of information he releases and trust and hope and remember.

Now she hears herself saying, 'OK,' but feels a sharp dart of worry that the landlord might be a con man, but then, she reasons, he came through the uni so must have had some checks done on him. She'd just have to trust Wilf on this occasion. 'Have you tried your dad?' she asks.

'Yes, he wasn't picking up.'

Typical, thinks Fern, he never does. She's cross for a second, but then remembers that her husband is a good man; he is loyal and hard-working and she shouldn't be feeling like this. She daren't think what his secrets might be, that he might have unresolved things hovering in the background, might watch women in bars and restaurants, like that waitress the other night, the one she'd told Jules about, and wonder, 'What if.'

'OK, I'll send him a text, get him to transfer the money as soon as he can, or if he can't do it today, I'll put cash in your account tomorrow. That clears immediately, doesn't it?'

'Yeah,' Wilf says again, his interest already waning. They'd transacted their business; he is ready to move on.

She can hear voices in the background, feels him being pulled away from her. What would

154

happen, she thinks, if he asked, 'Actually, Mum, how are *you*?'

What would she tell him? Would she say, 'Well, I met someone this morning who I haven't seen in years, and who, if things had been different, I probably would have married, and now I feel I'm in danger somehow, that I could actually mourn more than I celebrate, that I might have got it all wrong, fear I've done it all wrong, that I might not be able to do the next bit of this, the bit without you and Ed in it, the bit when it's just your dad and me.' Would he turn to her like she thought he might when she picked him up from the station the Friday before Mother's Day and actually judge her for these failings?

There has, she realises, been a pause, the static on the line is humming and she can hear the pottery wheels turning behind her; birds are singing and there is the distant beat of traffic.

'Well, I guess I'd better let you go,' she says into this gap of sound.

'OK,' her son says, 'and hey – thanks, Mum.'

He will, she knows, go spinning away and she will be left here and the phone line between them will be silent and she will have to dig deep and tell herself that in the face of everything she does have, this kind of loneliness doesn't matter, won't last.

She texts Jack to tell him about Wilf's call, scans the inbox but there are no new messages. She kind of hoped that there might be one from Elliott, something to hold on to during the next few hours, but the screen is blank and she returns the phone to her pocket.

Inside the studio Jules, Linda and Rachel are still busy at their wheels; Tom is skitting between them like a restless butterfly. He wants so much for them to do it right, for it to be as easy for them as it is for him, but it isn't, and the women lift their heads now and again and shrug at one another, their hands around their slippery clay. Some sense of the beauty of what they're doing seems to have gone.

'Right, now then, ladies,' Tom says as Fern climbs back on to her seat and pulls the sleeves of her overall up. 'It's time to learn how to do plates!'

They tidy up what they're doing and hover around him as he takes his place on what must be his favourite wheel. He chose this one before too.

'Firstly,' he says, 'you need to make a bat, a sort of a plate to go under your plate, so you can lift yours off.' It all looks so easy and logical as he centres his clay, almost whispers, 'You need to cone up,' and he holds the pill of clay steady and lifts both hands until an upside-down cone appears, it is almost phallic and it is moist and grey and Tom is lost to them now. 'Flatten it down, put your finger in the sweet spot and drag, drag it out, there, there, there she goes . . .'

Fern can't look at Jules. This time she wants to

laugh and cry both at the same time. This is like music, she thinks, so much like when Jack puts his fingers on her and circles until she cries out. But as she watches Tom score the underside of the bat and put it back on the wheel, she can't recall the last time Jack did this.

Repeating the process, Tom makes a plate on top of the bat. Again he clenches his muscles, dips his head almost lovingly as he drags. The result is a perfect circle, exactly the same size as the bat. Tom reaches over for his calliper, measures, nods, makes a small guttural noise in the back of his throat and then lifts his eyes to look at the women. How can I compete with this? Fern thinks as he says, 'Right, ladies. Your turn!'

She takes her clay, starts to wedge it, then throws it and as she bends to centre it, her phones buzzes again. Jack, she thinks. It'll be Jack about the money. This is what he's good at. If she'd said, 'Help me, I'm lonely. I've realised that I'm lost in these middle years,' he would look at her blankly and tell her to write a list of her worries, work through them, offer each one a solution, then park it. This is, he'll say, how he keeps his mind free, has space in which to breathe, and she will want to thump her fists against his ribs and cry, 'No, that's not the way. You don't understand me at all.' But he does understand the practical things, and if she's honest, he does know her too and this payment is something he can do. This is the balance they've worked out between them and it works just fine.

He has been a good father; has managed to keep his sense of self and has loved the boys justly and fairly, but would, she knows, take any risk to keep them safe. It was much the same with him and his father. Charles had been a good man too. He'd been quiet and steady, had played football in the park, helped Jack reconstruct a motorbike when he was seventeen, had commuted from Brighton to London each day for twenty-five years, then had retired and taken up golf with enthusiasm, but without fuss, and had slipped into his seventies with ease. But then the diagnosis came and, for a while, he had faltered. Fern had seen a flicker in her husband's father's eyes that said, 'This is not good. I don't know how to deal with this. I want to tell you everything, fill in all the gaps and make you understand who I really am.'

Rosemary had been equally uneasy; had twittered and fussed and clung on to Jack as though he could provide the cure. The cancer was operated on and then there were treatments that shrank Charles to the size of a boy, and he fought so hard that in the silent moments, when Fern would enter a room to find him asleep in an armchair with a blanket over his knees, she would search his face for the battle scars but find only exhaustion. He rallied briefly that last Christmas, but by January the pains were back and he was so much weaker this time. Rosemary showed Fern and Jack the letter. It didn't mention the word 'terminal', but talked instead about palliative care, the measures they could take to make him comfortable, how he should have time to get his affairs in order, and the boys had been bewildered and outraged in equal measure that their remote and romantic grandfather was inexorably being taken away from them.

He died in early February when there was snow on the ground. She and Jack and Rosemary had taken turns to sit with him during those last days and had listened to the rasping of his breath and seen the glimmer of a pulse under his paper-thin skin, and at six that last morning the nurse had come to the family room to wake Fern and Jack, said, 'It's time. It won't be long now,' and they had shuffled along the morning-still corridor to where Rosemary was sitting dry-eyed by her husband's bedside, her warm hand on his cold one. There'd been one last, long breath which had made Charles's body shudder and Fern think he had shaken off this demon that had hold of him and was coming back to them, but then it all just stopped: all the waiting and hoping, the fearing and grieving. For a few blissful seconds there had been nothing but an overwhelming sense of peace as the snow fell in slow motion outside the window.

Jack has never, Fern thinks now as she watches the clay spin, really talked about it. It had happened, they'd had the funeral, he'd sorted out the paper-work and she had helped him bag up the clothes and take them to a distant charity shop, and he had spoken to his mother twice a week for a while and then the calls had dwindled and his mother had bought the Mini and had her hair cut and his father's absence became a solid, unquestionable thing; as though it was always meant to be like this.

She'll check the message later, she tells herself as she prepares her wheel to start again. It must be about three o'clock by now. They have an hour or so left and then this bit of her day will be over and she will have to move on, move nearer the time when Elliott might text or ring, saying, 'I'll be at Paddington at seven. Shall we meet for a drink?'

CHAPTER 10

When Hywel Morgan looks up at his son, Elliott is surprised by how familiar this man is to him. In the times between visits, whether purposefully or not, Elliott seems to distance himself from his father; both the man he was and the man he is now. Therefore, seeing his face in front of him is a shock. It's a shock both because his dad appears to be so unchanged, but also because he is so much like an older version of Elliott that looking at him is like looking in some kind of time-distorting mirror. The two men have the same grey-green eyes, and the same creases running from temple to cheek, although the old man's are deeper and the bristles of his beard are white.

His dad appears puzzled by the man who is pulling up a chair to sit near him. Elliott can almost see the thoughts journey across his father's face.

'Dad?' he says, his voice croaky with lack of use. The minutes that have passed since his conversation with the manager seemed to have stretched into hours. 'It's me – Elliott. You need a shave,' he adds, wishing at once that he hadn't. It sounded

161

like a criticism, just one more reminder that his father can no longer do these things for himself.

Elliott had so wanted it not to be like this.

The old man shuffles in his chair, looks forlornly at his slippers and then raises those eyes to Elliott. 'I have a son called that,' he says.

In all the research Elliott's done and all the conversations he's had with his father's doctors and carers, he knows the one thing to remember is not to contradict, not to put blockages in the way of the already blocked thoughts. It is better to be encouraging, to let the memories flow, however wrong and wonky they might be. So Elliott has to say, 'Ah, do you? That's nice.'

'He was a good boy,' his dad says. 'Used to read a lot, if I remember.'

There is a pause, and out of the window Elliott can see an elderly lady walking slowly across the lawn, a carer by her side. The old lady is wearing a floral patterned dress, much like the ones his mother used to wear, a beige mac over it and her arm is hooked through the carer's; they are taking bird-like steps across the grass. There is something easy about the partnership; an aura of acceptance and a small amount of joy.

'Would you like to go for a walk, Dad?' Elliott asks. 'It's a lovely day out there.'

'No, thank you. Thank you so much, but it's almost teatime, I think,' his father replies, looking at the clock on the wall and squinting.

Elliott has no idea whether he can see the

numbers or knows what time tea is served or is making this up. His dad had, unwittingly it seemed, become a very good actor, especially towards the end when he was trying to carry on living on his own in the house.

It had been Peggy who'd called Elliott in the end. 'It's your dad,' she'd said, and her voice on the other end of the line had trembled. 'He's not so good. I think you ought to come.'

How had Elliott not known? He still asks himself this a hundred times a day. Had the signs been there even when his mother was alive or was it, was it, his mother's death which had started it all off? Had he wished the signs away, covering up the memory lapses and lost keys as innocent, isolated incidents? He's even sometimes wondered whether it is better for it to be like this or for his dad, if he has to suffer at all, to have something physically wrong with him, like heart disease or cancer; something that can be fought, not this awful deterioration.

'Are you staying for tea?' his dad asks. 'It's custard creams today.'

At that moment a carer wheels in a trolley. The cups chink on their saucers and, yes, there's a plate of biscuits and Elliott peers over, wanting it so much to be true. Yes! It's custard creams. Elliott watches the trolley progress around the room and at last it comes to him and his father. He hasn't known what to talk about, so has stayed quiet.

'Ah, Mr Morgan,' the carer says. 'Tea?' She is

ample and smells of soap; she has rosy cheeks and soft grey hair that falls in curls around her neck. Her feet are, Elliott notices, swollen in their crêpe-soled shoes.

His father nods enthusiastically.

'Your favourite biscuits today!' she says, putting two in the saucer alongside the cup she's passing him. She looks at Elliott as if to say, 'Every day is custard cream day. It's just easier this way.'

'Thank you, Gladys,' Hywel says.

Elliott wants to ask if that really is her name, but he doesn't because he's afraid of the answer. If it is, then maybe, just maybe, there is more of his dad left than he'd thought and then maybe, just maybe, it is a matter of choice what he does and doesn't remember. And if it's not? Well, if it's not her name, then that is just so fucking sad.

'Would you like a cup?' the woman whose name might or might not be Gladys asks Elliott.

'Yes, please.'

'It's nice to see you here,' she adds. 'He so likes the company.'

How does she know? Elliott thinks. How can she have any idea what this man in his too-loose trousers and old-man cardigan likes or doesn't like? Did she know him when he stood on the touchline and watched Elliott play rugby every Saturday morning, calling out, 'Man on,' and, 'Pick it up and run with it, boy,' and, 'Pass it!' and then, win or lose, they'd travel home in silence because that was just how they were?

All his dad would say when they got back to the house was, 'Make sure you clean your boots right now, son. The wax is in the drawer,' and he'd go out into the back garden to busy himself with his daffodils or a fence repair while Mum made the lunch and Elliott stood at the tap in the yard washing his boots, the water cold on his hands.

Then there was the time when Elliott got up in the night to get a drink of water. He must have been eleven or so, almost old enough to understand, and a noise had made him hesitate outside his parents' bedroom door; it had been his mother's laughter, a soft, gentle-edged sound, and then there'd been a silence, just the rustle of bedclothes and his father asking, 'Like that, Annie? Is that it?' and her murmured response, 'Yes, yes.' Did this carer know about this?

The morning after he'd heard this, Elliott had tried to notice if there was anything different about his parents, but they had sat at the breakfast table as they always did; his mother in her dressing gown, his father in his vest, trousers and braces, and they had buttered their toast without talking. Of course now, now Elliott knows about the secret language spoken by husbands and wives, about the worlds they keep separate from their children, and he knows about all the rest of it and envies his parents their version. They were far more successful at it than he ever was.

'There you are then, Mr Morgan,' the carer adds, tipping her head towards Elliott as she bustles away to the next resident, who is sitting on his own, staring into space.

Elliott has no idea what to say, but watches fascinated as his father sips his tea.

'Dan sends his love,' he says at length.

Hywel frowns. The name must be familiar then, Elliott thinks. As he stirs his own tea absent-mindedly, he tries some more information.

'He says it's been a lovely spring in New York this year. The blossom has been wonderful.'

He waits for this information to sink in, but what happens next surprises him. His father leans forward suddenly, grabs Elliott's arm with his free hand and pins him with a fierce look. Some tea slops out of the cup into the saucer. 'Did I ever tell you,' his dad asks, his voice creaky and urgent, 'of the time I spent in New York?'

'No!' Elliott stammers the word out, dreading what might come next. His father had never, to his knowledge, been to New York, never been further than London, if the truth were told.

'Remind me to tell you about it next time you come. We need to be somewhere more private. Walls have ears, you know.' The old man lets go of Elliott's arm and taps the side of his own nose solemnly.

'OK,' Elliott says.

'I have to be so careful, what with my history as a . . .' Hywel looks furtively around the room, 'spy,' he whispers. 'My enemies have very long memories, you know.'

'I'm sure they do,' Elliott answers, wishing somehow that even a tiny part of what his father is saying to him could be true. Then he says, 'Here, have you finished with your tea, Dad?' He can't help using the term, even though he fears it will only confuse his father further. It is an instinctive thing.

'Thank you, son,' Hywel says, handing Elliott his cup and saucer which he puts on the small table by his father's chair, and for a second Elliott's heart jumps, thinking that with the word 'son' his dad has recognised who he is. But then, then he remembers.

His dad called everyone 'son'; all Elliott's friends, even those of Dan he didn't approve of; the 'rough boys' from the estate, as he called them. This would be about the time when Dan was starting to break free; something neither his brother nor his father had really wanted to happen. But from the time Dan had been a small boy, with grazes on his knees and a fire in his belly, it had seemed ordained that the two of them, father and son, would clash and that Elliott would be left in the middle, loving both of them, not knowing what to do.

The battles had been over the usual things like staying out late, worrying their mother, not getting homework in on time. The teachers at school had been on Dan's case from an early age too; they seemed to recognise the free spirit in him and wanted to quash it rather than let it soar, and Dan would square up to them and his father, both as a bony-limbed twelve-year-old and a muscled nineteen-year-old, until he left for good that rainy October day when their mother had wept noiselessly over the sink and Elliott had had no idea how to comfort her.

Dan had drifted for a number of years after that; there'd been the odd postcard and infrequent visits when he'd turn up, far too thin, his hair matted and with a hollow-eyed girl in tow, and they'd crash down on Elliott's student-room floor and sleep for what seemed like days.

Then he disappeared completely; no calls, no letters, and an awkward heaviness grew around his absence. Elliott didn't mention his brother to his parents and they didn't talk about him to Elliott. However, he did imagine them deep in the night, their voices muffled by their pillows, sharing a sort of nameless grief. Even now Elliott finds it difficult to forgive Dan for this.

'Will you be staying here long?' his dad asks him now, his face polite, as if he was talking to a stranger.

'Just a little while longer, then I have to go.'

'Where will you be going to?'

Elliott doesn't want to have to explain about trains and London and Hastings and Meryl and Chloe and especially about Fern, so he says, 'I have a meeting to get to, Dad.'

'Ah, I see.' Hywel rests his head back and closes his eyes. It seems the visit is at an end.

There is so much Elliott hasn't said. Some part of him wanted to talk about the house, the furniture, his worries about money and how Dan is in New York, now so successful after putting himself through college during the silent years, buying a suit and learning how to see through the crap to the essence of things. These skills have made him marketable and he now hunts through the welter of rubbish that's thrown up around news stories in America for the one handle, the different view which will make the most impact for the news channel, and he's good at it, very good at it. Even so, there are times like earlier and now when Elliott is standing up, ready to walk away from their father, that he wishes his brother were here with him to share the responsibility and of having their dad's grey-green eyes look up at both of them, sure he should know who these men in front of him are.

'I'll get going then,' Elliott says, and bending down, touches his dad's knee. The old man sighs. 'It's been good to see you. Take care now and make sure you get your quota of custard creams.' It is a naff thing to say, but then the whole situation is naff. It shouldn't have to be like this at all.

Elliott hates leaving; he's done it countless times but it never gets any easier, each time as difficult as the last. Some of the other residents watch him go, there is a murmur of conversation in the room which he hasn't noticed until now and the lemon sun is still shining silkily in the entrance hall. It feels as though he's been here for a very long time, but it's only been half an hour. He still has the rest of the day, the week, the month, the year to get through and, as he pops his head around the office door to ask the manager to call a cab for him, he is overwhelmed by a hard grey wave of loneliness.

The manager looks up from her computer screen and for a second he recognises in her eyes a look of despair, of panic. Are her suit, tidy shoes, crisp white shirt just covering up something raw and beating, like his clothes cover his own grief? 'Yes?' she says, almost sharply. Then she recovers. 'Sorry, Elliott. It's been a bit of a day.' She folds her arms, tilts her head to one side and smiles politely at him. 'How was he?' she asks.

'Much the same.' It's not a good answer, but it will do. There's no way he can sum up how his dad is today, no way he can reconcile himself to what's happening to the man who once stood so tall in front of him. 'I was wondering,' Elliott asks, wanting to look away but not quite able to, 'if you could get me a cab?'

'Of course,' she replies, all bustle and efficiency now. 'Where to?'

'Think I might pop into Cowbridge, and then it'll be back to Cardiff for the train.'

'You going home tonight?'

It's an oddly personal question and one he

doesn't want to answer because he has no idea where home is right now.

He nods briefly and says, 'I'll wait in the garden, if that's OK.'

'Sure.' She is already dialling. He has no right to be here, to interfere with her work; his function is to pay and worry from afar. Hers is to shepherd and cajole, to constantly rearrange the pieces on the chessboard to make sure no one actually ever loses, or wins either. It's not that sort of game.

He steps out into the garden. The breeze is less strong here than by the beach, but it still carries the sea with it. He breathes in deeply, then out again, wishes he could bottle some of the air and take it back to Hastings; the air there seems thinner, like it has no depth, no roundness to it. He starts to walk, keeping to the edge of the lawns, pretending to scrutinise the borders. The azaleas are starting to bud and an early magnolia is in flower. Its petals are waxy; slightly obscene. Birds are singing and there is the chatter of seagulls. The gardens slope gently and he feels he's being drawn down into something; he has to get to the bottom in order to turn and make his way back up to the top. This is his mission now. Only this. He doesn't want to think about his father, not peer up to The Grange and try to pick out the window behind which the old man is sitting; nor does he want to think about Fern. Not quite at this moment. This moment is too filled with guilt and shame. He'd hoped that some of it would have dissipated by now, but no, it's all still there; in full technicolour.

He thinks instead of Chloe. Not the girl she is now, but the soft-limbed baby the nurse handed to him a few seconds after she was born. She was wrapped in a pink blanket, her tiny mouth pursed in, what Elliott imagined, was disbelief. 'What am I doing here?' she seemed to be saying. Tiny bubbles were spilling from her lips and her fists were clenched. Then she opened her eyes; they were mysterious, cloudy, full of thought and wonder, and she'd looked at him and he at her, and he had fallen from a height he hadn't known he'd climbed to. He must have been, he thought later, somewhere cloud-high to have fallen with such speed and heaviness into a love that took him utterly by surprise. The fact that he fell so completely has made their current relationship even harder to bear. But maybe it was all much harder because of the first baby, the one he and Meryl never had. Maybe he'd hardened his heart against the potential pain of losing this one. But whatever the reason, he just hadn't been prepared for the shock of that first meeting: the awesome responsibility and magnificence of it.

'Here,' he'd said, offering his daughter to his wife. 'She's beautiful.'

And Meryl had frowned slightly as she'd looked at the bundle in her arms, then had looked at Elliott and said, 'I don't know if I'm ready for this.'

'That's quite natural,' said a nurse, bustling over

and straightening the sheet under Meryl's arm. 'You're in a kind of shock. It'll pass. You'll be fine.'

But the truth was that Meryl wasn't actually ever really fine with it all. Yes, she'd done the nurturing and caring, but there always seemed to be something missing. Elliott had never witnessed in her the same sort of breathless panic or surging love that he felt whenever he bent over their daughter's crib and watched the gentle rise and fall of her chest, studied the faint blush of pink on her cheek.

As the years passed, Meryl and Chloe seemed to settle into some sort of almost adult relationship. Rather than being mother and child, they were more like sisters, wary of one another, competitive, overly polite even. So it puzzles Elliott now that Chloe should be so angry with him and so forgiving of her mother.

He's at the end of the gardens now. There is a row of laurel bushes bordering the neighbouring field. They are about ten feet high and have been trimmed to look like a wall, a battlement almost. The leaves are dark and shiny, and Elliott suddenly wants to push his way through them, to escape to he doesn't know where, and just keep walking.

But he doesn't. He turns and starts back up to the house, not wanting to think what it would have been like before, when a real family lived here. There must have been servants and aspidistra plants and hems brushing the wooden floors and life might have been slower and there were no telephones or emails and people would have had more space. Or maybe he's just fantasising, and the people who lived here were as full of doubt and insecurities as he is now as he finds himself on the driveway where there is a car waiting. It is a white saloon, with a light on the top with the taxi firm's number emblazoned on it. Its engine is purring.

Elliott taps on the front window. The driver presses a button to lower it and looks at him. He is about sixty with grey hair and eyes the colour of moss. 'Yes, mate?' he asks.

'Cowbridge? Love Lane?'

He hadn't known why he wanted to go into Cowbridge until he said this. He'd known that he wanted to, that there was a reason why he was impelled to go there while he's here in Wales today, but the words 'Love Lane' just popped into his head, taking him by surprise.

'No problem, mate.'

'Actually,' Elliott says, shutting the door and reaching for his seat belt, 'I'm not sure I actually want to get out and, you know, walk about, visit anyone. Just take me there to have a look and then I'll probably just want to get going back to Cardiff, to the station if that's OK.'

'Right you are,' the driver says amenably.

Elliott leans back his head and closes his eyes just like his father had done earlier. It is, he thinks from behind his eyelids, a sign. It is a 'Fuck off and leave me alone' sign, and it works. The driver doesn't try to talk to him and Elliott is glad about this.

He must have dozed, because when the taxi stops he's taken by surprise.

'Here we are. What number did you want?'

Elliott tells him. The car creeps forward. 'Shall I pull over?'

'Yes, please.'

They park on the wide grass verge and Elliott stares out of the window. The house hasn't changed much. The render is still painted off-white, the windows are still small but the driveway has been block-paved and there is a satellite dish on the end eave.

He wonders if the back garden has been altered. He rather suspects it has. This was where he'd worked that summer. This is the house where it happened.

He'd answered an advert in the newsagent's in Llantwit. 'Temporary gardener needed,' it had said, 'reasonable rates. References required.' He'd rung, had spoken to a Mrs Williams and agreed to go round for an interview, a reference from his rugby coach in his pocket. He'd been seventeen, halfway through his A levels. He'd also been burning with a rough, raw kind of energy. Every day had been a struggle to find some kind of balance, and he'd thought that a job and some cash would help. He hoped it would.

'You OK?' the driver asks. 'Are you getting out or do you want to just stay here?'

175

'No, sorry. Can we just stay here for a minute?'

'Your money,' he says dismissively and opens his window, leans his elbow on it and rests his head in his hand. Then his phone buzzes and he plucks it from its holder on the dashboard and starts tapping the keys. It reminds Elliott of his own phone. He should check his messages soon as well, but for now, now he just wants to sit here and remember.

'Elliott?' Mrs Williams said as she opened the door.

He'd nodded, overcome with shyness. He'd followed her through the house. It was, he thought, strangely silent; almost eerily so. Nothing seemed out of place and everything was spotless. Then she opened the back door and an overgrown wilderness faced him. It seemed like he'd stepped on to a film set.

She laughed, looking over her shoulder at him. She was, he realised, very pretty, and younger than he'd first thought, had a sinuous, feline grace, was dressed in jeans and a loose T-shirt and was wearing flip-flops. He felt embarrassed; it was strangely intimate being able to see her toes. They were painted with a pale pink nail varnish, he remembers. 'I'm sorry,' she said gesturing towards the garden. 'It's a bit of a mess!'

He tried to smile back but wasn't sure it had worked very well. 'Will you . . .' he managed to say, 'will you be getting a skip or something and can I use your tools, or do I have to bring my own?' The sentence exhausted him and he bent down, picked up a stick from the path and tossed it into the bush on his right.

'I'll get a skip, and there are some tools in the shed,' she said, pointing to a ramshackle lean-to up against the fence between hers and next door's garden. 'Take a look and see what you think. Just let me know if you need anything else and I'll get them. It's not a problem. I just want it cleared so I can see what's there. You know, paths, real trees, that sort of thing!'

And so it had started. She'd come and gone that first week, flitting in and out of the house, Elliott had no idea where she went or why and then when she was home she would make him cool drinks and sandwiches which she'd leave on the doorstep and he'd sit with his back to the house and drink and eat and think of her. He would think about her legs and her breasts and the soft sweep of her smile and he would imagine what it would be like to touch her hair. At home, at night, he would slip out of bed and, in the darkness of the bathroom, he would wank and think of her again, think of her watching him from the kitchen window, think of her hands holding his empty glass and plate.

She wasn't married, at least not that he could tell. When he looked around the house on his way to the loo or when he got himself a drink when she wasn't there, he would search for signs of aftershave or pairs of men's socks; anything to help him understand. But there was nothing. Just flowers and pictures and some of her clothes in a dry-cleaner's bag hanging on a peg in the hall.

By the second week he had cleared most of the top half of the garden and they'd started to have halting conversations about school and the weather and he longed to tell her everything, about his parents and Dan and the ache in his groin and his fears about what the future would bring.

He'd filled one skip and it had been taken away and another one had arrived. His hands were calloused and his limbs ached and when he laid back in the bath at the end of the day he would feel a good type of tiredness. He would let the water lap over him and look forward to going back the next day to just be near her, be able to talk to her, watch how her mouth moved and how the light danced in her eyes.

It took a month to finish the job, and on the last day she said, 'Show me.' And so they'd walked down the garden together, her just a little in front of him, and she exclaimed at a shrub he'd uncovered, at the remains of a stone bird bath, and she'd turned to look back at the house, her hands on her hips, and said, 'It's lovely, Elliott. Thank you so much.'

There was a pause. It was heavy and puzzling and he felt uneasy as if she was about to say something for which he wasn't prepared. Then she said, 'Why don't you come back tomorrow? I'll have the rest of your money then and perhaps you can help me pick out some new plants. I've got a book from the library . . .' Her voice trailed away in the heat of the afternoon and they made their way back to the house in silence.

He went the next day. He rang the bell; much like he had the first time, but now there was a difference, he felt different. She answered the door and looked at him and somehow he knew. To this day he doesn't know how he knew, but he did. He went inside. As soon as the door shut behind him, she just stepped towards him; that's all it took. There was, he could see, an envelope on the hall table with his name on it, but then she reached up and touched his face. Her fingers were light and delicate. 'Do you want to?' she asked.

It sounds corny now, he guesses, but it was as though his head was filled with bells pealing and clanging and then absolute silence, absolute still-ness. He followed her upstairs, she closed the bedroom curtains. The light in the room was rose coloured and she slipped out of her clothes until she was standing in front of him. It was odd, but thinking back, he can't recall them actually speaking to one another. He guesses they must have done, but it seemed there was no need for words. She lifted up his T-shirt and tugged it over his head, letting it fall on to the carpet. She ran her hands over his chest and shoulders. He was hard, so hard. He was aware of the brown circles of her nipples, the gentle curve of her breasts, the shadows beneath them and the round of her hips, the dark triangle of hair. She was gentle with him, guiding him to the bed and pulling him down on to her, into her. She was wet inside and she threw her head back so that he could see the pale skin of her neck and he came quickly and completely, shuddering into her. He wanted to cry but he didn't and, with his cock still in her, she took his hand and placed his finger on the mound above her cunt and whispered, 'Just circle me, circle me gently,' and he had felt her grow rigid and then pulse like a heartbeat and then she was quiet.

It was, he knows now, a gift. That was the only time. She paid him for the garden, they didn't choose any plants that day and he never went back. He knew somehow that he wouldn't be welcome again. But now, sitting in a taxi outside the house that used to be hers, he remembers her with fondness and an overwhelming sense of thankfulness.

It is right to come back here today; it is fitting after seeing Fern again this morning that he should pay homage to the woman who showed him how to be that first time with Fern, and really all the times that followed. It is, he hopes, some part of his atonement for the wrong he did to Fern and the wrongs he's done to Meryl too.

'OK,' he says to the driver. 'Can we go now, please?'

CHAPTER 11

Back in the studio Tom is leaning over Linda as she sits at her wheel; his arms are wrapped around hers and their faces are touching as together they too try to centre the clay. After a minute or so he releases her and steps back to watch her work. She smiles sheepishly at her daughter and Tom says to no one in particular and to everyone in general, 'If anyone's not actually working on something, could they possibly pop to the house and see if Mary has the extra towels ready? I think,' he says, scanning the room and letting his gaze rest on the sink in the corner, 'we're going to need fresh supplies!'

His voice is bright and forced and it is still, Ferns thinks, like he's reading from a script; the stage directions possibly being:

'The potter turns to his students, puts his hands on his hips and, with a kind of artificial cheerfulness, says, "If anyone's not actually working . . ."'

'I can go,' she replies, slipping off her seat with an eagerness that surprises her; she hadn't realised just how much she needs to leave the studio. She is, she realises, jealous; jealous of the attention

Tom was giving Linda, jealous of all the things she doesn't know. She tells herself to stop being so stupid, but there's something about being in this room with these people that has shaken her. It seems ages since she's felt more than a mere witness to her life and the sharp edges that have suddenly appeared around this day are refreshing. They are energising, are full of colour and meaning, but they are also unsettling; it's as though she's not quite sure who she is any more, where she should go next, what she should do and, as she gets to the door, she wonders whether this is because of Elliott, or whether it would have happened anyway in this place, on this day, and she does not know the answer.

'OK, thanks,' Tom says. 'Mary said she'd have them done by now.'

And his attention is drawn back to the clay and to the turning of the wheels and Fern slips out of the studio and into the afternoon.

It's three thirty and the grass seems dustier than before; the air busier. Mary must have collected her daughter from school because there's a young girl playing in the garden with Benjamin. Their voices drift amongst the leaves and Fern can see their shadows on the lawn. She has no idea what game they are playing, but the girl is issuing instructions and Benjamin is following in her wake, trailing a pale yellow blanket behind him, the type used to cover babies in prams. Toys are scattered everywhere; it resembles a war zone.

Fern leaves the bustle of the garden behind her and walks through the conservatory and the dining room into the darkness of the house. She finds Mary standing in the kitchen and is about to say, 'Hi, Tom sent me . . .' but she doesn't. There is something so still and sad about the way Mary is standing that stops Fern in her tracks.

This is a tableau she recognises and, amongst the pans and plates and laundry, Fern waits for the other woman to come back from wherever it is she's gone to. It's only a few seconds before Mary lets out a breath and moves very slightly but these seconds are, Fern knows, fundamental. They are, when the boys were small, what she used to call her 'bridge moments'; those in-between times, the ones during which she used to try to remember who she was or who she could have been.

'Oh,' Mary says, 'sorry, I didn't see you there.'

'It's OK,' Fern replies, stepping into the kitchen and nearer to Mary.

Mary looks around so that she's staring directly at Fern, and Fern can see the exhaustion in the younger woman's face; it is etched on to it like a drawing.

'I . . .' Mary falters. She tries again. 'I didn't know it was going to be like this.'

'I know.' Fern wants to move closer, but doesn't. There's a sense of brittleness in the room, of something which could, if pulled, snap.

'I feel so eroded. My children are . . .'

'Exhausting, I know,' Fern says quickly. 'They are at this age.'

Mary runs a hand through her tousled hair. Fern can see the outline of her ribs under the thin material of her T-shirt. She wishes it was otherwise.

The two women are motionless but here, into the space between them, arrives the conversation they nearly had earlier.

'I never thought it would be easy,' Mary says, 'but when I married Tom, it was just us, you know? Just me and him and we made the rules and we had nothing, not really, to speak of anyway. It didn't matter then though. But now, now we seem to need all this.' She sweeps an arm to encompass the kitchen, the house and garden, Tom in his studio with Jules, Linda and Rachel and even Fern in the kitchen, in her clay-splattered overalls. 'We need this just to survive. And the kids – I love them so much but they are diminishing me. As they grow bigger, I seem to be getting smaller. They take up so much energy. Do you understand? Am I . . .?' she falters again. 'Does this mean I'm bad, a bad mother, a bad person?'

There are tears in Mary's eyes now and Fern risks taking a step closer. 'No, of course not. It doesn't. I . . .' Here Fern stalls too. What should she say? Should she say that this is what it's like and it never really gets any easier, or should she say it will pass, it will be OK? 'I . . .' she says again, 'I understand. It's just a stage. It gets easier as they get older. They know themselves better, and it allows you to know yourself better too. They stop diluting you so much, after a while at least.'

But, she thinks, do they? What would Mary think if she came back to Fern's house right now and listened to the silence and looked into her sons' empty rooms and saw the scatterings of belongings that they have no need of any more? Could she imagine the height and breadth of these boys, the timbre of their voices and how sunlight falls on them, making a flicker like scales on a fish, as they swim away and away? Would she feel any less diluted than Fern feels right now, any less sure of who she once was?

'Do they?' Mary asks. 'Do they really?'

'Yes.' Fern says it softly, puzzles over what to say next and decides to say nothing. Like Fern and her mother before her, Mary will have to learn to flex; it's just how it is.

'I'm sorry.' Mary tears off a sheet of kitchen roll and blows her nose noisily into it.

'It's OK, really it is.'

'But here am I being silly, and you a customer and everything!'

'Oh, it's OK, don't worry. I've been there, where you are. That's all. I do understand.'

'Did you . . .' Mary bends down to pick up a bright red plastic lorry from the floor and stands cradling it in her arms, 'did you want something, when you came in just now and caught me like this?' She studies the truck as if it contains some sort of answer.

Fern asks her about the towels and says that she assumes they'll be tidying up and going soon and Mary tucks the crumpled piece of kitchen roll into the pocket of her jeans and with her free hand picks out two towels from a pile on the kitchen table and hands them to Fern. The transaction is businesslike and over in a flash, but deep down, at the level of blood and wishes, they both know something they didn't quite understand before; that this grief they feel for all they have lost and gained is elemental and that they could not imagine it to be any other way: it is the price all mothers pay. But despite being certain about this, the other certainties, the ones that surrounded Fern that morning, in the hours before she met Elliott again, are crumbling and, she finally admits to herself, the day she is living now is being, has been, will be altered because of this. Fern is beginning to learn that there is a distinction between these things.

'Thank you,' she says, bundling the towels under her arm and making ready to go.

'No, thank you, for listening and . . .'

Mary doesn't finish her sentence and Fern doesn't want her to. It is best left like this, with Mary holding onto a red plastic lorry and Fern with her arms full of towels, and so Fern leaves the kitchen, walks back through the dining room and the conservatory and, as she steps into the

186

garden she hears Mary tap on the kitchen window and shout, 'Hey, Benjamin, Jasmine, do you want a drink and a biscuit?' and then the children rush towards the house in a blur of blond hair and blue gingham.

She knows she shouldn't, but Fern can't help stopping in the quiet of the garden, with her bundle of towels, to think about her own parents and the weaving they must have done to make Fern's childhood the one it was.

It had been a normal one – well, as normal as she imagines normal to be. They'd lived in a 1930s semi on an estate of 1930s semis and Dad had, over the years, worked as a production manager in factories making cosmetics, hair conditioners and suntan creams in a number of different towns nearby and Mum had stayed at home for a while and then had gone to work as a receptionist at a doctor's surgery. She'd been in when Fern got home from school and there'd been food on the table each evening and Dad had liked to sit in his armchair after supper and listen to classical records; he'd seemed to like Beethoven the most. And Fern had worn beige cords and striped tank tops and had played outside with her friends, and at school she'd sat tests and later done her exams and had made and un-made friendships, had fancied boys and had had dreams in the night about one day being beautiful and being touched.

Then she'd gone to university and met Jules and Elliott and the alignment of her world had shifted and she'd started to see her parents only from a distance, had grown impatient with them. They were just so pedestrian, she'd thought. Her mother was small, grey-haired, ordinary, and her father, well, he was just her father, there in the background listening to his music, tending his garden and saying, 'That was lovely, as usual,' after each meal.

She'd read somewhere that the relationship between parent and child is never easy and never over. It's the relationship that lasts longer than any other; it starts earlier and endures and it is, Fern thinks, as she stands under the trees in Tom and Mary's garden, the hardest one she's ever had to negotiate because, at each stage, she has been so known. Her parents have never just seen her as who she is now at this moment; to them she has always been and always will be like a character in a film, constantly moving from who she was, to who she is and who she will be. There is, she realises, never enough acceptance; never enough forgiveness for this type of love to work properly. She shivers, clutches hold of the towels and tells herself that she must call her mum later, say, 'Hello,' at least try to be the child she hopes her children will one day become.

This thought of her sons pulls her up short. Do they, she wonders, think of her the way she thinks of her mother? Is she merely the frame in which they have lived their lives so far and from which they will want, inevitably, to break free?

How come it's so bloody hard to let go, to be let go of? And then Benjamin and his sister rocket out of the house, shouting and laughing into the spring afternoon, and Fern realises, as she sees Mary's face at the kitchen window, that this is why; all these tiny, pinprick moments of squash and biscuits and toys and running and the familiarity of arms and smiles and voices are why.

Inside Tom is scuttling from wheel to wheel asking each woman which two pieces they want to be fired and glazed and sent on. 'It's part of the price of the day,' he adds breezily, 'apart from the postage, that is!' He laughs self-consciously as Linda and Rachel start discussing which of their creations they want to keep.

'What about you?' Jules asks Fern. 'Which ones do you want?'

'Um,' she answers, hanging the towels she's carried from the Mary's kitchen on two hooks beside the sink, 'I think I'd like to keep my first bowl and –' she pauses – 'my plate.'

'Right, put the ones you've chosen on the shelf above your wheel, write your name on the shelf in pencil and then we need to tidy up. Make sure,' Tom adds, a little breathless now, 'you still have your chamois leathers!'

He shows them how to clean their wheels and there is a sloshing of water and studiousness in the room that reminds Fern of school; each woman, it seems, doesn't want to disappoint Tom, wants to get the most marks for doing it right.

'There!' Jules says triumphantly, standing back and admiring her wheel.

'It's perfect, thank you.' Tom is standing next to her and he places a hand on the arm of her overall. It leaves a faint handprint and surprisingly Jules blushes. Fern sees this from the other side of the studio. It is one of the first times she has ever seen her friend look flustered.

Within seconds it's four o'clock and the day, or this part of it at least, is over. Fern had felt earlier that time was going at just the right speed, but now it's quickened and she feels a hint of unease at the base of her throat. She doesn't want to go on to the next bit. She doesn't want to have to check her phone and read the text from Jack about the money for Wilf's deposit, and she doesn't want to have to wonder if Elliott will get in touch again and suggest meeting later. Suddenly this seems a risky and wrong thing to do; not innocent like it did earlier when they'd sat at Paddington and had coffee and had tried, unsuccessfully, to fill in the gaps in each other's lives like Robert and Francesca tried to do that night in *The Bridges of Madison County*, the one when Robert said something like, 'I don't think I can do this, try to live a whole life between now and Friday,' and then they'd danced and someone had played jazz.

But now they have taken off their overalls and the goodbyes are all said quickly and efficiently. Mary waves at them from the kitchen and the children look up from their games in the garden but are not curious and don't call out. Tom seems relieved that the women are going as he folds up their dirty overalls and presses a business card into their clean hands, and says, 'Keep in touch!' and promises to send the finished pots on as soon as possible, and Fern doesn't blame him. It must be hard to have had them there, taking up his space, doing it all wrong, stopping him from making exquisite things.

At the gate the four women linger for a moment and exchange pleasantries. Linda points to a blue car parked a little way down the road and says, 'Well, that's us. Guess we'd better be going. It's been a pleasure to meet you,' and then she and Rachel link arms and walk away, their shoulders touching, their steps matching one another, and Fern can't watch them go. It seems too brutal a departure. Thank God, she thinks, that Jules is still here, that Jules and I will leave here together, go somewhere on Chiswick High Road for a glass of wine and I can be the person I've always been with her. But then Fern wonders if it will be as easy as she hopes. What will happen if she tells Jules about this morning, about Elliott? What will Jules say if Fern was to tell her that even now, even after everything, she thinks there is a possibility, an unwelcome and unexpected one admittedly, that she could still love the man who broke her heart so savagely, so long ago?

'Right,' Jules says, making to move off. 'That was fun, but I need a drink!'

'So do I!' Fern replies, closing the gate behind her, looking up briefly at the window and the blossom and forcing herself not to think of the room she and Elliott rented, and of their belongings scattered on the floor, and of finding him there with that girl early one morning when she was supposed to be still at her parents' house, and of the rip this made in the fabric of her life.

'Thank you.' Jules nudges Fern as she says this as they walk back down Merton Avenue and on to the High Road. The traffic bumbles by and people saunter or hurry and mothers push buggies and there's a young man on a bicycle. He stops briefly as a set of traffic lights turns red and Fern can see his chest rise and fall and the sweat gathering on his top lip. She wonders what his name is, where he's going, what his secret thoughts might be.

In All Bar One they're shown to a table by the window by a waitress dressed in black; she is doll-sized and smiles shyly at them and, as Fern wonders whether she is robust enough to survive a shift in this place, she hands them a menu each and says, 'I'll be back in a jiffy,' and then disappears off between the other tables.

It's the word 'jiffy' that gives Fern comfort; it's going to be OK after all. The waitress will come back, they will order, Jules will put her lime-green scarf down on the seat and cross her long legs and tap the table leg with a turquoise boot and it will be twenty-five years ago again.

'So!' Jules says, resting her elbows on the table and her chin on her fists. 'What's really going on?'

'What do you mean?'

'I mean I've been watching you today and there's something different about you; you seem preoccupied. I've not seen you like that for a long time. It tells me . . .' The waitress comes back. They order their wine and a platter of cheese and biscuits to share and the waitress taps the keys on a hand-held device which, once she's finished, she slips back into a belt around her waist. It looks almost too heavy for her to carry and then she's gone again and Fern wishes she would stay, wishes she would stop Jules from saying whatever it is she's going to say. 'It tells me,' Jules says again, 'that you're keeping something from me.'

How is it that Jules knows me so well? Fern asks herself, shaking her head slightly and looking at her friend and remembering what it was like to live with her every day when they were students, to have her presence in her life like a light.

The wine arrives. It is cold and the colour of honey and it tastes of vanilla and it numbs Fern's tongue and makes her feel like weeping. 'I met Elliott this morning. By accident. At Paddington. As I was going to the Tube,' she says.

'Ha!' The word explodes out of Jules's mouth and she puts her glass down with a surprisingly loud thump. The people at the next table look over and then look away. 'I *knew* there was something,' she says.

'It wasn't a big deal,' Fern says, knowing she's lying but not able to stop herself. 'We just said hello, grabbed a quick coffee and then I came to Victoria to meet you and he –' she pauses, struck by how familiar this all sounds: her talking about him and the word 'he' meaning Elliott, not Jack, not Wilf, not Ed, not her father, nor Jack's father, nor anyone other than Elliott and all he once meant to her – 'was going to Wales,' she finishes the sentence in a rush.

'And?' Jules leans across the table, fixes Fern with a stare which is clear and hard and knowing.

'And nothing. I'm here. He went to Wales to visit his dad. He's in a home now apparently.'

Fern's being defensive and coy and she doesn't like herself for this. She doesn't want to question why this is so.

'You seeing him again? What did he say? Did he say sorry?'

There are too many questions being asked too quickly.

'I'm not sure –' she picks up the wine bottle and tops up their glasses – 'how I feel about it all yet. I don't really want to talk about it. It took me by surprise, that's all.'

'I bet it did!' Jules laughs – a little unkindly, Fern thinks.

Suddenly it's not twenty-five years ago again but it's now, it's relentlessly now, and there's been a whole lifetime between who they were and who they are. For a second Fern can't recognise the person standing on Jules's doorstep that morning when Elliott had run after her, met her at the corner, let her go.

But it had been her, dressed in jeans and her Doc Marten's, a lace bandana wound through her hair, its ends trailing over her shoulders, her eyes smudged with tiredness after leaving her parents' house at dawn to travel back to Elliott because she missed him so much.

She hadn't rung him because she'd wanted to surprise him, and she'd certainly done that! She will never forget the look on his face as she swung open the door of their room, and he turned his head towards her, away from the dark-haired girl sitting up in the bed next to him, her nipples brown and large, and his mouth half open, steeped in a desire she recognised so completely. She had seen it a hundred times before.

And then she'd run, her feet pounding on the stairs, through the hallway, down the path and on to the street. She didn't feel as if she was breathing, but she must have been, and he'd put some clothes on and followed, but at a distance and too slowly. He caught up with her at the corner and they had spoken and he had left, walking quickly away from her, leaving her to stumble to Jules's, to ring on the doorbell and to say when Jules opened it, 'Let me in. Just let me in.'

'My God!' Jules had said. 'What the fuck's happened to you?'

And Fern had told her and Jules had wrapped

her arms around her friend and Fern had savoured the smoky smell of Jules's jumper and had felt so tired, so very tired.

'Come on,' Jules had said then, leading Fern into the house she shared with three other students; one she'd moved into when Fern had taken the room with Elliott in the house with the window like Tom and Mary's window.

Neither of them had been sure about this change. In their first year they'd had rooms next to one another in halls, in the second year they'd shared the flat with the Christian girls and Fern had met Elliott, and now, in their third year, they lived on different roads, in different parts of town, and saw each other on campus and in the evenings, but Elliott had come between them, had changed the dynamic of their friendship, and Fern knew this and knew also, as she followed Jules into the house, that Jules had not really forgiven either of them for it.

Jules made Fern sit at the table in the kitchen and poured her some warm white wine out of a bottle on the counter. It tasted bitter and unpleasant and Fern felt like retching, but it helped numb the pain, a bit anyway.

Later, Fern slept. Jules covered her with a blanket as she lay on the sofa and the people in the house all spoke in whispers and they waited, without really understanding why, for something else to happen. Fern dreamed that Elliott came. Over and over again he walked up to the door, rang the bell, came to sit by her while she slept, and then she woke and Elliott wasn't there and he never came and even now, as she sits opposite Jules in All Bar One, she doesn't understand why not.

'So what are you going to do?' Jules asks Fern, slicing off a piece of cheese and popping it into her mouth. She licks her fingers and shifts in her chair. 'Did he take your number this morning?'

'Yes. He suggested we meet later maybe, on our way back through Paddington. If he comes back tonight, that is.' Fern wishes now that she hadn't told Jules, wishes she didn't have to explain all this. It had been something she could control when it had been inside her head, but now, in the open, it seems to be taking on a life of its own, to be growing larger, more significant, more threatening with each passing second.

'And will you? Meet him, I mean. If he contacts you?'

'I don't know. I really don't know.'

And Fern doesn't. She wants to check her phone again, see the indelible letters of Jack's text, maybe even call him, hear his voice, but she also wants to be near Elliott again, watch for the expressions she recognises, see him tilt his head, push back his hair in the way he always did. He's been a memory for so long that she wants to be reminded that what she once felt had been real, that he had been real.

'Just be careful, that's all,' Jules says, taking a sip of wine and shaking out her hair with the confidence of someone who has only really ever loved once and who has never been torn like Fern is being torn now, she's remembering both the joy and pain of being with Elliott, of losing him, of living with his absence and of working so hard to learn to trust again. Such a small word, 'trust'. Such a huge thing to lose.

Before this morning Fern had forgotten much of this, but now the memories are back, and they are unshakeable and permanent. 'I will,' she says. 'Don't worry about me. I'll be OK.'

Her phone is in her bag. Her bag is resting up against her thigh and she can feel a vibration from within it. Someone is texting her. Please let it be Jack again, or Wilf, or Ed. Don't let it be Elliott. Please let it be Elliott, she thinks as she raises her glass and smiles uncertainly at Jules.

CHAPTER 12

To Elliott this day is about magnets. It's like he'd been drawn like an iron filing to Love Lane and now, without really understanding why, as the taxi speeds along the A48, he knows he's heading to the hospital and he can hear his mother say, 'You'd better take her to the Heath, Elliott.'

The taxi drops him outside. Elliott pays the driver and watches him pull away. He feels very alone now, but also relieved. It's odd, but he'd started to wonder if this particular driver could see inside his mind.

The hospital's changed, of course it has. There's a new entrance and signage and different people are walking in and out of the doors, but there's something about being here that is so familiar, so right. Maybe it's the slant of the sun on the windows, the slightly sweet smell in the main corridor down which he is walking, the sound his shoes make on the floor. Whatever it is, he's back to when it happened and the weight that has been at the base of his heart ever since is growing heavier.

He finds a small garden in between two build-ings and pushes open the door leading on to it; the metal of the handle is surprisingly cold to the touch. There's a bench and gravel and small tended plants in bright blue pots; it's an odd place, a kind of suspended place. He guesses it might have been a smokers' garden in the days before the ban. He sits down and closes his eyes. It's sheltered here, but the only patch of sun is way off in one corner and there's a slight chill in the air, so he tugs at his jacket, pulling it tighter across his chest, and forces himself to remember.

There'd been that first time with Meryl, the time Fern found them, and then there'd been a second time, later that same week. Why she came back, he's not sure. Why he let her in, he's even less sure. He'd been in a daze then, not quite in control. It makes him sound weak, now, at this distance, but back then his mind had been full of this strange white noise and he'd not been thinking straight. There were his exams and the red wine he'd found in the kitchen which he seemed to drink without stopping and his dissertation to finish and this huge slug of remorse that hit him every time he thought of Fern. And then there was Meryl in his room again, that evening, promising to make it better. Had he let her in because he thought he'd lost Fern anyway, had no grounds to make amends with her, and Meryl was, therefore, the only source of solace? Maybe. Maybe it was just instinct. His cock versus his heart and his cock won, obviously.

Jules had come to take Fern's stuff away. She'd been like a Fury, avenging and thin-lipped. They'd hardly spoken. After all, what was there to say? But he remembers her hair and her outrage and the bags she brought with her into which she stuffed Fern's clothes and books and cosmetics. Without these things the room suddenly became shabby and very male; it was like someone had come with an eraser and rubbed Fern out of his life. He still can't quite work out whether this had been the best way or whether there might have been a better, quieter, more tender way it could have been done if he'd been more in control of himself, more able to think straight.

He's also not sure what happened about the rent. He guesses they must have sorted it somehow, but it's one of the things he's blanked out. It got subsumed in the greater matter of Fern's total absence, of Meryl's presence and the bizarre comfort it seemed to offer him, at the time at least.

So Meryl was there again, under him, her legs wrapped round him, a glint of triumph in her eyes which he tried not to notice, and he came in her and she said, 'It's OK. It's safe,' and afterwards he had showered, the water scalding his skin, and he hated himself for what he'd done to her and to himself, and to Fern of course.

And from then on Meryl insinuated herself into his life, seemed to Velcro herself on to him. She was there in the library when he was trying to revise, there in the pub and on the touchline when he played rugby and he carried the thought of her about with him constantly; she seemed to take up all the available space in his head, not allowing thoughts of Fern to break through, not allowing him to admit to himself just how fucking wrong he'd been.

And he'd taken Meryl home to Llantwit just before their finals and his mother had stood at the sink with her back to him and he'd known she knew he was trapped; that he'd made himself so, and that she didn't pity either of them – it would have been a waste of emotion. Instead her anger was hard and permanent and Elliott had felt reduced by it.

On the last day of his exams he left the Main Hall feeling dizzy and afraid. He'd expected to feel elated, lifted by this bubble of relief, but instead it was like a canyon had opened up in front of him; he realised he had no real idea what was coming next. And then he saw Fern on the other side of the quad. She was walking slowly, carrying her bag over her right shoulder; her steps were measured and the sun made her hair shine like a beacon. He felt sick. There was a pain in his groin and he wanted to run after her, fold her into him, say, 'I'm sorry, sorry, sorry,' into the soft skin of her neck and draw in the scent of her. But he didn't. He just stood there and watched as she disappeared from sight. Even now it's hard to explain how and why he did it this way; it was as though someone had unplugged him, taken the power lead out of him and switched off the socket at the wall. There was nothing he could do about it.

The letter from HP arrived the next day, offering him a traineeship, conditional upon him getting a 2:1. It gave him hope, though, it was something to hold on to, but it came on the same day that Meryl told him about the baby, so now, looking back, the two things are inviolably linked; one has become the other.

It was midday. The sun was beating hot and the whole word seemed doused in treacle. The post was sitting on the mat downstairs and Elliott woke with a hangover the size of the Eiffel Tower; his tongue seemed vast and dry and his head thumped. 'Shit,' he said, turning over in bed, the sun burning his eyelids.

The pillow next to him was empty, but the sheets were still warm. He heard the toilet flush and Meryl's footsteps padding back along the landing.

'Morning,' she said, clambering back in beside him.

He made some sort of noise at the back of his throat and sighed heavily. He tried to go back to sleep but there was an atmosphere in the room he didn't recognise. Wearily he opened his eyes. Meryl was sitting upright in the bed, her arms wrapped around her knees, her chin resting on them. Her dark hair curled on her shoulders. She was dressed in one of his T-shirts. He would have liked to ask her to take it off, to return it to him, to leave. But he didn't. Of course he didn't. He could recall some of the previous night, but not much of it. There'd been too much beer and a curry and he and his mates had talked about stuff that seemed important at the time but probably wasn't and he'd looked for Fern everywhere and Meryl was waiting back at the room like some sort of sprite and he'd turned away from her in bed and not made love to her and hadn't minded at all.

'Elliott?' she said.

'Mmm.' He stretched. His limbs ached and he needed a pee.

'Elliott?'

'What?' he snapped. He knows he snapped. He remembers that this is how it was.

'We need to talk.'

Oh, fuck, he thought. This is like some bad B-rated movie.

'Mmm.'

'I'm pregnant, Elliott.'

There was a pause. He did not speak.

'About twelve weeks, I think.' She said this much, much more quietly.

Time seemed to stop after she said this, or if not stop, then slow to a crawl. He imagined a clock with a second hand and the second hand went tick and then it stopped and then it went tock and then it stopped and the whole thing, the whole journey of this hand around the clock face, would, he knew, take a lifetime. He lifted his head slowly, looked at her. She was looking down at him. Her face was small and her eyes were huge and afraid.

It was as though she could read his thoughts.

'Yes,' she said tightly, 'it's yours. Of course it's fucking yours.'

There'd been nothing in Elliott's life so far to prepare him for this; no banter in the school yard, no heart-to-hearts with mates at uni, nothing his dad had ever told him, but he knew that what he said next would be fundamentally important. It would, in a way, define him.

What he wanted to do was rave, say, 'But you said it was safe. I trusted you. How could you let this happen? This is going to fuck everything up.'

He didn't say this. Instead, he just asked, 'When?'

'That second time, I think. Looking at my dates, I think it must have been then.'

So, he thought. The second time. Not the first. Not the first, mad, unthinking time, but the second, the second, thought-out, deliberate, chosen time, the one when his heart had been bleeding because Fern had gone and it was all his fault. So the solace he'd sought had been razor-edged, it had cut him. But how had it happened? This he did not want to know. Had Meryl done it deliberately or had it been an accident? He was too exhausted to wonder that morning, became too afraid to do so later.

'And,' he was on autopilot now, 'how do you feel? Are you OK, I mean? Is there anything I can do?'

She cried then. Huge hot tears and her face became ugly with them, or at least this is how he remembers it. He hopes now, thinking back, that his thoughts would have been with the unborn child; the spark they'd made, the promise it contained.

'I'm keeping it,' she said, her breath raggedy.

'I thought as much. It's OK. We'll be OK,' he said, more to convince himself than her. In truth he wanted to run. This was way out of his league. But just as he hadn't said what he was really thinking earlier, now he didn't do what he really wanted to do. Instead he reached out and held her and she curled up inside his arms and the heat was unbearable and his head thumped and his world changed on a pinhead.

Sitting in the hospital garden now, he's aware that someone has sat down next to him. He looks across.

'Good afternoon,' the man says.

'Hello,' Elliott replies.

'Nice spot, this.' He seems to wait for Elliott to say something, but when there's no response he carries on. 'I often sit out here when visiting. It gives us both a rest,' the man adds.

Us? Elliott wonders who 'us' might be. The man is elderly, dressed in a tweed jacket and polished shoes. He has white hair and is clean-shaven. His hands are, Elliott notices, trembling slightly, spotted with age spots.

'It is nice here, yes,' Elliott says.

'Are you visiting someone?' The man obviously needs to talk, needs the company.

'Not really.'

The man frowns.

'I mean, not now. There's no one here now. But I lost a child once. Here, at this hospital. A baby. Not even a baby really – more the idea of a baby. She was only just pregnant when it happened.'

Elliott doesn't know why he's telling this stranger this, but suddenly it's as though it's terribly important that he does, that he makes this man understand why he is here, in this garden, on this day. He's said so few words out loud today that he needs to talk, needs the words he's going to say to draw lines around him, make him into something definite and physical, give him a place in the world and what some writer somewhere had called 'the essential corroboration of others'.

The man inclines his head towards Elliott and Elliott starts talking, saying things he's never told anyone else. It's as if he's thinking out loud, and the relief is vast and wonderful.

'We were visiting my parents in Llantwit. Do you know it?'

'Yes, yes. Of course.'

'And she came down to breakfast. It was years ago, but I didn't really love her then either, you see. That's the awful thing. She wasn't really supposed to be the one. I guess that makes me bad, doesn't it?'

The man doesn't answer. Elliott feels like Forrest

Gump again, but this time on his seat, with his box of chocolates, and he can't stop. He needs to say this.

'We were students, had just finished our degrees and we were going to get married. I knew we would have to, because of the baby, you see. So we went back to my parents' house to tell them and she came down to breakfast looking pale and unwell and I said, "You OK?" and she said, "Not really. I feel a bit odd," and my mother said, "Yes, you do look peaky." She didn't say "dear" – my mother never really liked her, you see – and we ate our breakfast and didn't say much and then later that day she, Meryl, my girlfriend, I suppose you would call her, told me she had started bleeding and that it looked wrong, the wrong sort of blood.'

The man shifts uncomfortably in his chair, but Elliott can't stop.

'I asked her, "What shall we do? Shall we go to the chemist?" and she said, "I think I might need to see a doctor." And I said, "Well, perhaps we ought to talk to Mum first. What do you think?" "Do we have to?" she replied. "It'll be OK, I promise," I said.

'So we told Mum and she knew, like mums do, and she said, "You'd better take her to the Heath, Elliott," and so we came here, on a hot day in July, and they told her that the baby had gone.'

Elliott expects the man to say something, an 'I'm sorry' or something similar, but he doesn't and

Elliott doesn't risk looking over at him. Maybe, he thinks, this man is carrying too much grief of his own to have room for another's, maybe the reason why he's here is hard enough for him to cope with without taking on the reasons of others. However, Elliott can still remember that day, that moment when he went into Meryl's hospital room and saw her lying in the bed. Her eyes were closed and there was, he sensed, a weight of despair in the room which, when she opened her eyes and looked directly at him, seemed to say, 'Here, take it, this despair. It's your fault anyway. Have it, keep it. I don't want it any more.'

And he had; he has it still.

'I wish . . .' he says as an orderly pushes a trolley along the corridor behind where he and the old man are sitting. The wheels of the trolley squeak and he can hear the distant murmur of voices. 'I wish we'd talked about it more at the time, learnt how to mourn properly, but we didn't. She seemed so closed down after it, wouldn't let me near her, but I had to go through with my promise to marry her, I had to. You see that, don't you?'

Any vestige of pride has gone now and Elliott is a boy again, wanting comfort, wanting to be told that everything will be OK. He has no mother now, nor father really, and his brother is a world away and he's lost Meryl completely and is holding on to Chloe by his fingernails. Who else is there, he thinks, who can tell me it wasn't all my fault? Who else can understand that when Meryl had the D&C

and they took what they said were 'the products of conception' away, that these 'products' had been his baby, a person he could have shared that lifetime with? And why, after these 'products' had been examined under a microscope for the reasons why the baby hadn't grown, didn't stay, wasn't born, why was he never given an explanation as he surely should have been? It would have given them something to hold on to, made it easier the next time to take the risk. It took them years to do so and now there's Chloe and he feels almost as distant from her as he does from the child that never was.

There's no one, he thinks, not this man sitting next to him, nor his friends or colleagues at work, and especially not Fern, who can tell him he wasn't to blame. He actually doubts Fern ever knew the real reason why he never tried to find her again afterwards. Shame, he knows, is a powerful force and it kept him away from her and it kept him with Meryl and, as he sits on this bench in a hospital garden, he knows now he should not have done either of these things.

'Yes,' the old man says.

'Pardon?'

'You asked me whether I understood why you had to marry her anyway, and yes, I do.'

'Oh.'

'It's never easy, is it?'

Elliott glances at the man; he's looking off into the middle distance and seems miles away. 'What isn't?' he asks.

'Knowing if you've done the right thing or not. You never get a chance to try a different path, do you?'

'No, I guess not.'

'We, my wife and I, we've been married for nearly sixty years, but we never had children and I sometimes wonder what it would have been like if we had. Did you –' the man uncrosses and recrosses his legs, and a tannoy sounds somewhere in the heart of the hospital – 'did you have other children, after the one you lost?'

'Yes, a daughter. She's nearly twenty now.'

'You're lucky then. My wife, she's in there –' he points behind him. 'She's dying. Cancer, of course, and it's too soon, much too soon for her to go. We have, despite everything, so much more to do.'

With this unexpected conversation, Elliott feels as though he has given and been given a gift. It is something magical. Never in his wildest dreams would he have expected to be here like this, sharing these thoughts with this stranger, and it is so cleansing, such a relief, and he hopes his companion feels it too.

'I hope,' he says, then falters. What is the right thing to say? 'I hope,' he tries again, 'that she's not in pain, that she's comfortable, I mean.'

'They're doing what they can. She has been, is, very angry. It's not been easy.' He pauses and then fixes Elliott with a stare, his eyes are intense and crowded with thoughts, 'I'm in pain though. I shall,' he says, 'miss her so much.'

Now Elliott wants to say, 'I'm sorry,' but he doesn't. It is such a meagre phrase for such a massive loss.

The man continues, 'Be careful,' he says, reaching out to touch Elliott's hand. The feel of his fingers is a shock. 'Be careful you don't waste a moment. When I think back, it's all gone so quickly and now we're here, like this, and it hurts; it hurts.'

They are both quiet for a while, each preoccupied. Elliott can feel his phone vibrating with another email and he thinks about Meryl and the hard set of her mouth these days and how, when he stands on the doorstep of what used to be his home, he feels no pull, no hint of affection; it's as though all the years he spent there with her, the life they lived together, their wedding and the well of bitterness she seemed to dip into even before they found out about the baby and then lost the baby, were just one huge fucking waste of time. Chloe is, he thinks, the only positive, but even she seems to be something he hasn't got quite right.

'You will, won't you?' the man says, withdrawing his hand.

'What?'

'Do whatever it is you need to do to make it right, now, before it's too late.'

How does he know? Elliott thinks. Maybe it's a universal condition, this need to make amends. No one, he realises, is without regret; we are all driven by the thoughts of 'What if'. What if he'd fought for Fern, made Meryl leave? What if he'd not listened to his head but done what his heart had told him was the right thing to do?

'I will,' he says. 'I'll try.'

'I'd better get back,' the man says. He looks disappointed in Elliott, but this is a promise Elliott can't make, not right now anyway. He can try, but it might not work, too much time might have passed. He might have lost his chance. 'She's probably woken up and is wondering where I am,' his companion says.

'I hope . . .' Elliott starts to say, but what does he hope? He can't wish that this man's wife will get better, because she won't, but he can hope that the end will be painless, merciful, not too drawn out, but give them enough time to say whatever goodbyes they need to say. 'I hope,' he says again, but more lamely this time, 'that she's as comfortable as possible.'

'Thank you,' the man says, standing up. He takes a moment to balance himself and then moves away. He limps slightly as he walks, and when he gets to the door he turns and lifts his hand. Elliott waves back and they try to smile at one another, but neither do it properly. All they can do look into the other's eyes and acknowledge the grief and say, 'Here, now, I understand.' It is all that can be hoped for.

Elliott picks his phone out of his pocket. The email is from Ryan Edwards at Foxtons about the house. It says that the draft details are attached for Elliott to approve. That was quick, Elliott thinks. It is almost too quick. How can they have got them anywhere near right in so short a time? He can't open the attachment on his BlackBerry but forwards it to Dan anyway; he'll have to look at them when he gets back to the office or on his laptop in the flat. For now he'll have to reply to Ryan, saying thank you and that he'll be in touch. But really what he wants to say is, 'Fuck off, leave me alone, leave my home alone, preserve it just as it was when I was a boy, back then before I did the things that made everything wrong.'

He wonders where the old man is by now, whether he's reached his wife's bedside, what he's saying to her, and he checks the time. It's just after half past four. He starts a text, 'Hey,' he writes, 'hope you're having a good day. I'm just starting my journey back. Is there any chance we can meet later, about 7.30 or 8 at Paddington? If you're around then, that is?' He signs his name, picks Fern's number from the cache and presses Send. He doesn't say, 'I hope so!' or 'please' but the words are ricocheting around in his head and it seems like the message has wings made of lead as it travels through the ether and he imagines it landing in Fern's inbox with a thud and her reading it, barely thinking about it, deleting it. It's what he deserves after all. However, the part of him that remembers the old man's warning hopes against hope that she doesn't, that he has a chance to put right some of the wrong he has done and reduce the weight of grief he feels back here in

214

Wales, with the memories of his childhood and the smell of the sea. Could seeing Fern again perhaps erase some of the pain he feels at being back at this hospital with the ghosts of his unborn child and the wife who never forgave him for this loss?

Miles ahead
our love's loose ends, blurred
to cigarettes, an unmade bed.

I often think of you in thread.

'In Thread', David Tait

CHAPTER 13

In All Bar One the tiny waitress is back.

'Can I get you anything else?' she asks Fern and Jules.

They look at one another. Fern would love another glass of wine, but she knows it wouldn't be wise. The message that might be sitting on her phone is burning a hole in her bag. She can see the texts blurring into one. What would happen if she replied to the wrong one? If there's one from Elliott about meeting up later, would she get confused and send the reply to Jack? If there's one from Jack about Wilf's money, would she thank Elliott for getting it sorted; let him have a glimpse through the window and into how her life is now, all its routines, its details?

'I think I'll just have a coffee,' she says, looking up the waitress, noticing the dark shadows under her eyes. She wonders what, if any, demons this girl might be battling or if she's been to too many late night parties with friends, what she last said to her mother.

'Me too,' Jules add. 'I'll have an espresso. Fern?'

'Black filter for me, thanks.'

The waitress clears away the wine bottle and empty cheese platter. The bar is humming with customers now, full of end-of-dayers: people on their way home from work, wives who've shopped the length of Chiswick High Road and are putting off the moment when they have to take their bags home and hide the credit-card slips from their husbands.

By the window, a young couple are sitting on a sofa; they are facing one another and as they talk, he reaches out to touch her, either on the arm or tenderly hooking a stray tendril of hair over an ear. They're laughing and drinking beer from long glasses, are impervious to everyone else in the room. Fern remembers when it had been like that for her, but the memory is blurred and the man on the sofa opposite her could be Jack or it could be Elliott; she's not sure which, but is sure that she should know.

'So?' Jules asks, leaning across the table towards Fern. What did he look like?'

'Who?'

'Elliott, of course!'

'Oh, much the same. A bit greyer, but still tall, obviously, with all his hair!' Fern laughs, then claps her hand over her mouth. 'Oh, God. Sorry!' she says.

'Don't worry yourself! Bernard's hair went south years ago, as you know. It's partly why I love him. I love the feel of the skin on the top of his head.'

'Enough with the detail!' Fern says. 'I don't want to think of you two like that!'

The women smile and their coffees arrive and Jules picks up her spoon to stir hers. The spoon seems massive in the tiny cup. To Fern her friendship with Jules is like living with a scrapbook open on her knees, detailing the threads of the years they've known one another. On each page there is a picture, a sound, a smell that shouts, 'Jules.' Jules is the person she trusts more than any other and, in her more sentimental moments, she's reminded of Bette Midler and Barbara Hershey in *Beaches*, but she's never been brave enough to work out which of them is which.

In this scrapbook there's a page of walks along the seafront in Kent: Herne Bay, Whitstable and Reculver Beach with its ruined church. Fern can hear the shingle slip under their feet, the breathing of the waves and the wheeling of seagulls. There are beach huts and children in sandals and the wise, dark wood of the breakwaters, and the wind is in their faces, snatching at their words as they argue about books and politics and Melvyn Bragg.

'But nothing actually happens!' Jules is saying. 'Surely in a book something's got to happen. The hero, or whatever he is, because he's hardly heroic, just stands still, lets things eddy around him!'

'That's the whole point!' Fern replies, tapping her bag in which Anne Tyler's novel *Noah's Compass* is nestling amongst the tissues and lipstick and Fern's purse with its photographs of Jack and the boys. 'Noah didn't need a compass because he wasn't going anywhere! Surely you can see that? The whole thing is ironic.'

'Of course I can, but still, where's the tension, the drama? There's not even any sex, not really, not to speak of!'

Fern winds her arm through Jules's and they lower their heads, forging ahead into the late October afternoon. It's overcast and squally; the clouds are lowering. One of Jules's dogs bounds up to them, his tongue red and his eyes soulful. He dances around the women, the fur on his coat swirling in the wind. He's barking and the waves crash and just for a second Fern wishes she was like Liam in the book, wishes she was static and ponderous because just now, with the salt spray and tide being drawn out to sea, she feels that if she was not holding on to Jules, she would lift up and fly away.

Later, back at the house they visit the stables while something bubbles in the oven. The kitchen is full of the scent of herbs and lamb and the bustle of Mrs Bridges, who comes up from the village to 'help out'. 'You are an angel,' Jules tells her each time Mrs Bridges picks up her bag at the end of the day, shrugs on her coat and steps out on to the drive, into her Nissan Micra to drive the half a mile to her house. And Mrs Bridges looks at Jules as if to say, 'I know I am, my dear.'

The horses nudge Jules in turn as she leans into their boxes. Fern follows, laying her hand on the curve of each horse's nose. She greets them in turn. Their coats are warm and musty. The horses snicker in reply and stamp their feet.

Bernard is on his way home from London and Jack has probably just got in at home and is reading her note about dinner. He will turn on the oven as instructed and check his emails while it warms up. He might even take or make a phone call, but he won't call her. There's no need to. She's there anyway in the small things: the keys on the hook by the back door, the iron she used earlier and left cooling on the side, the hasty note she's written to remind herself to buy toothpaste, the books in the bookcase and the pictures on the wall. All these shout, 'Fern lives here,' and the boys will be in their bedrooms and the world will have stopped at their doors until it's time to eat and Jack will sit at the table with them and marvel and fear them and Fern will be in their features and bones. Fern knows this as if she can see it, and this is what keeps her fixed to the ground. Despite the efforts of the wind and the sea, she's helped by Jules and by the heat of horses, by the sweet smell of straw and dung and feed and saddle soap and, as it gets dark and cold and they leave the stables and go back into the house to drink wine and eat and listen to Bernard talk about his day, Fern can't imagine how her life could be any different than this.

'I guess we'd better get going,' Jules says as she finishes her coffee in All Bar One on Chiswick High Road on the day they have learnt how to be potters.

'Yes, we should,' Fern says, draining the last of her drink and waving to the waitress for the bill.

And in the scrapbook they are in other wine bars and pubs; there is cigarette smoke and Jules's wedding and the day Fern first met her.

'Hi.' Jules is tall and broad and she pushes her way into Fern's room in hall and stands staring straight at her. 'My name's Jules. Well, Juliet really. Looks like we're going to be neighbours!' She shakes out her hair and beams at Fern.

'Fern,' Fern says, holding out her hand. Jules takes it and her flesh is warm and her skin is hard.

'Horses!' she says by way of explanation. 'Not very ladylike, I know!'

They go to the bar that first night and do the whole A-level, boyfriend, family questionnaire thing and other people seem to leave them alone, sensing that they have no need of company. And they didn't.

They make other friends on their courses and there are small snapshots of these people in the margins of the scrapbook. Then there are the girls in the flat in their second year and the atmosphere of pent-up fury, and Fern and Jules try, they honestly do, to make amends, but then there's the party and Elliott and the dynamic changes, and now there's Bernard, his mother, his boat and there's Jack, Rosemary, Wilf and Ed and Jules's life in the village and Fern's job in the shop and suddenly there's Elliott again; another picture of him in the album and, as the waitress brings the bill, both women seem to be pointing at it and saying, 'Ah, him again!'

'I need to go to the loo before we leave,' Fern says, leaving her money on the saucer.

'OK!' Jules says breezily, picking up her lime-green scarf and wrapping it around her neck.

Fern doesn't look back when she reaches the toilets, but she can sense Jules is watching her, wondering. Will there be a text from Elliott, Fern thinks, and if there is, what will I do?

A mirror runs the whole length of the wall in the ladies' and the lights are hot and fierce. The taps shine and there's music playing.

The first text is from Jack. 'No problem,' it says. 'Will sort.'

This is what she expects and this is why she loves him. He is solid and steady; he rarely falters.

The next text is from a number she kind of recognises. It arrived at four thirty-five. She presses the button.

'Hey,' it says, 'hope you're having a good day. I'm just starting my journey back. Is there any chance we can meet later, about 7.30 or 8 at Paddington? If you're around then, that is?' He's signed it 'Elliott'. There's no 'please' or 'I hope so', and she's glad about this. The way he's written it is businesslike, between acquaintances, but she doesn't answer it; she doesn't know what to say.

She goes back out into the bar. Jules is waiting by the door. They will step out into the late afternoon, turn left and head to the Tube. It's like being on a conveyor belt, Fern thinks, and just for a second she longs for Jules's house, the chink of cutlery on crockery, the patience of horses nearby and a dog sleeping at her feet. She also wants the distant sea; the push and pull of it. Despite the efforts of the sea and the wind, she feels she knew better who she was when she was there.

'Right,' she says to Jules. 'Time to go, I guess.'

The Tube is crowded and hot and people are impatient and narky. There's a scuffle between two passengers at Earl's Court; one trying to get on, one trying to get off, and Jules raises her eyebrows at Fern and Fern smiles back. There is nothing left to say.

At Victoria they are released into the fresher air of the station concourse and busy themselves choosing a train for Jules. The rush hour crowds swirl about them.

'Oh, shit,' she says. 'I've just remembered. Bernard's mother's coming round this evening for dinner and a "nice chat, dear".' Jules makes quotation marks in the air and grimaces. 'That means two things: one, I have to think about dinner – let's hope Mrs Bridges has got something ready; and two, it means listening to his mother's latest views on topics from super-injunctions and the state of the economy to her bunions and the challenge of finding a new gardener. Of course, it's all linked to the fact that Mrs Thatcher's no longer in power. If she was, we wouldn't be in the state we're in, blah, blah, blah!' Jules laughs and looks up at the departure board. 'There's one in ten minutes. I think I'll go for that one. OK?'

'OK,' Fern says. But it doesn't feel OK. She doesn't want Jules to go; it's too soon. She isn't ready.

'Just be careful,' Jules says, fishing in her bag for her ticket. 'With Elliott, I mean.'

Fern stays silent.

'I know you'll see him again. You have to, don't you? It's too good an opportunity to pass up. About time you got the chance to hold him to account, eh?!'

Fern nods. 'I guess so,' she says. 'It does seem to make sense.' But it doesn't. She shouldn't have to. It shouldn't still matter.

'Just take care, that's all, and give my love to Jack and the boys.'

It's a timely addition. Of course Fern will go home to Jack tonight and give him Jules's love. She will tell him about the pottery and mention that she bumped into an old friend from university, Elliott, his name was, and they will talk about Wilf's rent and Ed might text and the cat will need feeding and he'll rub against Fern's legs and make that small guttural noise he makes when he's happy, and later Fern will lie next to Jack in bed and Jack will rest his hand on her thigh and she will think back on this day and catalogue it precisely in the right place in her memory. It will have tidy edges and she will be able to close the cover on it and sleep. Yes, this is what will happen.

'Of course I will,' she says to Jules, 'and you give my love to Bernard, and his mother.'

The women laugh and hug and suddenly Jules is gone, striding towards the turnstile. She looks back and waves and Fern watches as her bright hair, her scarf and her red jumper disappear into the crowd of passengers walking down the platform. Fern imagines Jules making a soft fallumphing noise as she takes her seat, that she'll gaze fearlessly at the other passengers and then rest her chin on her hand and gaze out of the window. She might think of Fern and Elliott, or she might not. She might think of the children she's never had, or she might think of Mrs Bridges and the supper she's hopefully prepared, and of the horses in the yard, the stable hands they employ, and of Bernard, of course. She will imagine his energy and the bright brown flares in his eyes and the fact that, despite everything, he still loves her, and she loves him.

Meanwhile, Fern is standing on the concourse and is suddenly bereft. The layer of protection that Jules's presence afforded is gone and she feels exposed and at risk. She should ignore Elliott's message and go back to Reading, go back to her house with the ivy growing by the front door, the magnolia blossom on the tree Jack planted for her thirtieth birthday, to the sympathy card she has to write and deliver to her friend whose mother died last week. Yes, these are the things she should do.

She takes out her phone, reads Elliott's message again, types a reply. 'OK,' it says.

There are a couple of hours to fill. Despite everything, she should see him again. She has to, doesn't she? It's an odd feeling this, like she's suspended. However, if she hurries, she could be home in that time: the Underground to Paddington, the train to Reading, the taxi home. She could be opening her front door, putting her bag in the hall while Elliott is waiting for her, watching for her face in the crowd. Would that make it better? Would that be an appropriate kind of revenge?

But, she thinks, as she turns away from the departure board and starts to walk to the Tube, would that be fair? Doesn't he, after all this time, deserve the chance to explain? Does he?

At Paddington she goes back to the Sloe Bar, buys another coffee, sits in a deep leather seat by a window and gets out her book. She could leave at any moment. The trains are displayed on a screen above the bar; there are two fast ones to Reading leaving in the next twenty minutes. She could be on either of these. The book rests on her lap; her hand hovers on its cover. She's reading *To Kill a Mockingbird* again. This book is like a religion to her and she thinks of Scout and Jem and Atticus and of her own boys, wondering how she will ever be able to tell Elliott about all that they are, all they mean to her. She scans the lounge for Elliott, knows of course he won't be there but somehow imagines that he still could be. It's almost as though they're both there somehow, it's still morning and they are drinking coffee.

She shakes these thoughts from her mind and concentrates. It's a bit like having the scrapbook open again, the one with the pictures of Jules in. This time the pages are full of the threads of her life with Wilf and Ed instead and she's looking at it backwards. There's the first time Ed bought a girl home. He's standing awkwardly next to her in the kitchen by the door and they are looking at Fern, waiting for her to say something. 'Are you both staying for dinner?' she says. Ed's shoulders relax; he reaches for the girl's hand. Her name's Hannah, Fern remembers, and it's the word 'both' that's done it. It's her way of saying, 'It's OK. I can accept this new situation.' But inside she's reeling. This boy, her boy, is still so young. Behind him, in his shadow, is him posing for a photograph with the Under 8s' football team when he was awarded 'Man of the Match', his first day at school, him curled asleep on her lap while *Thomas the Tank Engine* plays on the TV, Man of the Match? she thinks now; even then, even when he was seven, she had already started to lose him. This is what it must have been like for her parents too, she acknowledges. Maybe it happens to every generation. Maybe she shouldn't be so angry with her mum and dad for not being able to let go of who she once was.

Then there's Wilf in hospital with appendicitis and her sitting waiting for him to come out of surgery, holding on to his teddy bear as if it was a talisman. As soon as she's told that she can, she hurries down to the recovery room. She wants to tell everyone en route: 'My boy, my boy's down there.' She wants to say, 'He's Wilf, he's wonderful.' And then there he is, sleepy, floppy, so small, and she nestles the bear under his chin and whispers, 'It's Mummy. I'm here.'

Watching him wake is like watching a miracle. Atom by atom he returns. Hers has to be the first face he sees, and he opens his eyes and she recognises him, all of him.

'I feel sick,' he says.

'It's OK, you're supposed to. That's a good sign,' she answers.

She wants to cry, but can't let him see her do so.

Jack is coming. He's been away in Scotland on business and is hurrying back.

'Daddy's coming,' she says, and Wilf nods and falls asleep again and Jack is there when Wilf wakes properly and her mother brings Ed into the hospital to visit and they hover by Wilf's bed and say he is brave and wonderful and that night, while Wilf sleeps and she lies on the camp bed by his side, listening to the sounds of the ward, she gives thanks but also knows that this thing that Wilf has done, he has done without her. It is another step closer to him being the man he's going to become; the one that hops into the car next to her at the station when he comes home from university and says, 'Hi, Mum, thanks for this.'

Then there's school: pale blue shirts, grey shorts, black shoes. They have reading books and there's handwriting practice after tea and at the start of each day she hangs their coats on low pegs, each with their name above it. Ed's first, then Wilf's, then time passes and they run into the classrooms without her and she stands in the playground with the other mums and watches them go.

She does her duty: helps with craft lessons, school trips, swimming lessons. The children are always hot and busy and vague. She makes a game of 'find the shoe' when Wilf's friend Peter loses his every single week when they're getting changed. The towels are damp and flung on the floor, trunks are twisted around legs and she unravels and sorts and puts it all in order and the boys emerge, sticky with chlorine and full of 'Did you see . . .?' and 'My mum says . . .' and then they go back into the classroom and she hangs their swimming bags on their pegs and tells Wilf she'll see him at the end of school and she has to leave. She has no further right to stay.

And there's them at two and four: Wilf just out of nappies, Ed already wise. They are in the sandpit, sifting sand, being diggers and builders like their dad, and the sun is low. She is like Mary Westbourne and has to pause before she calls out, 'Time for tea,' and they run inside.

Then they are babies. The scrapbook pages are full of pictures of them: their creased hospital faces, their small butterfly hearts. Even now, sitting in this chair, with an empty cup of coffee in front of her and her novel unopened on her lap, she can feel the heaviness of their heads as she cradles them. She remembers the total surrender of their sleep and how their cries pierced her in the night.

Finally there is their conception; Jack's weight on her, in her, and the quickening in her belly. She knows it's probably just hindsight, but she thinks she can recall the times, can pinpoint the exact seconds they started to arrive, and she remembers the months she carried them; how she loved their company, the promise of them and how impatient she was to meet them; how when they arrived, bloody, crumpled, mysterious, she had never been so full of wonder and fear.

And now? Well, now they've mostly gone. Her time with them is over. They are moving on and, like a point on a map, they will always know where to find her. She has her place and they have theirs. This is how it's meant to be, but it doesn't make it any easier, doesn't make the memories any less difficult to file and sort and, because she doesn't really know what to do next, there is still a part of her that wishes she could do it all over again.

She sighs as she looks up; a waiter is hovering, asking if he can clear away her cup.

'Can I get you anything else?' he asks.

'Not for the minute, thanks,' she replies.

He looks meaningfully at the screen, seems to be

233

making sure she knows she can't stay indefinitely. Most people here, he seems to say, have somewhere else to go.

It's six thirty and she could still go home; there's time to text Elliott and say that it's not OK any more, that something's come up and she's had to go. She fishes out her phone, rereads the text from Jack, presses his number. It's ringing and for once he picks up.

'Hello, love,' he says. 'How are you?'

CHAPTER 14

When Elliott gets to Cardiff Station he is, he realises, famished. He's also relieved that the taxi that brought him from the hospital is one of the last ones he'll have to take today. He's stopped being curious about the drivers, but he's still fearful that they'll pry into the whys and wherefores of his journeys, most likely because he's not quite sure of them himself any more, would not know how to answer them.

There's a Burger King opposite the station. He knows he shouldn't, but his hunger is raw and immediate. He gives his order to a smiling youth and leans his hands on the counter. He carries the brown paper bag back on to the concourse like it's some sort of hand grenade, and there, just outside WH Smith's, he eats. The food sits like lead in his stomach as he gazes up at the boards to see when the next train to London is. There's one at five twenty-five, which should get him in just after seven thirty. Fern hasn't replied to his last text and he doesn't know how he feels about this, but at least she hasn't said no. However, he

235

reasons, as he pops his rubbish in the bag hanging off the back of a passing cleaner's trolley, she hasn't said yes either.

He buys a coffee at Upper Crust and makes his way to his train. It's rush hour and the station is heaving; people eddy about him, there are the muffled sounds of tiredness and wanting-to-get-homeness and he wishes he was back on Llantwit Beach with the wind and the sea and the gulls making jagged patterns in the sky. He doesn't want to be here, to have done all he's done today. He just wants to stop.

But he can't. Emails buzz in every few minutes; someone brushes past him, their bag knocking into him. They don't look back to say sorry. Their footsteps are hurried and fractious and he hopes he won't end up sitting next to them on the train. He finds a seat in the Quiet Carriage and for this he's grateful. He can avoid calls and conversations this way, be cocooned. Maybe he'll even sleep.

He settles into his seat, switches his phone to silent, checks some emails, answers a couple. One's from the ubiquitous Susan about the quiz night at the pub on Friday. The company is fielding a team and she wants to know if they can partner up for the 'answer this in pairs' questions. He says something non-committal in reply, like, 'Let's see who else is around. You might find a better partner.' This will be a disappointment to her, he knows, but just at that second his head is full of Fern again and there are flashes and there is pain and there is beauty and he has no idea how to handle any of it.

His coffee is almost finished and he's feeling better now he's eaten, and although he still wishes it hadn't been a burger, it served its purpose. He feels almost ready for anything now!

Then he sees that a text has arrived. It's Fern's number. He hesitates before opening it, thinks about the sound of trees falling in woods if no one is there to hear them. Perhaps, if he doesn't read it . . . Then he makes a small noise in the back of his throat and the lad sitting opposite him in a fake football shirt and backwards-facing cap looks up as if to say, 'Poor old fuck,' and he presses a button. 'OK,' it says. He releases a breath and smiles. He hadn't realised just how worried he'd been she might say no. He looks at the window and his reflection in the glass smiles back at him. The boy on the other side of the table shuffles in his seat and nervously touches a bulky chain he's wearing around his neck. There's a disc hanging from it, with the word 'SOUL' on it.

Elliott types a reply: 'Meet you in The Mad Bishop & Bear upstairs at Paddington about 7.45? I fancy a real drink, how about you?!' He presses Send.

There's no immediate reply – perhaps she's on the Underground now, he thinks. He doesn't want to wonder if he's been too precise, too definite. There's a world of difference between the idea of something and its reality. He knows this; he learnt about this the hard way.

The boy has his eyes closed now and Elliott too puts his head back and eases the stiffness in his neck. This day has stretched him, not in the traditional sense of being too difficult, too challenging, but it has made parts of him longer, thinner, more transparent, and he wonders if he's strong enough to face Fern and the reminders she will bring with her, in her turns of phrase, in the chocolate brown of her eyes, in her ultimate unknowability.

As they pull out of the station, heavy rain starts to fall. It is noisy and he can't see past it. It streams and twists down the window and of course it makes him remember.

It had rained that day too. He'd come in from his lecture on Keynesian economics and was soaked. It was cold, drenching rain, the type that bounces off the pavement. Their room was a tip. Fern had said she would tidy it, but she obviously hadn't. He'd made his way to the kitchen, said something indistinct to the girl who rented the room on the top floor and who was sitting at the table eating a chocolate biscuit and reading a paper, and made himself a cup of tea.

Back upstairs, he put down the mug on the table next to Fern's side of the bed on top of the lifestyle supplement from last Sunday's *Observer* and sat down to pull off his shoes. The sheets were crumpled and dirty; he couldn't remember the last time they'd changed them, or the last time he had felt the touch of clean linen. He really would have to get organised and get them down to the launderette before the weekend. Maybe it would help.

It wasn't easy, living like this. He'd thought it would be. When he'd met Fern everything had seemed possible. It was him and her and they started to make an 'us' out of the things they did; the conversations and arguments and the sex of course. That was fucking brilliant. He'd never had it so good. She was small, and had so much energy. She was tight and always wet and he loved the way his cock felt in her, the release when he came, the way she moved under him, on top of him. She would stretch up and he would study the contours of her small round breasts, would pull her to him and her nipples would taste sweet and he would circle her clit with his fingers and his cock and she would cry out and smile at him when it was all over. But it was more than just sex. He knew this, of course he did. It was this 'us' thing they had; the things they did together, like making cheese on toast at two in the morning, like knowing she would put just the right amount of sugar in his tea, the familiarity of her clothes, the way she always hummed when she did her teeth.

Yes, these were the things that bound them, but in that binding he knew there lay the seeds of a problem. What would they/could they do next? The choices hung over them like swords and some-times, like that day in January when it had snowed, and now today, he didn't want to think about it.

He shrugged out of his soaked jeans and pulled

on some jogging trousers and shuffled up the bed and arranged the pillows behind his head. He leant over and picked up his mug of tea, resting it against his chest. He had the feeling that Fern would be back soon and he wasn't sure he was quite ready to face her yet; he wanted some time to himself.

That was what was hard, living here with her. The room was spacious, with a high ceiling and a large bay window, but it was full of their stuff, and sometimes at night when he looked across at her sleeping, her face creamy in the light from the street lamp shining through the curtains, he felt he couldn't breathe.

Then there were her footsteps coming up the stairs; he recognised them and concentrated hard, tried to gauge what sort of mood she was in. She'd had a meeting with her tutor about her dissertation and neither thing was going well, neither the dissertation nor her relationship with her tutor.

'Fuck him, fuck him, fuck him,' she'd said to Elliott the night before as she stood at the window, her hands on her hips and, when she'd turned to look at Elliott, he had seen something in her eyes that he hadn't been able to name but hadn't quite liked.

Now, on the train back from Wales, travelling at speed towards the thoughts of who she'd been then and the idea of who she might be now, Elliott knows that back then he hadn't known much, but he'd known enough to wonder what he would think in years to come about those months in that room with Fern. He's sure he would have found a way to reconcile how he felt; it would have just been a phase on their journey together, and years later they would have sat in their garden on a summer's evening, with a bottle of wine, maybe even with a family, and said, 'Hey, do you remember when we rented that awful room in our last year at uni? It was hard, wasn't it?' And they would look together at all they have now and feel glad, safe and wise.

Maybe he even thought this as he sat on the bed with his wet jeans in a heap on the floor and his hands around a mug of tea as Fern came up the stairs? But maybe it was also then that he started to doubt whether this was what he actually wanted, or had the doubt had always been there, or did none of it matter because he loved her and she loved him? He wasn't ready to make up his mind about any of this, not ready at all.

'Hi,' she said, coming in the door and throwing her bag on the floor. Her tone was flat and expressionless.

'Hi,' he said. 'It's a shit day.'

'Yes.' She peeled off her jacket and hung it on the back of the chair in front of what was supposed to be a desk. It was so covered with books and make-up and a pair of Elliott's socks that there was no room to work there. The rain dripped off her jacket on to the carpet, making plip, plip noises that seemed to fill the room.

'How was it? Do you want a cup of tea?' Elliott

asked, shuffling over and patting the empty side of the bed.

She sat down on the end of the bed with her back to him.

'It was crap,' she said. 'He . . .' Here she stopped. 'I can't be bothered to go through it all now. Maybe later. OK?'

'OK,' he said. He wanted to put his mug down and wrap his arms around her but he couldn't, didn't. Maybe he should have done.

'Elliott?' she said. Her back was still turned towards him.

'Mmm.' He'd picked up his bag and was starting to rummage in it for a book he'd promised he'd look at tonight and get back to the library tomorrow. Someone else had reserved it apparently. He bent back the spine, smoothed the first page with his hand and tried to read.

'What's going to happen?'

'What do you mean?'

'You know what I mean.' Her voice was sullen and sounded very, very tired.

He wished she would just lie down next to him and sleep. He could cope better with her then.

'Next, after this. What are we going to do?'

Maybe he should have said, 'We will get our degrees, we will get jobs, we will rent a flat – a real flat with a kitchen of our own and a lounge and a bathroom we don't have to share – and we'll go for walks in the park at the weekend and keep goldfish maybe!' and she would laugh at the thought of them having goldfish and she would lie down next to him and it would be OK.

But he didn't say this. Instead he said, 'How should *I* know? I haven't got a fucking crystal ball. All we can do is just see what happens. Surely? Isn't it too soon to be making plans? I know I've applied for that training scheme with HP and you've thought about doing that archiving course, but we don't need to have it all mapped out now, not this afternoon, do we?'

'But don't you see,' she said, wheeling her head round to stare at him, her eyes huge with need and fury, 'that *I* do. *I* need to know. *I* can't go on living like this.'

Fuck, he thought. Not this *again*. Since January they'd been through this a gazillion times, or so it felt. Every time she had a bad day or it rained or they didn't have enough money for anything other than soup and bread, she would start, and he was fed up with it, pissed off by it.

'Look,' he said. 'I'll go and get you that tea.'

'It's not going to make it go away, you know,' she said. 'A "nice cup of tea, dear" is not going to make things better. We still won't know what's going to happen.' She was standing up now, looking down on him. He felt small and powerless and he didn't like it, didn't like being here like this, didn't like not having the answers she so plainly needed. How had it all changed so much? How could he both love and dislike her at the same time?

When he got back with her tea, she was packing.

'What are you doing?'

'I need to get away. I thought I might go home for a few days. Clear my head. I've got to rewrite that chapter which bloody Dr Thomas has just torn to pieces, and . . .' she paused, 'I think it would do us good. Don't you?'

Her voice had softened slightly as she asked this, but still he couldn't go to her, hold her like he'd always done before.

'Why home though? Why to your parents? Why not go and stay with Jules? *She* always seems to be available.'

It was a mean jibe, and one that neither Fern nor Jules deserved.

'If you must know,' Fern said, her brown eyes almost black in the gloom of the late afternoon light, 'Jules is on a week's work experience with the *FT* this week. At least *she* knows what she wants to do. And, in any case –' she stopped again, threw a jumper into her bag and shook out her jacket so that more raindrops fell on to the carpet – 'if I can't stay here and I can't go to Jules's right now, I have no place left to go but home, do I?'

He should have done something right there and then. He should have gone over to her with the mug of tea and made her hold it and then he should have put his head on her shoulder, or something, anything. Maybe he could even have kissed her on her forehead, or put his hand on her hair. Maybe that touch would have made all the difference. But he didn't. He put her tea down on the floor by the bed and sat back down on it and opened up his book again and started to read while she zipped up her bag and said, 'I'll see you then. Just a few days, OK?'

He nodded, didn't look up, didn't watch her go. He heard her go down the stairs, heard the front door close and the gate swing on its hinges. He put down the book and closed his eyes.

Waiting was hard; but he waited; ten minutes, twenty, thirty. Every second he expected the gate to squeak, the door to open and close, her footsteps to come back up the stairs. He pictured her popping her head around the door to their room and looking at him with those chocolate-coloured eyes and he would melt into them and it would all be OK again. And as he waited, he thought ahead to when they would have a proper home together. Their house would have big flat windows and a bright red door. There would be hanging baskets and pots of plants, large-leafed palms and exotic herbs. On summer evenings as he watered them, he would look through one of the big flat windows and see her moving about inside and he would be glad. Yes, this was how it was going to be.

But then, after a while, he got off the bed and went downstairs to the kitchen to make something to eat. She wasn't coming back, not yet anyway, and despite his earlier thoughts of houses and plants and windows, he was relieved. It was good to have a bit of space. He made beans on toast and, as he was carrying his plate upstairs, he passed the girl who'd been in the kitchen earlier. She was sitting on the stairs murmuring into the telephone. Elliott felt a moment's impatience; if she'd get off the line, maybe Fern would ring, say, 'Meet me at the station, I've changed my mind.' But the girl talked on and he carried on upstairs and that moment passed too.

Fern didn't call the next day either, nor the day after. Elliott went to lectures, chatted to friends, played a game of squash, came home at the end of the second day expecting a letter to be sitting on the shelf in the hall where such things were put. But there was nothing, only silence. Relief became mixed with a kind of anger as the days passed. What was he supposed to think? It was hard, hard holding on to the thoughts of her; it was like there was a layer of dust over everything and he couldn't see clearly.

Then, that last evening, that Monday when Fern had been away for over a week, he met Meryl in the students' union. She was small, cute, keen on him. She always had been, he'd believed. Fern had once said, 'She fancies you, that Meryl,' and he'd replied, 'Crap! Anyway, I'm yours, aren't I?' It was a corny conversation, but hadn't seemed so at the time.

A group of them were sitting in the alcove next to the bar. There was the hum of conversation and music was playing. Somehow Meryl was sitting next to him; he did not know how this had come to be, but he remembers them playing 'Never Gonna Give You Up' by Rick Astley and Michael Jackson's 'Man in the Mirror' and that it seemed that the place had a heartbeat and that he was in the middle of it and it felt good.

'So,' Meryl said, turning to face him and lifting her glass to her lips, 'what're you gonna do next year? After your finals?'

Say, 'We don't know yet,' Elliott told himself. Tell her in that one word *we* – that he's spoken for, half of a couple.

'I don't know,' he said. 'I've applied to HP's graduate training scheme, but if they offer me a place it'll be conditional on my results. You? What about you?'

'I've always wanted to go into events management. My parents already run a business, and they've said I can join them if I want to.'

'That's good.' He didn't know what else to say. She crossed her legs; her skirt crept up her thigh. She was bare-legged and her skin was smooth and slightly dark. Right at that moment she seemed to be everything Fern wasn't.

'Yes, but I'm still stressing over my exams.' She laughed as she said this. It was a nice sound: easy and fresh. Her eyes were bright and the light in them was dancing.

'Aren't we all?'

This was when it would have been the right time for her to ask where Fern was; after all, she knew about them, everyone did. But she didn't ask and he didn't say anything. Fern was a presence between them but, as he finished his beer and started to riffle in his pocket to see if he had the money for another, it was as though he could look straight through Fern at Meryl, and Meryl was smiling at him, saying, 'You having another drink then?'

'Yeah, think so,' he said. 'You?'

It was a stay-or-go moment. If he stayed, it would be a signal; if he went, he would be safe. He could change his mind, say, 'Actually, I'm knackered, think I'll turn in. See you around then.' And she would nod and turn away from him and talk to someone else and the moment would pass. Yes, that would be the wise thing to do.

But she nodded and someone opened the door to the bar at the same time and a soft light fell across her, across her face, shoulders, arms, legs and he wanted her. It wasn't anything to do with Fern or love; it was a basic instinct to fuck, one he hadn't felt in a long time.

'Come on,' he said, shuffling along the bench, and together they went up to the bar to order their drinks.

She stood close by him while they were waiting; he could feel the warmth of her, the buzz that came from her. They didn't rejoin the others, but stood apart in a dark corner, talking quietly, drinking. Her head came up to his chest and she had to look up to speak to him, and each time she did so, she would tip her head to one side and look at him from under her eyelashes, and she smiled a lot. She seemed uncomplicated, totally new and untried.

At closing time they hung back as the others left. If the lads he came with noticed, they didn't do or say anything; student rules were different from other rules. Elliott knows that now. It doesn't make what he did right, but it was a different time; a different template.

'You coming back?' he asked her as they stood outside the union. It was a night of dangerous, slightly warm air. The rain from earlier in the week had left the ground clean and washed. There was a hint of summer on the breeze.

'You sure it's OK?' she asked.

This was another junction, a point when he could have said, 'Actually . . .' and she'd have been a bit pissed off, and he would have gone home and had a wank, and the world would have continued on its set path, but he was annoyed with Fern and he wanted Meryl, and he liked that she wanted him now, without forcing him to decide their whole future, and he'd had a few drinks. It was easy to succumb.

'The room's a bit of a tip, I'm afraid, but . . .' He didn't finish the sentence because she stretched up and kissed him lightly on the lips and his brain filled with that white noise again.

They went back to the room. It doesn't matter now what they said en route, how they moved from the kitchen, where they made coffee, to the bed, but they did these things and if Meryl noticed Fern's things lying around, she didn't say anything. She fitted under him and held onto him tightly as he fucked her. The lips of her cunt were soft and ripe, and she said, 'It's OK, I'm on the pill,' as he lifted back his head at one point to look questioningly at her, and then he came and it was sweet and long and there was no guilt, no comparisons with Fern; it was just what it was. He put his mouth on her and she came, he could feel the pulse of her, her pubic hair was damp and soft on his face.

Afterwards they slept, she was curled in the crook of his arm, and there was a time in the depth of the night when, woken by the thread of an owl's cry from a nearby tree, he looked across and for a moment couldn't quite work out who it was sleeping next to him. She was about the same size and shape as Fern, but there was something different. The hair was too dark, she was slightly bonier and her breathing sounded odd; it was heavier than he was used to. But still there was no guilt. There should have been, there should have been.

In the morning she sat up next to him in the bed, her full breasts hanging down, their nipples dark, her shoulders thin and vulnerable and he kissed her, felt the smooth roundness of her breasts under his lips, tasted himself on them. She rested her chin on the top of his head and he could feel her abdomen tighten, knew she wanted to come again. His cock was hard, ready.

Buried in her skin he didn't hear the gate open, the front door open and close or footsteps climbing the stairs. He didn't hear the door to the room open, but he did hear the small cry and he lifted his lips from Meryl's breasts, lifted his eyes to see Fern standing in the doorway, a lace scarf tied in a bow in her hair, her eyes smudged with tiredness, and he heard the door slam and her running, running.

Outside the window of the train, Elliott sees signs announcing they're at Didcot. The train slows. The youth with the SOUL necklace is starting to stand up. Elliott doesn't meet his gaze. He's further on in his journey than he realised. Is there time, he wonders, to change his mind? How can he face Fern now? What can he say to make it up to her? Surely what he did back then was just so wrong, so huge, that there is no going back? Is he foolish even to try? The youth goes and Elliott picks up his empty coffee cup, studies it hard as if he'll find an answer there.

CHAPTER 15

'Hello, love,' Jack says to Fern. 'How are you?'

The phone is already hot in her hand. 'I'm fine,' she says. 'How was your day?'

'Good, thanks.'

He sounds distracted, but then he always does these days. She can hear rustling at the other end of the line. This, she thinks, is one of those times when she feels squeezed into the cracks of his life, not the fundamental part of it that she used to be. She has learnt, is still learning, not to mind about this because she knows that there are times when she takes him for granted too. But it doesn't make it any less painful; it just serves to remind her how much there is still left for them to say.

'How was the pottery course?' he asks. 'And Jules?'

She can tell he's proud that he's now remembered what she's been doing today, but he's probably not that interested in her answers. Why should he be?

She sees him sitting in his car, getting ready to drive home, recognises the creases in his trousers, his long fingers selecting a track on his iPod. She sees the sweep of his shoulders as he plugs it in because she's seen these things a hundred times before. She imagines him standing next to his client on site, a hard hat on his head, his new safety boots on his feet. He'll sway slightly as he talks, clear his throat and jingle the coins in his pocket. She hears him say 'C-o-l-e, as in Lloyd Cole . . .' when he's on a call, and thinks again that she should tell him that 'Ashley' or 'Cheryl' would mean more to people these days.

Despite everything, all the ordinariness of her life, she still wants her husband to be a hero and there are times when she fears she doesn't really know him at all and, after all the years they've been together, this surprises her. But then, this is a day of surprises. She is somewhere unplanned and she doesn't know how she should behave now she's here.

A tannoy announcement says that the train at Platform 8 is about to depart, and before she has time to answer his last questions, Jack says, 'Oh, you're at Paddington then? What time will you be home?'

'Not sure,' she says. It's time to come clean. She knows it will be fine. He won't mind because, and this is the awful bit, he trusts her so completely. 'I bumped into an old uni friend this morning and said I'd meet them for a drink on my way home. So . . .'

She doesn't have time to finish, to explain any further, because he says, 'Oh, that's nice.' There's a pause. She wonders if he's going to ask for more details, but he's already turned the music on. She doesn't recognise the band. 'Let me know when you're on the train then,' he says.

He hasn't asked who she's meeting. It's probably because he's not curious. She realises now that she didn't say, 'I'd meet *him* for a drink on my way home'; she said '*them*' and she doesn't want to think about the significance of this.

'OK. I will,' she says, and then on an out breath, adds, 'You spoke to Wilf then?'

This change of subject is welcome. This is a topic they're good at. Talking about the boys is safe. Sometimes it seems that they've lost the art of talking to one another. Years of text messages and voicemails saying, 'Home at 7', 'Can you feed the cat?', 'Don't forget to call your mum' have been laid over the early days of urgent, whispered conversations and phone calls in the night just to say hello. But, she tells herself, this is how it should be. Isn't this normal and healthy and right?

'Yep,' Jack answers, 'I transferred the money direct to the landlord. It seemed the easiest thing to do.'

'That's good then.'

It is good. They are lucky that they have the money and that their sons are OK. She's heard such awful stories about boys from school, boys she helped in the swimming-pool changing rooms when they were five and who have since grown into young men who live lives she doesn't understand, and whom she wouldn't recognise if she passed them in the street; maybe she wouldn't want to. She wouldn't know what to say to them, not any more.

She does, however, want to tell Jack about Tom and how the clay felt between her fingers. She wants her husband to understand what it was like to lift the pot, how it felt like sex, and she wants him to understand the joy being near Jules gives her even now, how scared she is about this evening, about what seeing Elliott again might bring. But how can she tell him these things?

On this day as she sits in the bar, waiting for the clock hand to move nearer half past seven, and as Elliott's train eats up the countryside and the years that separate them, she realises that there is so much she hasn't told her husband that to start now wouldn't make sense.

They were who they were then and are who they are now. Should it matter that there seems to be a vast tract of time in between which has disappeared? Yes, she says. It does matter. In her mind she's beating her fists against a wall, drilling the word 'remember' into her brain. She wants to remember all the tiny splinter-like things: Jack's footsteps on the stairs, the sun glinting off his hair in the garden, him at the other end of the table when they're entertaining, how they've made love so many different ways but each time it's the same. There's her and there's him and there's the safety of their marriage; this thing that seems to frame them, make sense of them, but, she thinks, there are times when, as well as holding her in, this structure, this grief she feels now the boys have left home, is keeping her out. There is a difference here and, despite all the wonder and joy of her life with him, it's not an entirely comfortable one. It seems she has lost the art of being who she's always thought she was. Would now be the time, she wonders, to start again, be someone without all the trappings of the past? Could she be this new person with Elliott? Is it now time?

She can hear Jack breathing on the other end of the line. He's started the car and is already planning to move on. When he gets home he will check his emails, maybe go to the gym, pick at some leftovers in the fridge, and he won't miss her, not really. It's not like that for her. When she's at home on her own, she feels suspended; waiting for the next time someone will need her. Despite all the things that bind them, this is one of the things that keep them apart even now, she thinks. And even though he's asked about her day, she won't tell him, she can't, and he won't imagine how it went either. It is not necessary for either of them to do this.

However, when the boys were small she remembers watching Jack leave the house one morning. He closed the front door and walked down the path to his car. She was halfway up the stairs, looking out of the landing window, probably carrying laundry or an armful of toys. He unlocked the car, put his briefcase on the front seat, took off his jacket and hung it on the hook above the passenger door. Then he flexed his shoulders and stood, just for a fraction of a second, with his hand on the door handle and she thought she could see herself, the boys, the corners of their house lift themselves up from around his neck and float away into the morning sky. In the car he bent his head and turned the radio on, put the car in gear, took the handbrake off and drove off. At the junction at the end of the road he looked left and right but he didn't look back at the house, didn't see her watching at the window, couldn't know that what she wanted more than anything was for him to come back, hold her, tell her that, yes, everything was going to be OK. Maybe it had been foolish of her to think that her life could have been anything other than this. After all, we are all fundamentally alone, aren't we?

'Well, I'll see you later?' Jack is saying now. The music in his car is drumming and a man walks by her trundling a case; the noises merge in her head until she can't think straight.

'Yes, I'll text when I'm on the train.'

Should she tell him she loves him? Will he say anything more before he hangs up? Should they need to? She thinks of the plants in their garden, how the eucalyptus tree rustles in the wind, the sturdy shapes of the shrubs, the delight the daffodils he planted in the bed by the front door bring her each year. Then there's how he turns to kiss her goodnight, how his face looks like a child's when he sleeps, how she has no idea what he dreams because he never tells her.

'OK,' he says.

'Bye, then,' she says. 'Drive carefully.'

'Will do.'

He hangs up. His music has gone; the man with the case is bumping it down the steps, its wheels making a metallic sound. It is twenty past seven, her book is lying on her lap, her coffee cup is empty and the waiter is looking at her again from behind the bar.

She waits a few minutes, then reads Elliott's text, is surprised by the preciseness of the plan. What had merely been a possibility is becoming more of a certainty. This is unnerving but also, in a strange way, satisfying.

'See you there!' she texts back. At this particular moment she has no idea who she is. If someone presented her with a story of her life since that morning when she'd run out of the room and Elliott had run out after her, she would struggle to know whether it was fact or fiction and this thought makes her angry. She must have worked hard enough; she must have enough to show for it.

It took months to begin to reconcile herself to the scene in the bedroom: Elliott's head bent low before that girl's breasts as if he was paying homage, or praying. It was a betrayal of everything she and Elliott could have had together. If Jack was unfaithful now, or if she was for that matter, it would be a different type of betrayal. If there was a judgement scale of these things, you know, a sort of scores-on-the-doors thing, which would be worse, she wonders as she packs her book away, pushes her cup across the table to give the waiter the sign that finally she's preparing to leave? Would it be Elliott's pre-betrayal or that other, the post-betrayal? What would be worse, a rejection of all the things that have been or of all the things that were yet to be?

How can she know the answer to this? What she does know is that in the story of her life that a stranger might present her with as she makes her away across the station to the pub and Elliott, there is the chapter where she met Jack, how she found out that she could love someone who wasn't Elliott and that it was different; it was a different kind of love, and she was different too.

This difference started almost immediately when she took her finals, camping in a room in Jules's house whose tenant was abroad on a work place-ment, and then starting work herself in the local library. She had felt safe amongst the books. It was their orderliness and the way that the public would shuffle in and out. She would relish the quiet moments before it opened, imagine the words on the pages of the books stretching their muscles, waiting to be chosen. But even better was the quiet at the end of the day: the weariness after activity, the way the dust settled back on to spines and covers. The world was a good place within those walls.

Meanwhile, Jules shot off into the stratosphere, becoming a cub reporter, then reporter, then features editor, finally working for the *FT* and it was then, when she interviewed Bernard, the short, fat, bald managing director of a hedge-fund company, that she fell in love, gave up her career to tend to horses of her own, tolerate his mother, breed dogs and keep Mrs Bridges busy while she waited for the babies that never came. Meanwhile Fern trained as an archivist, then as a curator and got a job planning the refurbishment of the museum in Reading's Victorian town hall.

She loved the building, with its russet-coloured bricks and grey-blue crenulations; loved the nineteenth-century footsteps she could hear echoing down its hallways and lodged in its rafters.

In calls home to her parents she sounded breezy and happy, 'Yes,' she'd say, 'I've found a lovely bedsit in Crowthorne; it's about twenty minutes from town. I park at the station, then get the train in. No, Mum, it's fine, really. The people at work are great too. My landlady? Her name's Mrs McHugh, she used to be a dancer at the Folies Bergère; the photos on the wall of her lounge are incredible. Yes, I have my own kitchen, well, kitchenette really, and bathroom and then a bedroom; it's fine, really. The job? Yes, that's great too. Everything's good, Mum, couldn't be better. And how are you and Dad? How are Dad's tomatoes doing this year?'

Looking back, Fern has forgotten much about Mrs McHugh, but she does remember that she was a stately battleship of a woman who would surge down the small garden of her converted house in Crowthorne to pick runner beans that her son-in-law had planted and tied to wigwams of canes for her. Fern has also forgotten the lonely nights in front of the small white plastic TV she rented from Radio Rentals, the innumerable tins of beans on toast she had for tea, the baths she took, waiting for tomorrow and the time when the empty museum would be full of hushed silence, with just her and her catalogue and her card-index systems.

And then there was Jack.

Adrian, the museum director, had planned a meeting about the refurbishment with the contractor and surveyor who'd been appointed by the council and had asked Fern to sit in, just in case she had any comments. Just in case?! she'd thought. By now these rooms were her rooms, the whole place was her territory and the displays were like children to her. She guessed at the time, and still believes now, that it has to be like this for it to work properly. The shop she works in now is a bit like that, not quite the same, but almost.

So there they were, these people around a table in the office. Fern had made coffee and there was a plate of biscuits and an overhead projector for the contractor's slides, if he had any. In the moments before the door opened and the visitors came in, Fern stood at the window and looked down at the heads of pedestrians in Market Place, watched how these people swung their shopping bags in time with their footsteps. The door opened.

'Here we are then,' said Adrian, leading the way. He was one of those pale, indistinct men who have hearts of gold and who love their families with a ferocity that is surprising. It shouldn't be, but it is.

Behind him followed two other men; one grey-haired, round-bellied, with a florid face, small piercing blue eyes and a wide smile. Fern didn't trust him; felt that he was the type of man who had secrets, did deals. His companion was young; tall and bendy with fair hair cut close to his scalp. He seemed to stoop a little and she presumed this was from years of bending down to hear what people were saying. There was no eye contact; Fern was just aware of him, like a light in the room, like a promise about to be made.

The details of that meeting are sketchy now; there was talk about timetables and access and health and safety and there were diagrams, and the florid man had a pen that turned into a laser pointer with which he proudly presented drawings on the OHP. This pointer seemed to be proof that this man had embraced technology and, after one particularly robust flourish, Fern glanced at the tall bendy man whose name she'd been told was Jack Cole, and found him smiling gently at her.

It had been a long time since she'd been smiled at that way; she recognised the type of smile immediately, had to reject it of course. After all, she'd told herself, never again was she going to put herself in a position where she could be hurt like she had been by Elliott.

But Jack had rung her the next day at work.

'Hello, Museum,' she'd said when she picked up the phone.

'Hi,' he said. 'It's Jack, Jack Cole, C-o-l-e, as in Lloyd Cole and the Commotions. We met yesterday at the planning meeting . . .?'

'Oh yes.' She tried to sound disinterested, but there was a small quiver in her voice – she knew it and cursed it.

'I was just wondering if you'd heard back from the council about the requirements for disabled access; how low the displays in the Green Space needed to be . . .' he tailed off. This wasn't why he was calling. These things had already been agreed; they were in the report, a copy of which she'd had sent over to him that morning.

'I think it's all in Section 3 of the papers you received this morning,' she said, tapping the desk with the tip of a pencil. She wished he would hang up; she wanted him to stay on the line forever.

'Right,' he said. 'Of course. I'll look it up, thank you.' There was a silence, it was heavy; it dripped between them in slow motion. 'I was also wondering,' he said at last, his voice surprisingly high suddenly, 'if you were free tonight. Perhaps we could meet for a drink, chat about the refurbishment. It would be nice to get a better understanding of it from your point of view.'

It was a strange request; was it a date or a business meeting? If she'd believed it was entirely the former, Fern would have said, 'Thanks, but I'm busy tonight. I'm sure we can cover this in our next scheduled meeting.' It would have been a brutal but safe answer. Instead, however, there was this small flutter in her chest, at the place in between her breasts where the bone seems hardest. She recalled the way he swayed as he walked, the way he moved his hands when he spoke, his smile. 'OK,' she said. 'That would be nice.'

The start of her and him was slow and hesitant, both of them skirting around the other, mostly fearful. They met in pubs and at the cinema, went to the theatre and for walks in the park. It was summer and they kissed one another hello and goodbye and once he came round to her bedsit for supper. She made spaghetti bolognese and they drank cheap red wine. Afterwards they watched TV and he put his arm around her and stroked the skin just under her ear. It was enough and not enough. Inside she was howling for him to touch her, to shift her under him and fuck her, but the distance between where they were and where she wanted them to be seemed too huge a space to bridge; Elliott was still there, still looking at her, still asking her to forgive him, and her fury was still there too, a hard and definite thing.

Then, just as she thought it was time to give up on this because neither of them was ever going to get it right, she met Jack in town one Saturday afternoon. Her mother wanted a new dressing gown for her birthday and he needed a new shirt for work, and it was there in British Home Stores as he stood in the queue to pay, the shirt over his arm, and she watched him from the lingerie department, that something hit her. It felt like thunder, it was green and bright, it had a tail of glowing amber and she realised that she wanted to be with this person forever. He was safe and kind, he bent down to listen when she spoke. He was gentle and good; he was all the things she'd thought Elliott had been.

As he walked back over to her with his shirt in a bag, he smiled at her, said, 'Right then, shall we go?'

She'd said, 'Yes, Jack. Let's go home.'

He'd known all along, of course. Later, when they told the boys the story of how she fell in love with him in BHS, he said that of course he'd known all along that she would eventually.

'Hindsight's a marvellous thing,' she'd said, and they'd laughed and the boys looked despairingly at one another and Wilf said, 'Yuck! Give it a rest, you two!'

That autumn was damp and safe. He moved into her bedsit and Mrs McHugh clucked and bustled around them and they slept in Fern's single bed and didn't mind.

When Jules met him, she took Fern to one side in the small kitchenette and said, 'Well done. Good girl' and Fern didn't mind that either.

Sex with Jack was then and still is a gift and a surrender. The first time was fraught and nervous and she didn't, couldn't come. It still seemed disloyal. But, like peeling back the layers of an onion, he was patient, undemanding. He kissed the curve of her hip, the shadows made by her ankle bones and she had felt herself unravelling. It was inexorable, this undoing, and when, after a handful of soft dark nights, he put his mouth on her, his tongue on the nub of her, she felt she was a cello, giving herself up to him, the strings giving out a kind of music she has carried in her head ever since.

Now she is halfway up the escalator towards The Mad Bishop and Bear and, if asked, she would have to sit down somewhere quiet to write out the chronology of what happened next. There was their wedding; she still has all the paperwork in a blue lever-arch file in the garage and her dress is in a box in the loft, the pale pink satin bows stuffed with acid-free tissue paper like they say to do in magazines, and there was their first house, with garden furniture in the lounge for the first three months and the previous owner's nicotine stains on the walls, and there was leaving for work and getting home and Jack building a rockery and it being so quiet in the night that she could hear her thoughts rumble and fizz.

And then there's now, and looking down on to the station concourse Fern thinks about chairs. The other night in bed she and Jack had counted the seats in their house and garden, had given up when they got to sixty-three.

'Why do we need so many?' she'd asked.

'I have no idea,' he answered, his voice light with laughter, and, turning over, he tucked the pillow under his head.

He is so different, she thought at the time, and yet so much the same. We have more than sixty-three seats, I can imagine him at a distance of miles, I would know him in the dark, but I can't hold on to all the moments we've lived together, can't sort them into patterns. They are just there; all of them, a whole world of thoughts and conversations and stacking the dishwasher and mowing the lawn and folding towels and driving away, driving back, making phone calls, being diluted by the people we know: his mother, his father's death, my parents, our children, the things we have to do, even the cat.

Maybe Elliott is in there somewhere too, she thinks as she walks into the bar. It is dark and noisy, the carpet is shouting at her. She'd not told Jack about Elliott, not then, not in detail. He was just someone in her past and Jules hadn't said anything either; it was like they'd both agreed to park it somewhere where it could not raise its head and shout, 'Hey, what about me?'

But now the carpet is shouting at her, Jack is on

his way home, their boys are grown up and she feels she's on a carousel which has spun so fast she can't see the world around her in detail; not the scenes she has already passed or those that will appear when she pays to go round again, the money bright and hard in her hand, the soundtrack playing on a constant loop, busy, insistent, slightly out of tune with the music in her head.

She scans the bar, but of course Elliott won't be there yet. She's early. There's still time for her to change her mind, for him not to come.

'Dry white wine, please,' she says to the bartender and takes the glass to a low sofa on the far side of the bar. She can see the door from here. She sips her drink. She waits.

I once heard that every life
has a point before which there is
always a looking forward,
afterwards a looking back.

'Thinking of Holland, III. The light on
the water at Rhenen', Will Kemp

CHAPTER 16

The other passengers are starting to shuffle and check their phones as the train passes through Old Oak Common on its approach into London. Elliott's heartbeat is irregular; he is impatient. It's not, he realises, just the thought of meeting Fern, but it's facing up to his own part in what happened that morning that's making him feel this way. For years he hasn't wanted to think about it and how it changed what came next, but this day has changed that, it has changed him.

Gazing out of the window at the sidings and depots he notices that the train is slowing. No, he thinks. Don't stop, not here. He's ready now, ready for what he might be told, what he might confess to. What he'd had with Fern, what he did to her that made him lose her, had mattered, it had mattered very much, and any delay might test his resolve to admit to this. He wants it done now; he has waited long enough.

The view outside the window is becoming clearer with each second; he starts to notice the buddleia plants between the tracks, the graffiti on the underside of a bridge, a beaten-up old car on its side in a compound surrounded by wire fencing. He shouldn't be able to see these things; the train should be going fast enough for them to be a blur, to be unremarkable.

Despite the 'Quiet Carriage' signs, or maybe because of them, the man opposite him says, 'Shit,' to the carriage in general and jabs angrily at his phone. 'Yes,' he barks into it. 'Sodding train is just *crawling* into Paddington. Looks like I'll be late. This is fucking ridiculous!' He's dressed in a suit, looks hot and tired. Why is he going to Paddington at this time of night? Elliott wonders. What can be so important to him?

Elliott's thoughts are interrupted by the train manager, who, in a strong Welsh accent and over a crackly intercom, announces, 'My apologies for the slow arrival into Paddington this evening. This is caused by a failed engine ahead which is blocking a platform. As soon as we're allocated a platform, we'll be underway. In the meantime, I am sorry for the obvious inconvenience this will cause to your onward journey.'

'Too bloody right,' the man says, sighing loudly and staring fixedly out of the window.

Everyone else busies themselves with their bags and coats in preparation anyway and, as if given permission by the train manager to do so, makes the necessary calls. The carriage is filled with the sound of murmuring. Elliott can hear the words 'broken-down train . . . don't know how long . . . yes, I know,' rumbling around him. He picks out his phone and texts Fern.

'Being held outside the station,' he wrote. 'Not sure how long we'll be. If you need to get off, I'll understand. We can always arrange to meet another time.'

He doesn't mean this, and he doesn't want for this to happen. Now is the right time for them to see one another again. He's spent the day building up to it. It would be such a let-down if, after all, it is not to be.

His phones buzzes immediately with a reply.

He reads it, lets out a sigh. Then he checks his email cache as the train's engines hum in the background. It's like I've been half asleep for years, he thinks, just moving from point to point, making money, trying to be nice to people, to Meryl and to Chloe and even to Susan at work, but all the time it's like there's been another Elliott tucked under the surface of this skin, clamouring to get out and now, well, now it's possible that this other Elliott, the real one, the one he hasn't acknowledged for more years than he can remember, is starting to burst through.

As he's looking at the screen, an email arrives from Dan. Elliott wonders where his brother is, who he's with. 'Great stuff,' it says. 'Thanks for sorting the house, etc. Let me know if there's anything I can do.'

He thinks of his brother, and so fixed in his

mind is the image of Dan as a boy, he worries momentarily that he wouldn't recognise him if he met him unexpectedly: Dan building a camp with sticks and bracken leaves, Dan's back silvery in the sea, his arms windmilling in joy. To Elliott, Dan is always laughing, throwing his laughter out into the air, careless of where it lands. How Elliott wishes he was more like this!

Before he can reply his phone rings. It's like buses, he thinks. Nothing for ages, then texts, emails, calls, all in the space of a few minutes. He wonders if anyone else in the carriage has noticed, has categorised him as someone who is busy, valued, needed. He hopes so. It seems to justify his presence here. We all carry a shield of activity around with us, he thinks, but no one is really interested in anyone else's; it's only when we bump into one another that we take notice, that it starts to count.

It's Chloe. His heart sinks. What now?

'Hello, you,' he says breezily into the mouthpiece. 'What's up?'

'Hi, Dad.' Her voice is bright, light and sunny. His spirits lift. Maybe it's going to be OK this time. 'Where are you?' she asks.

'On another train!' he replies. 'We're stuck just outside Paddington.'

She's not really interested. He can tell by the length of the pause between the end of his sentence and when she says, 'Dad?'

'Yes, Chloe.'

'A group of us are thinking of going to Greece in the summer. Baz's dad's got a villa out there he says we can use. So all I'll need are the flights and spending money. What do you think?'

He wants to shout at her. What's she asking him for? Why does she couch everything like it's his decision, not hers? She's almost an adult, should be making up her own mind about things like this. But, then, on the other hand, it's nice to be necessary, for it to have counted.

'How much do you think you'll need?' he asks quietly, conscious of the signs on the windows and not wanting the rest of the carriage to know that there are fundamental cracks in the shield that surrounds him.

She names a figure. 'It'll just be a loan,' she adds breathily. 'I can get a job over the summer and pay you back.'

'Have you spoken to Mum?' he says.

'Nah, not yet. Thought I'd see what you thought first.'

Sneaky, he thinks. She knows he'll be a softer touch than Meryl. He always has been.

'How's your laptop?' he asks to give himself time.

'Oh, it's OK. Dez has said I can borrow his old one until mine's fixed. It's no biggie.'

Baz? Dez? Who are these people who populate his daughter's life now, and how come what was HUGE this morning is now 'no biggie'? How he wishes he could reprioritise his worries like his daughter seems to do. If he could, he would shift his concerns about his dad's care and selling his childhood home to the bottom of the pile. They wouldn't intrude on him so much there. He would park his divorce from Meryl in a side street, cover it with tarpaulin and walk away. He would tuck the responsibility of running his own business and being the person accountable for other people's mortgages, food bills and holidays down the side of the car seat where he would only need to check them when the car got serviced. Finally, he would put the regret he still feels about how he treated Fern all that time ago in a box and he would close the lid on that box and put it high up in a cupboard in a room, draw the curtains and close the door on his way out. That way, all the things that bother him could stay out of sight and he could concentrate on listening to birdsong, drinking a cool beer in the evening, shagging Susan when he felt like it and for there to be no consequences to anything, anything at all.

'You still need me to come at the weekend?' he asks.

'It would be nice, but Dez has said he'll come with me to PC World.'

She's losing interest in this bit of the conversation. She wants to know about Greece; the laptop conversation is old news. She can already see herself stretched brown and smooth on a beach, dancing under lights in a town square, drinking cocktails. These are her ambitions now, and maybe, he thinks, as the train manager makes another announcement, telling them that they are now second in the queue and should be into Paddington within the next ten minutes, this is how it should be. These moments spin by so quickly. Let her have her time in the sun; there'll be years ahead of her when she will have to live the sort of life he's lived, make the choices he's had to make.

'Well,' he says, 'the money's OK with me. But check with your mum first. OK? In principle though, it's OK with me.'

'Oh, thanks, Dad. You're the best,' she says, laughing. It's a nice sound, this laughter; it's something he hasn't heard enough of lately.

'See you soon then?' he adds, hoping he doesn't sound needy.

'Yeah, sure, Dad.'

And she's gone. He knows he's been weak, giving in so easily, but he isn't sorry. Her laughter is enough recompense. The phone line is silent; the view outside the carriage window comes back into focus. The man opposite him is still fidgeting in his seat, has probably listened in for lack of anything else to do. Elliott is overcome with a desire to stand and smash his fist into the man's face. But he doesn't. Instead he slips his phone back into his pocket, pushes his hair out of his eyes with his hand. It flops back into place almost immediately, and for some unaccountable reason he remembers the sound of Fern's footsteps running down the stairs, the door slamming and how the sun had hit the window that March morning as if to proclaim that he had done something that was irrevocable.

Without wanting to be, he's back there with Meryl naked by his side and Fern's stricken face burnt into his eyelids. He looked across at Meryl, didn't like the expression on her face, said, 'I have to go after her.'

'Why?' she'd asked.

'I just do. Don't ask me not to.'

Meryl opened her mouth as if to say something, but then closed it again. For this he was glad. Then, 'Do you want me to be here when you get back?' she asked after a pause.

Her lips were thin and her eyes dark and beady. She didn't seem to be the same girl he'd met the night before. Shit, he thought to himself. Shit, shit, SHIT!

The sun still tapped on the window. Fern would be approaching the corner by now. He had no idea which way she would turn. If he was going, it had to be NOW.

'Perhaps it would be better if you weren't,' he said. 'Just in case.'

'In case of what?'

He had no idea. Would he be able to persuade Fern to come back with him? What would happen if Meryl decided, after all, to stay?

'I'll call you, I promise,' he said. 'It's just best if I'm on my own for a bit.'

She leant over and kissed him lightly on the lips. She still tasted of sex. It was the best thing she could have done.

Grabbing his keys, he slipped on his jeans and trainers, dragged a T-shirt over his head and ran. Thinking about it now, he still doesn't know if he was running away from Meryl or towards Fern. Perhaps it was neither, perhaps both. All he knows is that he ran out of the room, down the stairs, out of the front door, to the gate and into the road. There was no sun now. The clouds were heavy and the breeze was sharp; it whipped at his face, at the thin material of his top. He turned right, saw Fern's back as it disappeared around a brick wall. He ran.

And the running was primitive; it was about the chase, the capture. The blood thumped in his veins; the houses and gardens blurred and the sounds of cars were nothing but a faint hum. All he could see was Fern's back as it raced away from him. The lace bow in her hair had come undone and was trailing behind her, like some sort of broken wing. He had no idea what he was going to say or do if he caught up with her.

He tried to call her name. 'Fern!' But nothing came out. He tried to hold on to the bits of their shared past that were ricocheting around inside his head: the night they met, that morning in January, the pinprick moments of happiness he'd felt with her since, but it was like trying to hold sand in his fingers; grains kept slipping out, and if he'd looked behind him he felt he would have seen a trail of it on the pavement like some weird yellow river.

But he did catch up with her. She was tiring; she was slowing.

'Fern?' he called as she reached the corner. She looked back this time and there was something wild in her eyes like in an animal's; she reminded him of a hunted animal.

'Fern!' he called again. 'Stop, please, stop. Wait.'

And then he was standing before her. She was looking down at her feet, and her chest was heaving as she tried to catch her breath.

His legs ached and he had a stitch. 'Shit,' he said, 'I'm so not fit.'

Neither of them acknowledged this statement. It wasn't worth it.

Then, 'Oh my God, Fern,' he said. 'What can I say?'

And she raised her head and stared at him. Her eyes were fierce and hard. She looked as if she was wearing someone else's face. 'How should I know what you should say?' she asked, her voice low and vibrating. 'I'm not the one who's just fucked someone else, am I?'

This is the moment when he should have said, 'It meant nothing. Forgive me. I've been a fucking idiot. She's nothing to me. You are *everything. Everything.*'

But somehow the words got stuck between his brain and his mouth, frozen by shame and a type of paralysis he'd never felt before. Maybe he'd never really been sure about their great plans for the future, not sure enough about wanting to spend the rest of his life with her. Perhaps, after all, he didn't believe his own spin and this was the reason why he couldn't speak? Was this, therefore, the time to bail? Was this his get-out clause? As his mother used to say, rip the plaster off quickly; it'll hurt but for a shorter time.

'Am I?' she asked again, and this time she said it more quietly. It was as if she'd already surrendered.

So maybe now should have been the point when he took her in his arms and rested his chin on her head, his hands on the familiarity of her bones, and said, 'No, you're not. I am and I'm sorry, so sorry.'

But he didn't do this either. He just stood in front of her, his hands in his pockets, his stitch fading now, and couldn't find the words, didn't know what to say. Maybe this, therefore, was the turning point, the point between looking forward and looking back.

She'd once read him a poem, one a friend of hers had written. It was about trying to capture time and how in doing so rest the seeds of our inevitable failure. The poet had called this pinpoint of time 'the fingerslip' and, like the sand he'd imagined earlier, this pinpoint, this opportunity for reparation, slipped through his fingers too.

'Oh, Elliott,' she said, leaning back against a garden wall. It was low and built of brick and a plant was pressed up against it. As her weight landed on the wall, the scent of lavender rose into the air. He felt sick. It was either the lavender, or the running, or the guilt, or this strange suspension he was in. He bent over and retched.

'Oh, Elliott,' she said again, but this time her tone was not of pity, nor anger, it was more of disgust, distaste. It was like he was repulsive to her, and in truth this was how he felt too.

This is why, he thought. This is why I can't say what I should, do what I should. It's because I don't deserve it. I have no right to a second chance. I have fucked up and there is no way back.

Overhead a plane cut through the sky; the sound of it drowned out his thoughts, the noise of his heart beating in his chest; slower now, quieter, much, much sadder.

He stood back up, risked looking at her: still that same expression on her face; that stranger's face full of anger and a bottomless sadness.

'Why?' she asked, yet more quietly.

The plane had gone now, leaving just an echo, and the sun broke through the mercury-coloured clouds and for a second threw itself down on them, but it didn't seem like a blessing, more like a punishment, and it didn't warm him.

How could he answer her, when he didn't know himself? How could he describe his fear of the future, his fear of her, and that when Meryl's body had been under his he'd somehow felt that sex with her had been both an escape and a different type of prison?

He hadn't thought about afterwards; he knew now that he should have done. After all, he had enough imagination to foresee the implications of what he was doing, but he hadn't, and now he had no answer for Fern, none at all.

All he could say was, 'I don't know. I just don't know.'

'That's not good enough.'

'I don't expect it is.'

'Well, what happens now?'

'I don't know that either. What do you want?'

'What do *I* want?' The anger flashed back. Her body seemed to coil in on itself and then uncurl and he imagined her rising up like some monster and towering above him, throwing fire down at him with her hands. 'I want for this never to have happened. I want to go back to my parents' house, leave it again, walk into our room and find you on your own, waiting for me. Me. Me. Me. Not have that slut in your bed. That's what I want.'

He didn't answer. He couldn't, but somewhere deep down he felt something sting him. Maybe it was the word 'slut'. Maybe he should be defending Meryl? Wasn't this more his fault than hers?

'What have I done wrong?' Fern shifted her body. The scent of lavender broke over him again.

This was a different type of question, but he didn't know the answer to this either. Was it because her presence was suffocating him in the room they shared together? Was it because by being with her he hadn't had enough time on his own yet? Was it because he had to think about her future as well as his own, was responsible for her happiness as well as his own? He wasn't ready for any of this. This he knew now. He didn't want to live in small rooms with her, with anyone. He wanted to be free to breathe his own air. Maybe he'd never really loved her enough and, therefore, was the answer not what had she done wrong to cause this, but what had he done? Maybe he should never have allowed himself to get into this situation in the first place. He should have kept his distance, taken things more slowly. He should not have lain in bed with her that cold January morning and told her everything would be OK. That had been his mistake and now, here, was payback time.

He didn't want to say, 'It wasn't you. It was me,' because that would have been the mightiest cliché of all time, but it was the truth. He should never have allowed himself to be in this position, but he was, and, as they stood there on that corner that March morning, he had no idea which direction he should travel in next to make things better, easier, healed.

He could sense Fern's impatience growing. It was surging over her grief and confusion and if she'd been four years old she would probably have stamped her foot, turned and flounced away. As it was, all she said was, 'Well, when you do decide why you've done this, what I've done to deserve it and what you want to do next, you can try to let me know. Of course, I might have lost interest by then. You have destroyed so much, Elliott, so much.'

And with that she did turn and walk away and a part of him was relieved that she'd done it that way; not crying, not running, and that her last words were dignified and solid ones and that she was walking with her head held high.

He watched her go. She got smaller and smaller and soon she was gone altogether. He waited for her to come back, had thought she might, but she didn't. A lady with a pushchair came round the corner instead. She had a dog on a lead. It was straining, the muscles of its legs tight and bulging. Its eyes were excited and its tongue was lolling out of its mouth. Elliott waited for the woman, the pushchair and the dog to pass him by and then he turned and walked slowly back to the house.

Meryl had gone. She'd left him a note with her telephone number on it, nothing else, just her name and number and this was the best thing she could have done too. He pulled the bedding off the bed and left it in a heap on the floor. The mattress was cold and hard without it but he lay on it, his arms spread out, his legs curled up to his chest, his face turned away from the window, away from the tapestry of Fern's things – her clothes, books, make-up, shoes – and he closed his eyes. Surprisingly he slept.

He slept a lot in the days that followed; he drank wine, tried to revise. Elliott remembers this as the train finally pulls into Paddington. The brakes clank and hiss and there's a woman in a pink top waiting with a cleaning trolley. She's talking on her mobile to someone but he can't hear what she's saying through the glass, just sees her mouth moving. The man opposite him stands, says, 'At last! This country's a joke,' and strides down the carriage, his shoulder tense, a patch of sweat on the back of his shirt. Elliott wishes he'd put his jacket on to hide this but soon the man is gone, is marching along the platform and Elliott steps from the train, is swept along with the other passengers as they hurry to the turnstiles. When he gets there he hesitates, hangs back, looks up in the direction of the pub, imagines Fern waiting there for him, waiting for the explanation he wasn't able to give her all those years ago, waiting for him to say, 'I'm sorry, I was wrong. You were everything to me. I should never have let it happen. We should have had our life together like we planned.'

He puts his ticket into the machine, pushes himself through the barrier and walks across the concourse. It's almost eight o'clock.

It is so much like
the twist in the plotting of things she should
pass here

'In Athens', Bernard Spencer

CHAPTER 17

It's odd, Fern thinks, as she waits for Elliott, that she should be here, now, like this. When she got up this morning, fed the cat, put some laundry away, she had no idea that mere hours later she would be here, having rewound her life like she has and be waiting to face the man who, if it doesn't sound corny, broke her young and tender heart.

How is it, she wonders, that fate has dealt me this hand? She's reminded of a book of poems by a guy called Bernard Spencer. The title was *The Twist in the Plotting*, and that's how she feels now. It's like someone has come along and gathered together all the bits of her life that were resting quite nicely in the right order and were following the right script, and has thrown them up, high into the air and is standing with their hands on their hips watching them fall, waiting to see what pattern they will make on the ground when they land.

Her phone buzzes. It's a text from Elliott. 'Being held outside the station,' it says. 'Not sure how long we'll be. If you need to get off, I'll understand. We can always arrange to meet another time.'

She's furious. No! Why should she postpone this now? She wasn't expecting to meet him again, but now it's all in place, please let me see it through, she thinks. It wouldn't be fair to cut the cord. It's been tugging at her for years, and today, in a few minutes' time, she has the chance to wheel in the rope, see what really is at the other end of it.

Her glass is almost empty. This is not a good sign. 'No,' she writes, her fingers tapping crossly on the keypad, 'I'm fine for time. Will hang on here. Just keep me posted?'

She goes to the Ladies' and when she washes her hands she gazes at her reflection in the mirror. Whose face is she seeing? It doesn't feel like hers, doesn't look like hers. It's a surprise that Elliott actually recognised her this morning! The years concertina suddenly and, walking through the bar and sitting back down in the seat with a view of the door, she puts her bag on the floor and crosses her legs. The empty glass has gone. The minutes are ticking by. She can sense Elliott's train hovering outside the station, can see him on it, him pushing his hair out of his eyes with his hand, see his legs, the soft shadows in his eyes. How different is he? she asks herself. How changed is he really from the boy who did something so wrong? And, she thinks, as a couple walk by her hand in hand, how much of it was her fault?

It wasn't easy living in that room; all their stuff

scattered about, the daily grind of lectures and walking in the rain, having no money. There were good bits, of course there were, but there was also a sense of frustration that bubbled away in her veins. She guesses the unravelling started on that January day, the one with the snow when they'd woken, made love and then had tried to talk, but kept missing each other's meanings, patched it up by saying everything would be OK when perhaps they hadn't really believed that it would. Maybe it was the snow outside, the feeling of being trapped amidst the debris of their belongings, the wonder of his body, his nervousness and the splendour of *Paradise Lost* and all its promises. He'd tried to articulate what it was he wanted to do; all those dreams of political change, of making a difference, and she'd reduced these dreams with her talk of domesticity and cats! Why had she done that? Why had they been unable to see each other clearly that day? Had that been when his doubts had started in earnest? Should she have blamed him? They were both so young, so unformed. How could they have known what they'd wanted and, one final question, why wasn't she patient enough to wait to find out?

Then there was that other day, the one when it rained and she came back in a foul temper from her meeting with Dr Thomas. 'Flippant and unscholarly,' he'd called part of her dissertation! She'd wanted to bury him in his books for saying that. He was a small man, with hands of different

293

sizes and a head that seemed too large for his body. For some reason she couldn't explain, he annoyed her, made her want to argue with him over every fucking comma and full stop.

'I want you to rework the second section,' he'd said, 'make your references more telling, and when it's reshaped, bring it back to me.'

There were no laptops in those days; everything had to be done by hand and then typed up. 'Rework' wasn't just that, it was 'work', and in that mad March when the wind blustered and swaggered around the campus and everyone's heads were bent low against it, she wanted to raise her head and shout, 'Fuck off then! I don't want to do this any more.'

But giving up wasn't an option; neither giving up on her degree, nor on Elliott. It had seemed, as she climbed the stairs to their room that afternoon, like she was trapped.

And then Elliott was there, drinking tea, spread out on the bed, saying, 'Shall I get you a cup?' or something like that, as if tea would make everything better. No, the only things that would make things better would be space and time and the feel of warm sun on her back and a clear view of the future. Not this room with its weeks-old newspapers, empty plates, dirty socks and his wet jeans on the floor by the bed.

He'd asked her how her day had gone. 'It was crap,' she'd said. 'He . . .' Here she'd stopped. 'I can't be bothered to go through it all now. Maybe later. OK?'

And what she wanted more than anything then was for him to stand and hold her and tell her that everything was going to be all right. But he didn't and, like picking at a scab, she'd asked the 'What's going to happen?' question. She shouldn't have done; she knows that now. It shouldn't have mattered; she should have been able to cope with the uncertainty.

She checks her watch again; ten to eight.

It's all very well saying now that it shouldn't have mattered, now that she can look back through the vista of years, when she's learnt patience, when the years of being a mother have taught her how to put herself second. Perhaps, if she could actually rewind her life, she wouldn't have done what she'd done when he'd said those things and then gone to get her that bloody cup of tea, she wouldn't have grabbed her bag and started packing like the coward she was.

'What are you doing?' he'd asked when he got back.

'I need to get away. I thought I might go home for a few days. Clear my head,' she'd said. She said some other things too and it seemed like they were playing squash blindfolded and with a dead ball; each shot making a dull thwack on the wall; no one winning, no one losing.

And she left, hauling her wet jacket back on and going down the stairs. At the front door she paused, expecting him to have followed her, could feel his weight pressed against her, the taste of his breath in her hair and him saying, 'Don't go, stay. We can work this out.' But he didn't. She paused again at the gate, looked back up at the window, the window so like the one she saw today at Tom and Mary's house, could almost see him standing there a bit like in the TV programme she'd watched a child, based on the book by Joan G. Robinson, called *When Marnie Was There*. Elliott's imagined face, like Marnie's, has haunted her ever since.

His words about Jules were still stinging her as she got to the end of the road, but she could have forgiven him those had he just touched her, just tried to stop her. It was, she felt, like all the colour had drained out of the world that evening as she walked through the dark rush-hour rain to the station, her bag heavy on her shoulder, her head wet and cold and the words 'you stupid, stupid sod' bouncing around in her head. But who was the more stupid, her or him, she wasn't quite sure.

At the station she tried to call Elliott, but the line was engaged. She waited a couple of minutes, then tried again. Still engaged. The beeps were harsh and insistent, the handset and the phone box both cold, and she could still hear the tone in her head as the train rumbled into the station. While she was in the call box, she should have called her parents, warned them she was coming, but she was too tired so didn't, just sat in her damp clothes in the cold compartment, pressed up against a man clutching a briefcase, a sodden newspaper under his arm, with her head resting on the misted glass, and waited to arrive at her destination.

Elliott hadn't chased after her to the station, hadn't jumped on to the train and searched every carriage until he found her, and as each minute passed and he didn't come, her heart both hardened and softened until she didn't know how she felt about anything any more. It was as though someone had built a brick wall between who she was when she was with him and this other person, this stranger who was sitting on a train travelling at speed away from him.

Then why hadn't she contacted him while she was away? How had she expected him not to wonder whether or not she had gone for good? She'd said 'just a few days', but had she meant it? Had she really known where and when this running away would end? Of course, it wouldn't have happened that way these days. Any disputes between her sons and the girlfriends that have speckled their teenage years have been resolved via tentative texts or messages on Facebook. Just a smiley face sent by phone can mean the world, but she and Elliott didn't have such things. She could have written, or rung, or have gone back earlier than she did, but when she got home, it was as if she was paralysed. Whether it was by shame or by uncertainty she didn't know then and doesn't know now either. What was certain, however, was that she hid out at her parents' house for a few days and, as it turned out, stayed there for one day too many. If only she had gone back the evening before, found him in the bar drinking with his friends . . . If only . . .

But she hadn't; she stayed at home, hiding like a child, counting endlessly to one hundred in her head, waiting and hoping to be sought, to be found.

'Well?' her mother said the morning after she arrived.

'Well, what?' Fern replied, standing at the kitchen counter with her back to her mother and buttering a piece of toast. Her mother didn't answer and Fern was aware of her slipping out of the kitchen and for this she was glad. They were probably both too unsure of their ground to take the conversation any further; her mother didn't know what she should ask and, if she had, Fern would have had no idea how to answer.

Standing at the kitchen window, she ate the toast. Her father's garden was just taking its first cautious breaths after the winter, and somewhere deep down in her navel Fern felt a pulse of excitement; it was as unexpected as it was welcome; maybe it would be OK after all, she thought. But for now there was the work she had to do for Dr Thomas in the quiet and space of this house. This, more than anything, was what she needed.

Her mother came back into the kitchen. 'What are your plans today?' she asked Fern.

'My dissertation.'

'Oh, OK. You all right to get your own lunch? I've got to go out.'

'Sure.' Fern rinsed her plate and stacked it on the side with her father's breakfast things. No doubt Mum would wash it up later.

She passed her mother on the way out of the kitchen and, just like with Elliott, there seemed a huge distance between them. It was as though Fern was floating on an island of her own making, totally adrift in a fathomless ocean; constantly missing the landfall offered by those she believed loved her.

The days dragged by. One, two, three. She tried not to think about Elliott, but at night she would lie awake in her childhood bed and her body would miss his touch and she would write letters to him in her head. But come daybreak, that flinty feeling in her heart would reappear, drown out any of the stirrings of hope she'd felt on the first morning when she ate her toast overlooking the garden, and finally the rewrite was finished. She and her parents had danced around each other as much as they possibly could and so on that last night, as she stared out into the darkness of her room, picking out the contours of her childhood furniture lit by the thin strip of light from under the door, she knew she had to go back. There was a kind of inevitability about it, a facing-up to what would happen next. What this was she had no idea; all she knew was that she had to see Elliott again, stand near him, perhaps touch him, be touched by him, and then maybe, just maybe, whatever it was that has driven this wedge between them would dissolve and disappear and it would be like it was before, before January, before that wet afternoon when she ran away.

She left a note for her parents: 'Have gone back. See you at Easter. Lots of love, Fern,' and she crept out before dawn and caught the early train. She'd tied her hair up in a lace scarf, hadn't put her make-up on but had grabbed her stuff and left. As each mile sped by, her sense of excitement grew. The rewritten chapter was nestled in her bag, her approaching finals seemed doable for a change, and what did it matter, she thought, if she and Elliott didn't know for sure what was going to happen next? Surely finding out – finding out together – was what their life together was going to be about?

The house was silent when she arrived. She opened the gate slowly – its hinges didn't squeak for once – and she slipped her key into the lock and crept upstairs. In her mind's eye she could see Elliott as he lay sleeping, his head to one side, see the gentle rise and fall of his chest. Maybe the duvet had slipped off him and an arm or a leg was showing. Every part of him was familiar to her; he was like her second self, the thing that made her whole.

She opened the door and saw Elliott's head, but not turned to one side on the pillow, his dark hair flopped over his forehead, his eyes closed, his chest gently rising and falling. No, what she saw was Elliott's head tipped towards a girl's breasts and his eyes were the eyes that had looked at Fern during sex: hooded and full of desire. The girl's breasts were soft and ripe, her nipples dark brown and there, in her eyes, was a look of triumph that made Fern's heart flip in her ribcage and crash-land at what felt like a thousand miles per hour.

Fern ran. She ran down the stairs and out the front door. She hurled herself through the gate and ran to the corner, her bag thumping on her back, her lace scarf untied and streaming out behind her. With each heartbeat she imagined she could hear Elliott's footsteps following. She stopped at the corner and looked back. He wasn't there, and this was the fatal moment. If he had been – if she'd seen a look of contrition on his face as he hurtled towards her and swept her up in his arms whispering, 'I love you, only you,' into her hair – maybe she would have forgiven him. But he didn't do this; he wasn't there.

She was tiring; her footsteps were getting slower, weighed down by her bag, and then there he was, but the turning point had passed.

'Fern?' he called. Then, 'Fern!' He called again. 'Stop, please, stop. Wait.'

Their conversation took mere minutes but seemed to last a lifetime. The silences were limitless and whenever she leant back against the low garden wall, she brushed against a lavender bush and the air was filled with the scent of it.

He'd asked her what he should say. How should

she know? Why did it have to be up to her to provide the solution to this?

'How should I know what you should say?' she said. 'I'm not the one who's just fucked someone else, am I?'

There was something ridiculous about the situation. He was breathing deeply, complaining he wasn't fit. At one point he even retched. He repulsed her and she could see absolutely no way back to who they had been, the closeness they'd shared. His betrayal with that girl could have been forgiven, possibly, but what couldn't be forgiven was the fact that he made her stand there, on that corner, on that Tuesday morning in March, with the smell of lavender, and the sound of a plane overhead, and seemed to hold a coin in his hand, asking her to flip it but with the full knowledge that it was heads you lose, tails you lose. This is what she would never be able to forgive, or so she felt at the time.

She felt absurd and pitiful, never more so than when he asked her what she wanted and she told him, her heart exposed and beating pathetically. 'I want,' she said, 'for this never to have happened,' but it had and there was a tightness in her chest that she remembered from being a child and not being allowed to have the one thing she wanted more than anything. The silence stretched. There was so much he could have said but chose not to and so, eventually, she set the seal on their time together, said what a week ago would have seemed unsayable. She said, 'Well, when you do decide why you've done this, what I've done to deserve it and what you want to do next, you can try to let me know. Of course, I might have lost interest by then. You have destroyed so much, Elliott, so much.'

And she walked away, left him standing there, did not let herself look back. It took every ounce of muscle and every vein and sinew not to turn around and run back to him. Every fibre seemed to be screaming, 'Hold me, touch me, forgive *me*,' but she kept walking, his eyes burning a hole in the back of her jacket, the space between her legs singing a lament which had no beginning and no end.

She passed a woman pushing a buggy. The child in it was sleeping, its face was pale and smooth, its limbs cast asunder in helpless abandon. The mother looked harried; she had a dog on a leash. It was straining and panting as it walked. It was a scene of two halves. Fern didn't want to catch the woman's eye, was afraid if she did, the woman would be able to read in hers the failure Fern now carried around with her. From now on, Fern would be known as, and know herself as, the girl who had been stupid enough to believe that love was real, that love could last forever.

Jules answered the door, let her in, gave her warm white wine, made her sleep, spoke in whispers to her housemates. They both thought Elliott would come; they believed he would, but one day followed the next and he didn't. After a few days Jules went to the house and brought back Fern's things and Fern gathered these around her like wreckage and started slowly, slowly, to build the life that she has lived ever since.

The barman in The Mad Bishop and Bear looks over at her and smiles. She smiles back, is shocked to find herself here, now. The past had been so vivid; she could smell it, feel the shape of it in her hands, and suddenly she isn't ready to see Elliott again. What can she say? What can he say to make amends, to put the past right, make sense of who they are now? She looks over at the door; a man is walking through it. He is pushing his hair out of his eyes with his hand. It's almost eight o'clock.

                  and

thinking

that anything – a love affair, a marriage –
  could start
in the self-same way, even a simple walk
in the country; one step, one leap of the
  heart.

            'Marriage', David Harsent

CHAPTER 18

This is one way for this day to end.

Elliott walks over to where Fern is sitting. She starts to stand up but he stops her by placing a hand on her shoulder; touching her is like touching electricity and he snatches his hand away. She looks at him, surprised.

'You OK?' she asks, sitting back down, the cushions on the seat making a kerrumph sound which he hears over the pulse of music from the bar.

'Yes,' he says, 'sorry. I'm a bit . . .'

But he doesn't know what he is part of; it doesn't seem that he's really here at all. Throughout every minute of each hour since he met her that morning, he's imagined being with her again and yet hasn't been able to believe that it would really happen. After all, he doesn't deserve it, does he?

'How was your day?' she asks, shifting on the sofa and crossing her legs and at last he sits down too, facing her with his back to the bar. She looks tired, he thinks. Some more people walk in through the door, talking loudly to one another. He hears snatches of their conversation.

'It was difficult,' he says to Fern. 'Going back always is. Dad's . . . well, Dad's not really himself and nothing's the same. But I did what I had to do, so that was good, I suppose.'

'What was it? What did you have to do?'

So he tells her about the house and the estate agent and visiting his dad, but he doesn't tell her about Love Lane, nor how he's replayed what happened with her and with Meryl; how each mile he's travelled has been some sort of atonement, or justification or apology; he's still not quite sure which.

'That must have been hard,' she says, and for a moment he doesn't know what she means. How could she know, he wonders, what he's been thinking about today, how hard it's been looking back, seeing the mistakes he's made glaring at him in vibrant technicolour?

'Can I get you a drink?' she asks.

He realises he hasn't said anything in response and that he should have done.

'No, it's OK, I'll get them,' he says, standing up and picking his wallet out of his pocket. The remaining sticky labels come out with it. He hastily stuffs them back in, hopes she hasn't noticed. If she has, she doesn't comment.

She asks for a glass of dry white wine, which he orders along with a pint of London Pride for himself, and, as he carries the drinks back over to where she is sitting, finds he is transfixed by the way the bar's lights are dancing in her hair as she bends her head over her bag, picks out her phone, looks at the screen and then puts it away again.

'You sure you're OK for time?' he asks, putting the drinks on the table and sitting back down opposite her.

'Oh yes,' she says, 'perfectly OK.'

There's an awkward pause and then they both pick up their drinks, take a sip, swallow and start speaking at the same time. 'What . . .?' he says. 'Tell me . . .' she says. They both laugh, just a little, not much, not enough to change anything.

'What have you done today?' he says into the echoes of this small, not much, not enough laughter.

'I've been on a pottery course, with Jules,' she answers. 'It was a birthday present for her; it was supposed to be last week, but got moved to today. Just think . . .' she hesitates, takes another sip of her drink, 'if it hadn't been, moved that is, if it had gone ahead last week as planned, I might not have seen you this morning, and we might not be here like this now.' She speaks quickly, a little breathlessly.

'I know,' he says, wanting to reach across the table and try touching her again. He wants to hold her hand, feel the weave of her fingers through his; there is so much that is familiar about her, too much almost. 'I know, I've been thinking the same, all day actually. What if we hadn't met this morning? What if we'd done it differently back then?'

'Oh,' she laughs again, looks at him with her chocolate-brown eyes and for a split second he forgets that they are here, that they aren't back then. He's forgotten that she married someone else, that he married Meryl, that these marriages have produced children who are vibrant and shining people. 'Oh, there's no point,' she says. 'What is, is. We can't undo . . .' She puts down her glass. He notices her hand is shaking slightly.

'I guess you're right, but . . .'

'But?'

'But we can go on – forward, I mean. From today we can pick up where we left off, try again, can't we? It's not too late for that, is it? Tell me, Fern, is it?'

He sees the day he's just lived again; but this time it is speeded up. There's this morning on the station concourse, there's the beach at Llantwit, there's the house, Dad, Love Lane, the hospital, and there are miles and miles of train tracks and there's the room he lived in with Fern, their belongings scattered over the furniture and floors and there's the feel of her under him, next to him, all around him and his heart is poised as if on a cliff top; he can see the sparkling waters below, hear the gulls' distant cries, there's a bell tolling somewhere and Dan is there too, he's nearby and it's good to have him close, and then Fern leans over to him, across the low table, and touches his knee very gently.

His heart leaps as she says, 'No, it's not too late, Elliott. We can try again, we can.'

Or, another way for this day to end is this:

Elliott brings Fern a drink in the bar at Paddington Station. It's ten past eight and their conversation is stilted and uncomfortable. There is so much she wants to say, but finds that she doesn't know the right words. She wants to tell him about her house, how it clicks and creaks as she waits to fall asleep, as if it's talking to her. This, she feels, is the most important thing she should be telling him, but she can't.

Instead she tells him about the pottery. 'He made it look so easy,' she said, 'Tom, the potter, made it look so easy. But it wasn't. Both Jules and I—'

'How is Jules?' he asks.

He has stretched out his legs and is nestling his glass against his chest. He looks exhausted and she wants to touch the denim of his jeans, rub it between her fingers, but doesn't know why this should be.

'She's fine,' she says. 'Still the same. She never changes.'

'That's good to hear.'

There is a silence and she imagines he can see all the memories that have besieged her during the day that's just gone, like the camera she thought he had earlier, the one playing images of her to him, and it's like they are marching by him, saluting, saying, 'Here we are, look at us!' and he will inspect each and every one and give it a score. He will see the day in BHS with Jack; the nights she's crept into the boys' rooms and watched them sleeping; see her walking with Jules on the beaches of Kent and even in the hotel room with Lars, and he will know that with each beat of her heart she will have wondered what would have happened if, on that street corner years ago, they both had said different things, done different things.

She takes another sip of her drink. It tastes slightly bitter. The bar is getting crowded and she wishes for open spaces and fresher air. 'Well,' she says, 'I guess I'd better go, after this, I mean.' She nods towards her drink. 'Otherwise we'll both get in too late. You've got quite a distance still to travel, haven't you?'

'You could say that,' he answers with a short, brittle laugh. Then he adds, 'But, I've come a long way too. I mean, from that day, back then. I've often wondered what would have happened if we'd done it differently.'

She wishes he hadn't said this; she had thought it unsayable. It is, after all, a given, isn't it?

'Oh.' She tries to laugh and glances across at him. How difficult would it be to undo the years? Would it only take a few words, a sentence or two? But then she thinks of Jack, of her house and the sounds it makes, of her boys who are now men and of the cat who jumps softly on to her bed at dawn and curls up by her feet. She knows that these are things that can't be undone.

'Oh,' she says again, 'there's no point. What is, is. We can't undo . . .' She puts down her glass, notices her hand is shaking slightly.

'I guess you're right,' he says, 'but . . .'

'But?'

'But, we can go on – forward, I mean. From today we can pick up where we left off, try again, can't we? It's not too late for that, is it? Tell me, Fern, is it?'

Can she do it? she asks herself. The thoughts of what might happen next still scare her. She has no idea whether she is going to be able to be the woman Jack and the boys expect her to be. Would it therefore be easier to stop and start again, maybe with Elliott, maybe on her own? Is this the easier choice? Should she stay and be afraid that she will fail at the next bit, or go and forge a life separate from the past she's had with Jack, with her sons? Would this be the kinder thing to do?

But even as she hesitates before replying, she knows that although she's had her 'that was it' moments – the days her boys were born, even that morning on the corner of the street when Elliott hadn't said what she'd hoped he'd say, she will have yet more, of this she is certain; perhaps now more so than ever. And then she sees herself at her front door with the key in her hand. The porch light is shining and the cat is winding itself around her legs, purring at her. She's stepping into the house, sees Jack's briefcase at the bottom of the stairs – there's a message on the answer-phone; its red light is blinking at her and the TV's on in the lounge. It's a news programme, she guesses. There are pictures on the walls and a photograph of the boys on the dresser; she can remember the day the carpet was laid and how the hallway cupboard used to be full of large shoes and her sons' friends' coats. She wonders if Jack has eaten yet this evening, hears him calling, 'Hi there. You made good time.'

And now, sitting here with Elliott, her heart leaps as she says, 'Yes, it's too late, Elliott. We can't try again, we can't.'

Or, maybe this is how it really is.

A man is running across the concourse at Paddington Station. He is obviously late for something. Maybe he caught the eight sixteen instead of the eight ten from somewhere and so is hurrying towards the steps of the Underground, his suit jacket flapping like wings, his briefcase knocking against his thigh. At the moment he skirts the noticeboard alerting passengers to the fact that skating and cycling are forbidden and that thieves operate in this area, the girl, who is actually an art student from the University of Greenwich trying to earn some extra cash, and who is dressed, much to her distress, like something out of a Thomas Hardy novel, turns abruptly to walk back to the gazebo that bears the names of the company

314

who have decided to give out free yogurts on this March morning, thus bumping into the man, causing the tray she's carrying to crash to the floor, the man to shout, 'Oh!' and Elliott Morgan to glance up from his place under the departure boards.

He sees a cross-looking woman in a bright red coat at the top of the escalators. The woman's hair is just the wrong shade of copper; it's not a good look, he thinks, as he shifts his feet, wishing his train would be announced. His phone rings; it flashes the word 'Home' at him. He answers it.

'Hi,' he says. 'How are you?'

'I'm fine,' Fern says, 'just giving Harley his breakfast. Where are you?'

'At Paddington, waiting for my train.'

'I hope it goes OK for you today,' she says.

He loves the sound of her voice, its music and its familiarity. He remembers the warmth of her in bed that morning, her opening her dark eyes and looking at him and smiling, and wishes she had been able to come with him today; it was going to be tough going back to Wales, to the house. It's always tough going back.

'Thanks,' he says. 'I'll keep in touch and see you later, OK?'

'OK.'

'Give Harley a kiss from me.'

'Will do.'

'Bye, Fern.'

'Bye, Elliott.'

The girl has picked up the tray of yogurts; someone is hovering over the spot with a cleaning trolley. The man she'd bumped into has gone, as has the woman in the red coat. The swirl of people continues across the concourse and, looking up, he sees his train's boarding on Platform 1. He turns and strides towards it, passing the card shop and Costa, the statue and the three-faced clock and he gets on the train, takes a seat next to the window. Yes, he thinks, going back is never easy. There's always the awful weight of that 'What if' question. What if he'd been a different son, brother, friend when he was younger? What if he hadn't done what he'd done that moment, on that street corner, on a day very much like this one way back in March 1988 before he left university?

Fern's voice is still in his head and he can imagine her in the kitchen of their home with their grandson, Harley, in his highchair, waving his arms like semaphore and grinning gappily with his Weetabix breakfast smeared around his mouth.

Ellliott doesn't want the past to come back, but it does, it always does; that turning-point moment, the one that could have changed everything. He can remember the feel of that girl's breasts, that look in Fern's eyes, the sound of her steps running down the stairs, the front door closing behind her and then him following, running with the blood beating in his ears and him thinking he's shouting her name, but not able to hear over the sound of rushing in his head.

'Fern?' he called.

Then, 'Fern!' he called again. 'Stop, please, stop. Wait.'

He caught up with her on the corner; they were both panting. In some bizarre way their breathing reminded him of sex with her, of that hold-back moment just before . . . He had a stitch, said something lame to her and her eyes blazed up at him. Her feet were planted so firmly on the pavement he thought she might take root.

Then, 'Oh my God, Fern,' he said. 'What can I say?'

'Well,' she said in a voice he didn't recognise, 'how should I know what you should say? I'm not the one who's just fucked someone else, am I?'

His answer came in a heartbeat; it was instinctive and felt completely right. In later years he has wondered what might have happened had he said something else, done something else. The thought terrifies him still.

'What I've done is so utterly wrong, but you, you,' he said, wrapping his arms around her, resting his chin on the top of her head, feeling her rigid body slacken a fraction beneath him, 'you are everything. It was nothing, it was mindless.' He lifted her face towards his, he remembers his fingers being hot on her skin. 'It will *never* happen again,' he said. 'You have to forgive me, Fern. Fern? I am sorry, so sorry.'

She tensed and relaxed, tensed and relaxed in his grasp; it was like holding on to a wild animal. One part of him wanted to let her go free, let her fly so that he could see if she would fly back to him; the other part of him wanted to keep hold of her, steady her breathing with his like they did in those seconds after sex . . .

'Oh, Elliott,' she said, stepping out of his hold and leaning against a low garden wall. A scent of lavender filled the air. Her tone was unreadable and he was filled with panic; it seemed gold-coloured to him, and whatever it was moved very fast in front of his eyes. Did he deserve a second chance with her? he wondered. Did he?

The sounds of the morning leant in on them; an aeroplane up high, birdsong, traffic. In the distance someone shouted something that sounded like, 'Bastard!' and that's exactly how Elliott felt about himself. How could he have ever doubted her? Thinking back to that January morning when they talked about the future, when it had all seemed so scary and unfathomable, he wondered now how he could have ever have had such thoughts. Faced with a choice of staying and fighting for her or fleeing, his instinct was to stay, and that, that, he argued as she stood in front of him and he could still feel the heat from her body against the thin material of his T-shirt, that is the only answer he'd been looking for, the only answer there was. His future is with her, not with that girl he'd spent the night with, nor any other girl; what he had with Fern was precious, was worth preserving at all costs. That future was round and solid and bright. It was right.

'Oh, Elliott,' she said again. 'What is it that you want?'

He took a step nearer her. She pressed back against the lavender once more; the scent of it caught in the back of his throat. 'I want to rewind time,' he said, 'to go back and for last night never to have happened. I want it to be you next to me, for you never to have gone away, for us to live together until we are old and one day to look back on this as a blip, a missed heartbeat, nothing more. Can we do that, Fern? Can we?'

She was looking about her. Was she looking for a chance to run? he thought. He wouldn't blame her if she was. He watched her closely, carefully; saw the thoughts flash across her face like images on a cinema screen. A woman walked by them pushing a buggy, a dog straining on a leash by her side. As it passed them, the dog looked up at Elliott, its eyes dancing with energy and accusation. Yes, Elliott wanted to say, you are right. I am on the verge of fucking up what could be the very best thing in my life, and if I have, I will stand forever accused.

There is no way back to this moment, he thought, as Fern gazed down at her boots. His fingers itched to brush aside the lace scarf which had been in

319

her hair and which had unwound as she ran away from him so that it curled across the base of her neck like a collar. He wanted to feel the touch of her skin again, put his palm on the pulse below her ear.

'Can we?' he asked again.

'Yes,' she said softly, raising her eyes to his. 'Yes.' She inched towards him; her body had left an imprint in the lavender and he put a hand on each of her shoulders, bent his head and kissed her; she tasted of salt.

'Come on,' he said afterwards, 'let's go back.'

The walk back was quiet and slow; he guessed they were both anxious to know if Meryl would still be there, waiting for him. But she wasn't. She'd gone, leaving her number on a piece of paper by the bed. He wanted to say sorry to her, to try to explain, so he kept the number, didn't tell Fern but did make the call, then tore the paper into fragments and threw them away.

In the meantime, that morning when he took Fern back to the house and their room with its big window and the scattering of their belongings on the surfaces and floors, he stripped the sheets off the bed, bundled them into a bag and took them to the launderette. When he got back, Fern was curled asleep on the mattress, and he placed the clean bedding around her, wrapping her in it to keep her warm, to keep her safe, and sat next to her and watched her as she dreamed.

And now, as the train pulls out of Paddington, as it starts its journey to Wales, to the house where he grew up and today has to get ready to sell, to the father who looks at him and doesn't really know who he is, Elliott remembers Fern's sleeping face on that morning back when they were young. And he remembers it this morning when he watched her sleeping as dawn had spilled in around the edges of the curtains in their room in the house where they live with their daughter and her son, where he is surrounded by the evidence of his life with Fern, his years working at Hewlett-Packard and then, later, his years as an MP, treading the pavements, fighting small battles, making a little bit of a difference to some people's lives, and he knows he would not have had it any other way.

Fern is in their kitchen. She says, 'There now, wasn't that nice?' to her grandson as he bangs a plastic spoon on the tray of his highchair and beams up at her as she turns to the sink to rinse out his breakfast bowl and put it in the dishwasher.

Next she wipes his sticky mouth with a cloth and lifts him out, saying 'Here,' as she kisses him, 'that's from Grandpa,' and feeling the solid weight of him tucking itself into the curve between her armpit and her hip, and she remembers how it felt when their daughter was this age and how, every time she looked into her child's eyes she would feel a rushing under her ribs, as if she was holding something far too fragile, far too valuable, far too full of promise.

She and Elliott had been married just under a year when Tash had arrived; Natasha Awel Morgan, born 15th September 1990, weighing 7lb, 10oz, and Fern's life had spun around her daughter and husband. She'd shared her hopes and fears with Jules, watched Tash grow, felt that fragility and preciousness slipping through her fingers as the years spun by. And now she cares for the son her daughter bore after a one-night stand with a man who phones infrequently and visits even less often while her daughter works to save enough money for a flat of her own.

And as she places this child, their Harley, in his playpen, she remembers being witness to the changes in her daughter's body as the months of her pregnancy passed, marvelling at how her baby daughter could be so grown, surprised at the speed of years, thinking back to that moment on the corner on a March morning much like this one: this one when Elliott is on a train to Wales; when her daughter is on her way to work, having left half an hour ago, dressed in a dark suit and white blouse, her shoulders set in a tight line of grief at having to leave her son behind for yet another day; when Harley is thumping a toy on the floor of the lounge and gabbling in his own language at the windows and walls; and Jules is due to arrive at eleven; and the furniture in Fern's house is permanent and her garden is glowing in the spring sunlight and it is all because back then, at that moment when Elliott said, 'Can we do that, Fern? Can we?' she had, with one leap of the heart, said, 'Yes. Yes.'

CHAPTER 19

But there is a next day.

And on this day she irons in the lounge in front of the TV. She lifts up a shirt and lays it flat on the ironing board. She pauses. The thought is sudden and unexpected and it crashes against her chest like a shout. Her breaths are short, sharp; the furniture swells, the carpet starts to rise.

He walks into the room. Pictures are flickering on the screen. It's late afternoon. The rest of the house is quiet.

'You OK?'

She turns her head to look at him. 'Yes,' she says. 'It's just . . .'

His voice is soft, is kind, is so very familiar. 'Just what?' he asks.

'It's just that sometimes . . .' She presses down the iron so that the steam hisses. 'Sometimes I realise what a narrow line it is between what is and what could be, how many possibilities of us there could have been, how it all hinges on one moment. The thought terrifies me; it still terrifies me.'

'I know,' Jack says. He doesn't move closer to her. There is no need. Instead he says, 'I'll put the rubbish out now, I think.'

'OK,' she says, and hangs the shirt on a hanger, touches the cloth; it is still warm. She lifts another from the basket by her feet, hears the back door close behind him.

Outside, in the patch of sky above their garden, a red kite calls to its mate. Fern closes her eyes, can see the circles it draws with its wings, high up, out of reach.

THE END